RANGERS OF EL PASO

LAURAN PAINE

SAGEBRUSH
Large Print Westerns

Copyright © Mona Paine, 2009

First published in Great Britain by ISIS Publishing Ltd.
First published in the United States by Five Star

Published in Large Print 2014 by ISIS Publishing Ltd.,
7 Centremead, Osney Mead, Oxford OX2 0ES
by arrangement with
Golden West Literary Agency

CIP data is available for this title from the British Library

ISBN 978–0–7531–5367–3 (pb)

Printed and bound in Great Britain by
T. J. International Ltd., Padstow, Cornwall

CONTENTS

RANGERS OF EL PASO

CHAPTER
ONE

Captain Tomlinson had them up one at a time, and he gave the identical instructions to each man. "Go up to Valverde where you won't be known, stay clear of the law up there, settle in at the boarding house . . . and just sit back and wait. A man will look you up and show you a mate to this." Captain Tomlinson then handed each man a torn Confederate $100 note. "Don't nose around up there, don't look for anyone you might know, and don't act like anything but range men out of work. Clear?"

He sent Barney Glasser up to Valverde first, then Levi Holt, and finally Twenty-One McKinnon who had only just arrived at the El Paso Ranger barracks from down at Eagle Pass where Twenty-One's reputation had established him among both his own kind in the Ranger organization, and among his enemies south of the border who smuggled, raided, and rustled U.S. livestock, as a very good man to have as a friend.

There was one more Texas Ranger to be sent up to Valverde but so far Captain Tomlinson had had almost no luck at all in locating him.

His name was Cleve Hampshire and the last information Tomlinson had on him was that he'd gone pig hunting in the Staked Plains countryside with some Comanches, which made about as much sense to Captain Tomlinson as most of the stories that filtered back, sooner or later, about Cleve Hampshire.

Cleve was not a Ranger. He had been, but four years earlier he had been badly hurt in a brush fight with Mexican marauders and had resigned. Since then, however, he seemed to have fully recovered, otherwise half the things Tomlinson heard could not possibly have been done by Cleve Hampshire.

There was another man just as good at the kind of work that had to be done up at Valverde as Cleve Hampshire was, but he had been assigned as special bodyguard to a Mexican diplomat of high rank who was travelling between Texas and the District of Columbia, so that Ranger might just as well have been on the moon.

Charley Runnels, who had been on the force in its early days and who had worked under such notables as Jack Hays, visited Tomlinson at the El Paso barracks every now and then. In fact, it had been old Charley who had said Cleve Hampshire was peccary hunting with the Indians, and Charley would probably know because Cleve was his son-in-law.

Had been his son-in-law, and for all anyone now knew still was, but Charley's daughter, Cleve's wife, had died in the cholera epidemic over in Dallas where she'd gone to visit her sister. They had both died.

Cleve had never remarried. He was just able to be up and around again after his near-fatal injury along the border, when news had arrived that his wife had died.

Cleve had ridden away four days later and old Charley, instead of persuading the weak, sick Ranger to stay, had helped him catch his horse, roll his blankets, and rig up for travel.

"No man can stand that kind of agony," he had later told Tomlinson, "sitting down doing nothing."

"And he could faint out there somewhere and damned well die," the captain had replied, to which Charley had said — "He sure could at that, couldn't he?" — and had walked home without another word.

A lot of people were ultimately resigned to dying, a few less than that number guessed about when their time might be up, and fewer still did not give a copper-colored damn and Charley was one of those.

Captain Tomlinson was at the horse corrals out back in the cool early morning listening to all the reasons, valid as well as trumped-up, why the El Paso command of the border divisions of the Texas Rangers should be given a better horse allowance. Those working hardest to influence him on this were a pair of sunburned men who had just returned up out of Mexico with a bag of stolen jewels and the dirks, guns, and spurs of the six Mexican marauders who had ambushed the stage, shot the passengers, the driver, and gun guard, to plunder the stage and steal this particular bag of jewels from the strongbox.

Their particular protest was over the fact that, although they had in fact had two good horses shot from beneath them over the line and had been obliged to bushwhack their pursuers and steal a pair of riderless Mexican horses, the animals they had gotten home on were inferior, while the ones they'd lost in Mexico had been exemplary, Texas-bred animals whose loss, as well as whose keep, the Rangers had not been reimbursed for, and under present regulations were only going to be reimbursed for at the rate of a flat figure based on an incorrect assumption that everyone rode mustangs.

Captain Tomlinson did not say a word. Did not open his mouth. He listened to all the zealous Rangers had to say, and turned only when he heard someone approaching from the direction of the roadway.

It was Charley Runnels.

Tomlinson studied the old man's face all the while Runnels was crossing the yard, then he raised a hand to silence his pair of importuning Rangers, and walked out to Charley.

"You found him?" Tomlinson said.

"Not exactly," Charley replied. "I got a note from over by Valverde that he'd be along directly, that the hunt was a success, and he'd fetch us back some pig jerky."

Tomlinson said: "When?"

Charley didn't know precisely when Cleve Hampshire would arrive back in town. "Few days, I'd wager," he mumbled. "You know damned well he didn't say what *day* he'd ride in."

"The minute he gets here, Charley, you tell him I got to see him no matter if it's in the middle of the night. You hear?"

Charley was interested. "What is it, something serious, Captain?"

"Why no, Charley, I always like to see fellers I haven't seen in ages, even if it's got to be in the middle of the damned night." He looked steadily at old Runnels. "It's serious," he said, and turned away to avoid those importuning Rangers as well as Charley and walked quickly toward the back of the fortress-like low, old adobe structure that was the headquarters and officers' quarters of the El Paso barracks.

But he stopped stockstill six inches in front of the door. *Hampshire was over at Valverde?* He turned. "Charley, did you say he was over at Valverde?"

Runnels called back a trifle waspishly. "No. I said I got a note from him, over *by* Valverde."

"Where, exactly?"

Charley stood in the yard becoming annoyed. "What the hell's wrong with you? Where? Well, I don't know, but I'd guess maybe at the Chavez place at the south end of town. He's been their friend for a lot of years."

Tomlinson abruptly turned and hiked in the direction of the front roadway, avoiding the entrance to the building he had been about to use. He walked across to the way station, bought a seat on the noon stage for Valverde, then strolled back looking a lot less troubled than he'd looked before.

Charley Runnels went over to the saloon and told Ace Bedmann, who ran the place, that he thought maybe Elmer Tomlinson was beginning to get the desert complaint, a relatively common ailment, if one believed everyone who said someone else had it, among men who lived under the fierce southwest summer sun. It was said to be responsible for a giddiness,

7

forgetfulness, and irascibility in men, which was also symptomatic of an altogether different ailment in women.

Ace Bedmann neither agreed nor disagreed. He had over the years become such a tactful fence-straddler that he had picket marks on his rear. All Ace said was: "Hey, Charley, I haven't seen Cleve in a hell of a long while. I got to thinking about that yesterday. When's he comin' back to town?"

Charley raised his glass of beer and half drained it before fixing Ace Bedmann with a fierce glare and saying: "I'm not his god-damned keeper, how would I know?"

Ace blinked. "All I did was ask."

Charley finished the beer and shoved the glass forward. "Refill, Ace. By the way did you ever handle any of that corn beer the Tarahumaras make down in Chihuahua?"

Ace hadn't. "I never drank no Injun likker if I could help it," he averred. "It makes 'em all crazy in time, so why would a white man want to try it?"

"Never made me crazy," stated Charley, "and I drank my share of it when I was scoutin' for the Army during the Naná and Geronimo troubles."

Ace set up the refilled glass and grinned wickedly. "You sure?" he asked, then turned to go up the bar and wait on a youthful, long-legged cowboy who had walked in out of the sun blast looking dry as a bone and dusty from travel.

Charley took it well. He had been a Ranger too long in his earlier years not to be able to survive the rough variety of range country humor that passed for wit and cleverness throughout the Southwest. He drank his second beer more slowly. The second one never tasted as good as the first one, but its effect in a man as old and spare as Charley Runnels went right on building up until the second one was gone and Charley's spirits were pleasantly hoisted.

It was serious, otherwise Tomlinson would not have gone directly to the way station as soon as it occurred to him that he might be able to locate Cleve up at Valverde. Ranger captains didn't go off like that unless whatever was troubling them was serious.

Charley savored the last swallow of that second glass of beer and rolled a cigarette in the pleasant shade and peace of the saloon. A pair of perspiring, bearded big freighters ambled in for beer and a cool, quiet place to stand for a spell, and behind them another cowboy entered, also looking dehydrated and dusted over.

Charley left the saloon to go down to the shady bench out front of the blacksmith's building. This time of day there were usually three or four other older men down there. Sometimes the conversation lacked the essentials that might have earned it a classification as brilliant, but the humor, the anecdotes, and sometimes the scurrilous tales of long ago conquests south of the border kept it from ever being entirely boring.

Perhaps the most interesting aspect was that the children and grandchildren of those poor old men down there sitting in the shade whittling, smoking, and talking had no idea of how that conversation sometimes got down to the most amusing basics imaginable. The children and grandchildren thought those poor old men simply sat there and mournfully discussed past great events like their War Between the States, or maybe their lumbago and palsy and other ailments. If they could have heard some of those recitations, their hair would have jumped straight up.

Charley headed down there with his two tankards of beer pleasantly awash, and it occurred to him that he had never confided in his cronies his experience over the line down in Huamantla, the time the ardent *señorita* turned out to be a *señora*, and Charley had taken half a window sash with him as he'd fled out a bedroom in the dark with a roaring big black Mexican right behind him brandishing a huge old horse pistol.

CHAPTER
TWO

Valverde was in the border country without being actually considered a border town. For one thing it was thirty miles farther northward than all the genuine border communities, and for another thing it was in a variety of countryside that had trees as well as grass and water.

The territory was flat to rolling. In some parts it was bisected by low, thick barrancas, and there were any number of dry washes fringed by paloverdes, Spanish-bayonet, and ocotilla.

It was good low country. In fact, in its own way it was better than the purer grass territories farther northward, because it never snowed down at Valverde, and, in fact, there were many winters when it did not even get down to freezing, which meant that, short and tough though the grass might be, it was still there to nourish livestock when the longer-stemmed, more succulent grass of the northerly cattle ranges was under a foot or two of snow.

Valverde had started out as a military installation where border troopers had been trained. It had been a thriving community then, and now it was still a thriving community although there were no longer any soldiers up there. Valverde had become a very successful cattle country. Cattle interests fed the community's economy and some of the larger and more enduring cowmen even owned some of the business blocks in Valverde.

The string of structures along Main Street that included the saloon where Cleve Hampshire and Captain Elmer Tomlinson were relaxing at a table near the stove belonged to a cattleman of wealth and influence named Curt Brinkley.

It was partly with reference to this same Curt Brinkley that Tomlinson said: "It's not just stealing cattle, Cleve, it's evidently some kind of organized gang that has outlets for horses, too, and the Lord only knows what else. I've got a list of losses down at my office that all come together, and that's why I sent three men up here to be handy. It's Glasser, Holt and McKinnon."

Cleve Hampshire, who was a burly man of average height, gazed a trifle pensively at Captain Tomlinson as he said: "You know damned well those three don't need me, Cap."

Tomlinson made a gesture. "Cleve, if it turns out to be that I'm wrong, that the losses are just coincidental, you'll be plumb right, but right now it don't look like I'm wrong. If you could see the evidence . . . It's like some organization or other is systematically stripping the range up here."

"What kind of a loss are you talking about?" the burly man asked quietly. "Fifteen horses, fifty or sixty head of cattle?"

12

"Two hundred head of horses, Cleve, and close to a thousand head of cattle!"

Hampshire sat in silence staring at Tomlinson for a while. "If it's that big a loss," he eventually said, "why isn't Valverde up in arms over it? Why isn't there more noise being made and why aren't there range patrols?"

"Because I went to men like Brinkley and asked them to say as little as possible for a couple of weeks so's the Rangers'll have a chance. If they bust out in vigilante groups and catch some of the rustlers, they'll hang them and that's not what I want. Cleve, those rustlers aren't just all of a sudden, all at the same time, stealing choice animals and getting them out of the country. My point has been with the cowmen that, if they kill a few of the riders, they'll scare off the men who are really planning and ordering things, and maybe we'll never get another chance at them, or maybe they'll just hire new riders and keep right on raiding up here around Valverde. Cleve, I'm trying to run a completely clandestine operation. It's the only way we'll catch them . . . not the damned thieves, the leaders, the planners, the fellers who are behind it all . . . and you've got the skill and resourcefulness I need up here."

Hampshire did not decline. He said: "The cow interests have agreed to say nothing for another week or two?"

"Yes."

"And where are these stolen animals being taken? Mexico?"

Captain Tomlinson raised broad shoulders and dropped them. "If it's Mexico, they've got an

13

organization down there, too, because I had a couple of men loafing out over the territory down there watching for drives of U.S. branded animals, and they turned up with absolutely nothing. So . . . while I can't say it's not going on down there, I sure as hell can't swear that it is, either. And that's another thing I got to worry about, Cleve . . . not just where is it all going, but is there another damned organization, somewhere, receiving the livestock and whisking it away." Tomlinson leaned to hoist his beer glass. He looked squarely at the other man, the burly, blue-eyed, sun-bronzed man dressed as a range rider except that his hair was too long and his feet had moccasins instead of boots: "It's not going to stop, Cleve, I can promise you that. No one stops when he's got something like this working so damned well for him. If we don't stop him, he just isn't going to be stopped."

"The ranchers . . ."

"You know better. Like I just told you, Cleve, even if they catch and lynch a few of the riders, that's not going to help us get the head Indian, and until we nail him, this thing is going to keep right on functioning." Tomlinson drank, shoved the glass away, and leaned. "It'll be a damned sight more interesting than wild pig hunting with a band of . . ."

"How do you know that?" growled the burly man.

Tomlinson pulled back a little. "To me it would be. I think it will be more interesting to you. Cleve, you'll have three of the best men out of El Paso at your disposal." The Ranger captain reached into a pocket and placed an envelope upon the table between them.

"Inside are the torn halves of some Secesh hundred dollar bills. Holt, McKinnon, and Glasser will have the other halves. That's how you fellers will get to know each other."

Hampshire gazed at the envelope without making any move to pick it up. "Do they know I'll be looking them up?"

"Yes. Not by name, though. They're already at the rooming house up here, waiting. I told them to do nothing, to talk to no one and to look and act like footloose range men until someone showed up with the matching parts of their Secesh money. Cleve, they're some of the best men on the border. Believe me, they'll equal an army if it comes down to that."

"Which you expect it will," retorted the burly man wryly, "or you wouldn't have gone to all this trouble and planning."

Captain Tomlinson, who was a tall, thoughtful man with a knife scar into the hairline over his left temple, had rarely minimized difficulties and he did not minimize them now, when he said: "You know as much about an affair like this as I do. It's never like chopping the snake's head off to end all his wriggling. I don't know who is up at the top, how many men are in this thing, or what they might know about us. All I know, Cleve, is that one way or another they've got to be wasted." As though anticipating a particular argument, Tomlinson raised a hand. "I know you're out of it, and I know you've got a disability, and you sure as hell don't have to feel any obligation to me or to the unit." Tomlinson dropped his hand to the table top. He had said it all, and, if he continued to speak, there was nothing more to be added to what had already been said. He signaled for a bar man to bring two more glasses of beer.

Cleve Hampshire shook back his long hair, methodically rolled a cigarette that he lit and briefly savored, then he slowly turned as three range riders trooped noisily into the saloon and one of them said: "Hey, look yonder . . . there's old *pawhuska* hisself, old Long-Hair the squawman hisself."

The other two range men looked, then suddenly lost a little of their exuberance at the appearance of the two men at the little table, who were now stonily regarding them. The other two shouldered their friend along in the direction of the bar, but the bold-faced cowboy had to get off one more remark.

"Hey, Long-Hair, you been out eatin' beetles with the diggers?"

Cleve's eyes were narrowed against the trickle of fragrant smoke as he studied the youthful range rider. "You son-of-a-bitch," he called quietly, "I'd rather be out with the diggers than with scum like you."

The cowboy stiffened and jerked free of both his companions. The other two stepped wide watching those two seated men.

Behind them a voice said: "Fellers, you just turn around and settle against the bar, and don't even look like you're fixin' to say anything more."

Everyone in the saloon heard the deliberate cocking of a shotgun — twice.

16

The cowboy who was glaring at Cleve Hampshire had his right hand lightly atop his Colt handle, but his riding friends were already obeying the bartender behind them all with that sawed-off shotgun cocked and aimed in their direction.

Cleve said — "Draw it!" — and sat slouched in his chair, looking the least like a man about to kill another man as it was possible to look.

A doleful-faced cowboy walked in over at the roadside door, correctly assessed the situation instantly, and halted in the doorway eyeing the man over by the bar.

Captain Tomlinson spoke for the first time, addressing the yeasty man in front of the bar. "You'll never in this damned world get it done, mister, so you'd better just do like the bar man says, turn around, and have your beer . . . and keep your mouth closed the next time you walk into a saloon."

One of the other range men said: "Come on, Chad, what the hell . . . it's all over."

Chad had to turn away. Even if his friends had stood with him, the odds still would not have been so good. He glared at Cleve Hampshire, lifted his gun hand clear very carefully, and turned, red in the face, to look into the black bores of that shotgun.

The bar man eased down both dogs, replaced his weapon under the bar, and, as though nothing had happened, went after three glasses of beer, while the doleful-faced cowboy in the doorway finally moved over toward the bar, also, but made a wide sashay so that he

17

would not have to stand anywhere near those other three range men.

Tomlinson leaned with both hands clasped atop the table, watching the back of that troublesome cowboy, as he spoke to the burly man opposite him at the table. "I'll give you some advice," he said softly. "Go get a damned haircut."

Cleve chuckled. "Think I will." He was still grinning as he eyed the envelope atop the table between them. "Usual wages and expenses," he said, reaching to pick up the envelope and pocket it.

"Yes. And I'm working on a new horse-and-fodder allotment for men in the field."

"That's nice," Hampshire responded dryly. "How about ammunition and boot leather?"

"If a Ranger uses more than a box of bullets a year on his assignments, we figure he needs marksmanship training . . . what boot leather? Wonder that cowboy didn't say something about you wearing Comanch' slippers."

"Where will you be?"

"Down in El Paso where I'm supposed to be," stated Captain Tomlinson, and fished around in a pocket, then held out a closed fist. "Take it, you can use it to hold up your drawers if you've a mind to." He dropped the little nickel circlet with the star inside it into the palm of Cleve Hampshire. Then he smiled. "I'd swear you in, only I never could remember the whole oath. You want to walk down the road and have something to eat with me?"

Hampshire said: "You go. I'll get sheared first and maybe meet you later somewhere around town."

Tomlinson remained a moment or two longer. "Want me to tell Charley you won't be back to El Paso for a while?"

"Yeah. How is he?"

"Charley never changes, Cleve . . . he said you'd likely be out at the Chavez place, which is why I sent that messenger out there."

"You could have come yourself."

"Yeah, I know that. But . . . what difference does it make?"

"You knew my wife and you don't want to meet Eulalia Chavez, Captain. That's the difference it makes."

Tomlinson arose. "I'll be around town after you get that haircut," he said, and walked over to hand the bar man enough silver to cover their drinks, then he walked out of the saloon into the settling late day afternoon.

CHAPTER
THREE

Valverde was not as large as El Paso, but its night life was comparable on a smaller scale. There were several cafés in Valverde, as well as several saloons and pool halls and dance halls. The busiest night was Saturday, of course, but during the week there were usually enough range men in town to keep things moving.

It was Tuesday night when Captain Tomlinson had coffee with Clive Hampshire at the Palace Restaurant, which was where the cattlemen usually ate, and sometimes also transacted business. Cleve, freshly shorn and shaved, had supper. Tomlinson who had eaten earlier, was content to drink coffee and to sit in silence while Cleve said: "I got that envelope in case you'd like it back. It's empty." Cleve looked up. "I could never understand why everyone always says the Palace is the best place to eat in Valverde. This damned steak is as tough as last year's saddle blanket." He fished for the envelope and tossed it atop the table linen.

Tomlinson picked it up, looked inside, and dropped it. "How in hell did you make those contacts so fast?" he asked.

"If we're going to do this thing, we might as well get started so's we can end it, and I can go back for an antelope hunt the Indians are working up," stated Hampshire.

"Anybody who'd eat antelope," opined Captain Tomlinson, "would eat goat."

Cleve remained unperturbed. Anyone down in the border territories who had not eaten goat had to be some kind of rarity. Not only were the Indians fond of goat meat, but Mexicans also were. There was only one kind of red meat the Indians preferred to goat, and that was mule meat, hard to come by when it was no longer possible to raid a ranch or two when tribesmen ran low on meat supplies.

"What did you tell them?" asked Tomlinson, referring to McKinnon, Holt, and Glasser.

"To circulate, to try and get hired on by anyone they think might be worth cultivating on the range. To listen in every bar in town tonight and, after that, to sit on the porch of the rooming house until I come along so's we can palaver."

"That ought to keep them out of mischief," Tomlinson remarked dryly. "These are good men, Cleve, not messenger boys."

"If I need messenger boys, Cap, that's what they'll be," stated Hampshire, and finally put aside his eating utensils. "A man couldn't chew his way through this if he had steel teeth, and I'll tell you something else . . . they make the worst coffee in Texas in this place."

Tomlinson sighed. "You're cranky," he accused. "The older you're getting the crankier you're getting."

21

"You've got to have some ideas," said the burly man. "Some suspicions about who we're looking for around the Valverde countryside."

The Ranger captain threw up his hands. "That's the one thing I don't have any information about at all. Not a shred. Believe me, there is nothing I'd like better than to have just one name. All I've got is the rantings of some pretty darned mad range men."

"You mean to sit there and tell me that about a thousand head of livestock has been stolen around here, and none of the crews who've ridden out have turned up anything at all . . . not even any decent boot marks or horseshoe imprints, or *something?*"

"Nothing," stated Tomlinson.

"How about the constable up here?"

"Nothing again," stated the Ranger officer. "Cleve, if there was just one small damned thing, you know darned well I'd have handed it over to you . . . And that's just one more worry I've got. How in hell can they be so successful? I've been in this manhunting business most of my life, and for the first time . . . nothing. Not a lousy sighting or a lousy drunken word at the bar."

"But they're on the range," stated Cleve Hampshire. "There's no other way in the world to rustle livestock without being out where the livestock is. So . . . they're on the range, and, if riding crews swear up and down they can't turn up something, they are either blind or liars."

Tomlinson agreed. "Sure. One or the other. And that's what you've got to ferret out. McKinnon used to be one of the best top hands in the Eagle Pass country long before he was assigned that area as a Ranger. Levi Holt is from Arizona. They tell me he was a top hand, too, over there. If those lads can't turn up something . . ."

"What's Barney Glasser good for?" asked Hampshire.

"Get in a fight and you'll find out," said the Ranger captain. "That . . . and toss a rope. They say he's one of the best with a lariat in the unit."

"If I have to rope someone, I'll remember that," stated Hampshire. "First thing in the morning, if they haven't turned up anything around town tonight, out they go to different positions on the range. Cap, you don't look as though you approve?"

"Sure I approve," stated Tomlinson, "but just remember they're manhunters in the border country, they're not just former range hands."

"Quit telling me what I should and shouldn't do!" exclaimed Hampshire. "If we all live through this, your three border wizards will sure as hell be able to tell their grandchildren they got assigned to a bastard, one time, who'd work the butt off a brass monkey just to get results."

"They'll work, make no mistake about that," stated Tomlinson. "I just don't want you to alienate them by being overbearing. Cleve, you're going to need all the goodwill you can wring out of those three before too much longer, or I'll be a monkey's uncle."

Cleve yawned and made no attempt to disguise it. His gray, gun-metal eyes glinted sardonically upon Captain Tomlinson. "Have a nice ride back to El Paso," he said, "and don't forget to tell Charley I'll be on assignment for a few days, then I'll head for home."

Tomlinson nodded over all this, then arose as he said: "Let's go get a nightcap."

They left the café with a pair of cigars that they paused out front to bite into, then to light up as they stood and surveyed the flawless, balmy late springtime evening.

"Someone's range boss is sure as hell setting up the bunches to be hit," Cleve said thoughtfully. "No thousand head of cattle could begin to disappear, like you've made out they disappear, unless there was someone out there who knows when it's safe to raid a certain part of the range. Maybe it's more than one range boss, and maybe the riders who do the actual rustling are also local men."

"Find out," said Tomlinson simply, and headed for the bar he favored on his visits to Valverde.

When they entered the saloon, the place was half full, which probably was about as it should be on a weekday night. Tomlinson saw Twenty-One McKinnon at the bar by himself and over near a poker session was Barney Glasser, dark and self-assured-looking and expressionless as he glanced up and saw who was looking in his direction. Barney turned his back as casually as possible and continued to watch the poker game.

The bar man brought two glasses and a bottle, then hastened to take care of other customers. As Tomlinson poured, he said: "You got specific plans?"

24

Hampshire waited until the shot glass was full to the brim before reaching for it. "Yeah, put Glasser and the other two to work on local cow outfits if I can." Cleve hoisted the glass with considerable care in order not to spill a drop. As he did this, he also said: "You're right, Cap, there's no way for anything this big and successful to operate in a territory unless it's got plenty of local encouragement." He downed the whiskey and put the glass away from him. "If the local law's not mixed in, then he's got to be awful damned incompetent. Other folks have got to have heard about it, too." Cleve smiled. "A thousand head?" He gently shook his head. "The whole damned countryside's got to know *something* is going on."

Without warning a lanky range rider tapped Cleve's back. It was that same cowboy who'd been troublesome earlier, only now he was evidently by himself, and, also, he had clearly been drinking since the earlier unpleasantness. Neither Hampshire not Tomlinson had seen him when they'd entered the saloon.

Cleve turned slowly. He and the troublesome range rider gazed steadily at one another, then Cleve said — "Buy you a drink?" — and the cowboy half sneered his answer. "Don't try to butter up to me, you Injun-lovin' bastard."

Tomlinson turned, recognized the cowboy, and chopped outward from the waist with a powerful strike that caught the half-drunk range rider flush in his unprotected stomach, doubling him over.

Cleve caught the man on one side while the cowboy retched and gasped. Tomlinson caught him on the other

25

side and they began hurrying doorward with him. Behind them several bar patrons turned, incorrectly judged what was happening, and joined the bar man in yelling for Tomlinson and Hampshire to hurry. They did not want the retching man to be ill on the floor of the saloon.

Outside, Hampshire settled the cowboy upon a bolted, old scuffed wall bench and reached roughly to lift his head. The range rider's stomach had probably already been queasy as a result of the liquor he'd been pouring into it since earlier in the day, but even so the man would recover rapidly. He was youthful and lean and fit. He just was no match for the pair of men who were bending over him now, offering advice.

"If you work around here," said Cleve Hampshire, "get on your horse, sonny, and head for the bunkhouse. If you don't work around here, get on your horse and head north or south, it's up to you, and don't stop until you're at least fifty miles away. Mister, the third time I'll kill you on sight."

"Hit a man when he isn't watchin'," gasped the cowboy. "Just give me ten minutes."

A dark man appeared silently in the doorway, eyed the injured cowboy stolidly, then moved on through. It was Barney Glasser who was by nature self-assured, good-natured, and blessed with one of those sets of dark, swarthy features that should have belonged to a pirate but which in Barney's case had proved valuable any number of times. He looked mean and deadly, when he chose not to smile. Now, he gazed at the troublesome range man without smiling, and, after listening to Hampshire give the cowboy an additional warning, Barney stepped up and said: "You gents care to go back inside and finish your drinks, I'll take this man out back and shoot him, for two dollars."

The cowboy's tender midsection seemed abruptly to cease hurting him. He leaned to rise but Barney reached and pushed him back down. Then Barney nodded to the other pair of Rangers and they looked a trifle regretfully at the range man, then silently reëntered the saloon.

Barney leaned, pulled away the cowboy's six-gun, and gestured with it. "Around back," he said, "and if you don't get off your butt, I'll blow your god-damned head off right here. *Move!*"

The range man rose and turned southward to obey. At an opening between two buildings he came to a decision most men would have arrived at earlier. If he was going to be killed anyway, then it might as well happen while he was fighting his hardest. He turned and leaped back at Barney, but Glasser was to one side and still moving away. Barney was expecting exactly what happened, and he now systematically went to work overhauling the youthful, sinewy range man. Barney had been brawling all his life on one side or the other side of the border and in two-thirds of the cow towns of west Texas. His opponent had desperation and fear, and a none-too-steady set of legs. He was no match at all for the very dark man who went to work like an axe man felling a tree. Barney hit the cowboy in every place were it would still hurt tomorrow. He beat him badly without putting the man down.

27

When the cowboy tasted his own blood from a smashed mouth, and, through the singing sound in his head from too many blows high up, he knew he was outmatched but he could not stop, so he kept wading in. When Barney figured the cowboy had been through enough, he closed fast, laced in a powerful pair of lefts and rights, then stood and watched the range man's legs turn loose and slowly let him crumple.

Barney leaned, shoved the pistol back in its holster, and turned away just as a pair of riders turned in out front of the saloon and looked down where the prone man was sprawling.

Barney spoke with clear disgust. "If a man can't hold it, he ought not to drink it, should he, gents?"

The strangers agreed heartily as they swung down and stepped ahead to tie their horses. If a man couldn't handle his whiskey, he shouldn't go near a saloon, and that was a plumb fact!

CHAPTER
FOUR

It was still early when Cleve walked up to the porch of the rooming house. He'd had his nightcap, had also survived some inadvertent adventures, and now was ready for the palaver with the other three Rangers. He made a smoke, selected the deepest chair, got as comfortable as he could, cocked both thick legs atop the porch railing, and sat in silence and bland darkness until a lanky man ambled up nearby, pulled a chair around, and said: "My name is Levi Holt. I just had a few words with Cap Tomlinson. I expect Barney and Twenty-One will be along directly. What you got in mind, Mister Hampshire?"

"Just plain Cleve, to start with," replied Hampshire. "You know why we're all up here?"

"Not exactly," stated Holt. "Rustling, maybe?"

"On a scale I never heard of before," Cleve replied. "Fifty to a hundred head, both horses and cattle, stolen at a time. So far, about a thousand head stolen."

The lanky man looked skeptical. "Did you say a thousand head?"

"That's right. Up to now about a thousand head."

"Why aren't the cow outfits up on their hind legs?"

Cleve was watching a thick shadow amble up in the direction of the rooming house as he formed his reply. "They *are* on their hind legs, but for now they've promised Cap Tomlinson to say nothing so's we'll have a chance."

That oncoming shadow turned out to be Barney Glasser. A dozen or so yards behind Barney there was another stroller. Cleve Hampshire did not recognize Twenty-One McKinnon until he and Barney were on the porch only a few yards distant, then Cleve nodded and motioned for the others to drag chairs up.

He explained what he and Levi Holt had been discussing, then he said: "You boys circulate among the cow outfits tomorrow, see if you can get hired on. I'm going to stay here in town. Somewhere, either out yonder or right here in Valverde, there is a wedge we can use to open up this darned affair a little. All we need right now is someone's name, or maybe some story about someone having too much money or having been gone for a few days when he was supposed to be working. Mostly the name."

Twenty-One said: "You goin' to stay on here at the rooming house?"

Cleve nodded. "Yeah. And I'll be in plain sight around town most of the time. All the same, if you come looking for me wait until it's about this time of night. I doubt that anyone'll recognize any of us as Rangers, but a man don't have to be very bright to figure out there is something going on when a cowboy rides into town at night and goes over to the rooming house to hold a secret meetin' with someone else.

Maybe normally this wouldn't arouse too much interest, but if this rustling organization is as big and widespread and well-organized as Cap seems to think it is, I'll lay you big odds they've got eyes and ears all over this darned countryside, and in Valverde as well."

Levi Holt yawned. "You got any ideas about how we're going to get hired on this late in the riding season?"

"Yeah, I got an idea," replied Cleve. "You visit every damned cow camp around here and ask for work. That's my idea." Cleve looked from one of them to the other. "We're going to come up with something within the next few days," he said. "Gents, that's all." He rose and without another glance at any of them entered the rooming house.

Behind him on the porch three seasoned Texas Rangers looked at one another. Twenty-One McKinnon said: "Hell, I heard some time back that he was a hard man to work with." McKinnon sounded disgusted.

"There are worse," put in Holt, inhaling, then trickling smoke. "I worked for Chet Devlin the year before he caught it in Sonora, and he had to be about the most disagreeable man to work with in the world."

Barney Glasser, slouching in his chair, feet cocked up onto the railing with his hat tipped down, spoke in a detached manner. "No one said I got to like Hampshire. All they said in El Paso was that we got to work with someone they'd send up with half a Rebel hunnert dollar note. That's him just went inside. Tomorrow I got to try and find work at some damned cow outfit. So I'll do it. After that I got to try and pick up whatever information I can about a livestock stealin' outfit. Simple." Barney yawned and got more comfortable in the chair. "Tomlinson liked Hampshire, which is good enough for me." He peered darkly from beneath his hat brim. "You fellers want to sit out here all night?"

Inside the doorway and to one side of it in the shadows, Cleve Hampshire grinned to himself, then turned and tiptoed down to his room. The attitude of the men he would be working with was important only to the extent that it would contribute to their respect for him and their willingness to get this assignment concluded.

Cleve wanted to go on that hunt with the Indians as soon as he could shake loose of this present assignment. And the blasted Comanches wouldn't wait; when they figured the signs were right, including the position of the new moon, they'd saddle up and ride off. If he was late, he would miss out and that was all there was to it.

Cleve retired and slept as he always did, with his naked Colt within four inches of his hand, although this was hardly the customary way to sleep in a town. Maybe it was on the range, or southward down along the border, but not in Valverde or El Paso.

When he awakened next morning, he felt fully rested and as hungry as a bear fresh out of his den in the springtime. By the time he got down to the restaurant — and he avoided the Palace now that he was alone and could dine where he chose — there was streaky sunshine across the azure skies. Valverde looked pleasant and substantial and well shaded in broad daylight. It also looked dusty even though this was not yet full summer.

When Cleve finished breakfast and returned to the front roadway, he saw a large, thick man approaching from the north part of town, and was interested only because the large man wore a constable's badge on his vest front. They nodded because their glances crossed, then the constable headed on into the café, and that was somewhat reassuring. If the local lawman himself ate in the café Cleve had just emerged from, the café had to have something in its favor besides just ordinary food.

A range man walked his horse northward up Main Street on his way out of town. Cleve watched with veiled interest because that horseman had been Twenty-One. Presumably the other two men had already ridden out. Twenty-One McKinnon did not look at Cleve, except in a glancing manner just once, the same as he gazed elsewhere among the people upon the early morning plank walks. Cleve grunted to himself and turned.

Later, when Cleve was at the livery barn looking in on his saddle animal, he again encountered the local lawman. When he went out front to stand in shade, the lawman also came out there, and this time the constable grinned, shook his head a trifle ruefully, and said: "Mister, either I'm turning into your shadow or you're turning into mine." He extended a large hand. "I'm Tom Porter, constable hereabouts."

"Bob Warner," lied Cleve Hampshire. "Been loafing around the Valverde countryside for a few days. It's a nice town."

"For a fact," stated Constable Porter, looking up the roadway where tree shade was already, this early in the day, providing coolness. Porter turned back. "You don't look like no range man, Mister Warner."

"Cattle buyer, Constable. Cattle and horses. Mules I make a specialty of, but they tell me in all the Valverde countryside there aren't more'n half a handful of mules."

"Not much need for 'em," conceded Tom Porter. "It's mostly all done in this country by horseback. Even the wagons don't use mules much."

"Pity," mourned Cleve Hampshire. "There's no horse alive can outpull, outthink, nor outperform a good strong mule, Mister Porter. And you can work cattle off their backs. Don't believe what folks tell you about that. I've done it plenty of times, just to prove mules make as good saddle stock for working around, as horses make."

The constable yawned behind his hand and looked up and down his roadway again as though he should be somewhere else. "It was nice talkin' to you," he said.

Cleve agreed. "Yeah, nice to meet you. By the way, some fellers offered to sell me a bunch of horses south of here a couple days back, Constable. I'm new to the area, so I didn't know any of the brands, but they didn't all come from one outfit . . . I was just wonderin'. In my business it don't pay to turn up in some town and buy horses that'll turn out to be stolen. You show up

with stolen horses where folks don't know you ..."
Cleve grinned at the heavy man.

Constable Porter listened with interest, then made a little deprecatory gesture. "Probably was all right, Mister Warner. If they hit you up in broad daylight, it was probably a plumb legitimate matter. Lots of folks buy and sell livestock hereabouts. We got some mighty big and successful cow outfits in these parts, and, when horses commence to go downhill just a little, it don't pay 'em to keep the critters. It was most likely a plumb legitimate offer." Again the large man looked around, and this time he also began moving off. "I'll see you around town, Mister Warner," he said, and smiled as he moved away.

Behind Cleve in the cool, dark doorway of the livery barn a rough-voiced day man said: "Mister, he told you the plumb truth ... big cattle ranches hereabouts don't keep a horse if he just begins to hang in the bit a little more'n he'd ought to."

Cleve turned and studied the raffish, lined, and weathered face of the short, wiry man in the front barn opening. The hostler looked to be sixty, at least, but he was supple and sinewy and otherwise seemingly ageless. He had a sort of perpetual grin, a variety of fixed pleasant expressions that had probably never had enough spontaneity to look genuine, but most certainly did not look genuine now after so many years of daily use.

Cleve Hampshire's impression of the lawman was that Tom Porter was bear-like, able to keep the peace, otherwise none too observant, and lazy. His impression of the wiry little livery barn day man was not that neutral. If a man had ever existed who looked like a weasel in the face, it was the hostler. Everything about the man rang just a shade off key. He looked sly and devious and habitually dishonest.

Cleve smiled at the man and said: "Maybe I should have bought those horses, then, but right now I'm more in the market for mules."

"Not around Valverde," stated the day man. "I'll bet there ain't fifty, sixty right worthwhile good mules in the whole countryside. But horses . . . Mister, if you figure to stay around Valverde for long and got to make a living like most of us, you'd do better to forget the mules and get into the horse business."

Cleve accepted this gravely by nodding his head and saying: "You'd ought to know, friend. But it's a pity these folks don't have more mules. Well, if I'd bought those horses the other day, where would I have been able to pen 'em up?"

The day man jerked his thumb. "Out back there is a set of public corrals." He widened his perpetual and insincere smile. "Feed's cheap this time of year, too. Mister, I'd guess you went and missed the opportunity of your lifetime when you got skittery about them horses."

"Maybe," conceded Cleve. "But like I said, friend, I'm new to the area and for all I know you got rustlers operating out of every lousy cañon. I sure didn't like the notion of getting lynched because folks don't know me and I'm trailing along a few head of horses that got brands on 'em they shouldn't have." Cleve paused, then said: "You mean to tell me you folks don't have any rustling around Valverde?"

The hostler sucked his teeth for a moment, then spat aside before answering. "Every now and then someone turns up short a few head. Yeah, we got 'em just like every other area's got 'em. But like Constable Porter said, them wouldn't have been real horse thieves or they sure wouldn't still have been around here in broad daylight."

Cleve straightened up to move off. "Well, I'm not feeling too good about having missed that chance, so I'll amble on up to the saloon for an early morning pick-me-up." He nodded at the hostler and walked off. Behind him, the day man looked almost pityingly after Cleve Hampshire, fairly well convinced that he had just talked to a genuine fool.

The warmth arrived, finally, and it was just a shade more noticeable today than it had been yesterday or the day before. Summer was on its way.

CHAPTER
FIVE

Over a period of a week McKinnon, Holt, and Glasser reported in the night to the porch of the rooming house. Twenty-One and Levi had found riding jobs but Barney Glasser hadn't even been able to get hired on as a cook's helper. But he shrugged this off as he and Cleve Hampshire sat in darkness the last day of the week, discussing things in general.

"Maybe it's just as well," he opined. "It gives me a chance to do a lot of ridin' over the territory while I'm lookin' for work. So far I've discovered that a cowman by the name of Caldwell is sneaking out at night and riding over to see a widow woman named Hedges who owns a nearby ranch, and I've seen three range men who work for a cowman named Brinkley sneak out of the bunkhouse after all the lights are out and ride up into some foothills where they're setting up a still." Glasser smiled, his natural darkness coupled with the gloom of the rooming-house porch emphasizing the whiteness of his teeth. "Maybe, sooner or later, I'll come across a bunch of fellers sneakin' off with a band of someone's livestock."

The basic idea was good and Cleve said so. "All right, now that you've established yourself as a feller in search of work, just do that . . . just keep on riding and nosing around."

"There is something else," said Barney. "Just before heading for town this evening, I picked up the dust of a pretty fair-sized band of riders coming inland from the west of here."

"What of that?" asked Cleve.

"Well, if it's a herd of cattle being brought in . . . there wasn't enough dust. If it's a bunch of riders returning from a rails' end drive . . . it's too early for that. But maybe if it's something else, like raiders approaching ahead of dusk, why that ought to be interesting."

Cleve privately assumed Barney was reaching for a straw, but since he had nothing more substantial than a hunch, he said: "Go have a look in the morning."

Glasser was agreeable. "Figured to. What's interesting here in town?"

"Not a blessed thing," replied Cleve, "except that I think I got the constable convinced I'm a harmless sort of timid mule trader."

Barney looked around. "Mule trader? This is horse country from here to Abilene and back."

"Yeah I know," replied Cleve. "That's the idea. What's more harmless than someone who doesn't belong in the area where they're visiting?"

Barney sighed, shoved up to his feet, and asked about Holt and McKinnon.

"Both been hired, one on the east range, one off to the west of here. They were in earlier in the week . . . with nothing."

"You know," stated Barney thoughtfully, "maybe what we're lookin' for starts out from right here. From town. I realize the *riders* will almost likely come from the range, but it seems to me whoever is head Indian probably lives here in town."

"Maybe," said Cleve, also rising. "And maybe he lives at one of the ranches. Barney, keep lookin' and when you come up with anything . . . all right?"

They parted, Glasser to hike quietly around the side of the rooming house where he'd left his horse, and Cleve Hampshire to his room down the hall.

For Barney, who had no sensation of urgency, the ride back out to where he could make a night camp was pleasant because it was a warm, star-bright night. To Cleve, who got exasperated earlier than many men because he liked action, performance, the kinds of things anyone responsible for a success or a failure needed, this past week had been practically a total waste. He knew Valverde, and his men knew the cattle ranges beyond Valverde, but that was nothing of much importance, and he had known a family named Chavez up here for several years. Had, in fact, been out at the Chavez place when he'd first got word that Captain Tomlinson wanted to see him in town.

He went to bed with doubts, not about his ability to ferret something out, and not about the ability of McKinnon, Holt, and Glasser to perform their duties, but doubt that any such thing as an organized rustling combine existed.

He rose the next morning about to be convinced that some such connection did exist. He had finished breakfast and was outside in the thin warmth of post-dawn watching the town dray team haul the Valverde water wagon through, its drilled out lead pipe in back distributing a heavy spray of water over the dust to make the roadway damp enough to keep down the dust at least until about noon. He saw a ranch outfit jostling along accompanied by several horsemen, approaching town from the west, and over in front of the way station a hostler wheeled a mud wagon out and set the brake, climbed down, and handed the lines to a gun guard while the driver sauntered forth tugging on his gauntlets. Coach drivers were still "knights of the road". It was a glamorous occupation to small boys, and a great many who were not so small.

The water wagon went past, leaving the air smelling fresh. That elegant driver with his silver-ferruled drover's whip retrieved the lines and climbed to his high seat. The gun guard also climbed up there, but he was, for some reason, a much more drab individual than the whip.

Farther out, to the west, that escorted wagon got a little closer, and, as a man strolled forth behind Cleve from the café to ply his toothpick and also look out and around, he said: "Well, hell, that's one of the Brinkley outfit wagons. It's sure as hell awful early in the day for them to be comin' for supplies."

Cleve was indifferent. There was no special reason why some cow outfit couldn't dispatch riders and a wagon this early for . . . riders? He stared out there. Four horsemen were accompanying the supply wagon. *That* was unusual, unless the wagon was loaded with something very valuable, and Cleve could not imagine what that could be.

The water wagon turned off down by the livery barn and lumbered out of sight along the south wall of the barn. The mud wagon — called a stagecoach even by folks who knew better — finally responded to the high whistle of the driver. It only had two passengers, a pair of traveling salesmen, but on down the road it would probably pick up more people.

Cleve and the man behind him did not move as the transport vehicle went past with chain harness hanging loose and musically rattling. There was an ordinance against drivers busting out their hitches through town, even when the road had just been freshly damped down so they wouldn't stir clouds of dust.

The man behind Cleve said: "Sure a lot tamer than they were when I was a lad. You could hear whips and their rigs all over town and folks got a big thrill out of the way they arrived in a gallop and pulled out the same way. Darned shame, what's happened to people since those days."

Cleve turned. The speaker was Tom Porter, the constable. Cleve turned back to watching the mud wagon as it approached Valverde's lower environs. The whip was readying his hitch to break away. There was no need for speed, but there *was* a need for a member of a proud, colorful brotherhood to show townsfolk just how a stage should be led out of a town.

Westerly, those four horsemen and their wagon were swinging up and around so as to enter town by the north roadway, off the grasslands. Cleve paid little attention to this for a moment because the whip made his keening cry, cracked his whip, and the mud wagon lurched ahead in a spine-cracking lunge.

Constable Porter chuckled. "Darned near flung those salesmen out through the back," he said.

Cleve turned in response to the whistle of one of those horsemen. He had pulled ahead of his companions and was slow-loping on down the roadway in the direction of the café. Evidently at least one of those range men up there had good enough eyes to pick out Constable Porter standing out front of the café.

The rider kept his horse's head tucked up just right, kept his animal in its proper lead, and came rocketing along exactly like a centaur, more a part of his mount, than an individual separate from it. He turned in, dropped his reins, and looked past Cleve. "Tom, we got a bad hurt feller in the rig."

Constable Porter was equal to this occasion. "Get him down to Doc Henrickson. I'll be along directly."

"You better come now," said the bronzed, gray-eyed rider. "It don't look like this feller's goin' to make it. We was bringin' in the remuda and heard the distant gunshot, and got saddled to ride out and investigate."

Tom Porter said: "Shot? This feller was shot?"

The cowboy nodded. "Through the lights, and he's out of it about half the time. In and out of it. Like I said, maybe you'd ought to come along. So far he ain't told us nothing, but, like I just said, he drifts back and forth between bein' conscious and unconscious." The rider fished in a saddlebag and leaned to pass something over. "Mister Brinkley said to give you this.

43

We taken it out of the hurt feller's pants pocket. Mister Brinkley said it ought to interest you."

Cleve saw the badge drop onto the marshal's palm. Cleve's breath stopped in his chest. He recognized the badge, did not know whose carcass it had been taken off of, but as the wagon came slowly down the roadway, Cleve walked out into the damp roadway.

The man on the wagon seat looked blankly at Cleve Hampshire, but he drew back the lines a little because Constable Porter was also approaching, along with that lanky bronzed cowboy who had come on ahead.

It was Barney Glasser. Cleve looked steadily downward and Barney gazed upward. Their eyes met and held, then Barney's head rolled slightly to one side.

There was a bandage around Glasser's chest, crude and loose, but at least cleaner than his shirt would have been. His black hair and swarthy features looked even darker under the new day paleness upon a light blanket someone at Brinkley's ranch had put under him.

Tom Porter looked, and leaned upon the sideboards and scowled. "I think I've seen this feller," he said slowly. "Seems to me I saw him around town a week or so back."

The bronzed horseman made a dry comment. "If you keep him lyin' here much longer, Tom, you won't have to worry about ever seeing him again." Without additional comment the range rider jerked his head for the wagon man to drive onward.

Cleve stood out there as the little cavalcade headed on a diagonal course for a small house midway along that sat back a few yards behind a white picket fence.

There was a small shingle hanging beside the name that said, *Jerome A. Henrickson, M.D.* The lettering was in gold and had been very elegantly scrolled. That sign, in fact, had cost Dr. Henrickson a bottle of good whiskey fifteen years earlier, and three years earlier he had signed the death certificate of the talented wastrel who had made the sign for him. If a man had two livers like he had two lungs and eyes and a lot of other things, he could drink twice as much and take twice as long to kill himself with drinking.

Cleve went back to the eastside plank walk, rolled a cigarette, and from time to time raised his eyes to watch Constable Porter and the other men very carefully lift Barney Glasser out past the tailgate of the old ranch wagon, and start through the picket fence with him.

The man in the doorway, fully dressed but looking a little less than wide awake yet, and who called instructions to the men carrying Barney, was tall and raw-boned with a full head of gray hair and a lined, long face. As a medical doctor he was as good as people wanted him to be because he was the only medical man northeast of El Paso who was also a surgeon.

Cleve lit up and walked over to sit upon a bench out front of the jailhouse. He could not very well go down there and just shoulder his way in. Barney would get the best possible care whether Cleve was down there with him or not.

When Tom Porter returned to his office at the jailhouse building, Cleve would get the first-hand account, which he very badly wanted.

It seemed that they finally had their opening in this rustling assignment throughout the Valverde countryside, but at a hell of a cost. If it all went this way, that doctor down the road would have a houseful, directly.

CHAPTER
SIX

All Tom Porter told Cleve was that the wound would probably not prove fatal — at least that was Dr. Henrickson's guess.

"How did he get shot?" Cleve wanted to know, and the lawman simply shook his head. "Didn't tell me, exactly, except to say he was ridin' out of a dry camp early this morning and someone up and shot him off his horse, then, when he rolled over waitin' for them to come up and finish the job, they never arrived. That's all. Interesting, isn't it?"

Cleve agreed. "Yeah, interesting as all hell. What kind of a country you got hereabouts, a man can't ride through, some son-of-a-bitch don't dump him out of his saddle?"

"Like any other country," stated the lawman imperturbably. "You go nosing around where folks don't think you got a right . . . and bang!"

Cleve had to be satisfied with this. At least he had to give the appearance that he was satisfied with it in order to continue the charade he and his associates had embarked upon, so he left the constable and went over to the saloon that was opposite the stage stop.

The bar man over there didn't know anything at all, which was a surprise. Ordinarily barmen in a cow town knew more gossip than anyone else. The difficulty, apparently, was that this particular shooting had happened too recently. It was still early morning, and at breakfast time saloons did not do any business at all.

Later, Cleve got saddled up down at the livery barn and rode out over the westerly range. He asked no directions, nor did he have to, the tracks of those steel wagon tires were the best of all guides when a man chose not to have a companion.

He had a fair idea when he reached Brinkley range. The brand on the animals he saw was a big Circle B on the right ribs. He eventually topped a rim and saw the sprawling structures, corrals, and holding pastures down below in a big meadow. There were old poplars around the buildings, suggesting that the Brinkley ranch was old, along with being successful and well established.

He reined back down the near side of the rim and made a big half circle around the headquarters place, then tried to guess about where Barney had been shot using what little information that Brinkley rider had offered out front of the café at breakfast time. It was difficult. For one thing there were shod horse tracks everywhere on this westerly range, as though perhaps the Brinkley outfit was working this particular part of their grasslands.

Cleve sashayed back and forth, abandoning all hope of being able to backtrack the men who had located Barney after the shooting, and went instead in search of a fresh camp with, hopefully, char and the other elements of a recent layover.

He found such a place almost two miles southwest of the Brinkley Ranch headquarters, found where hobbled horses wearing shoes had cropped the grass short, and found where several bedrolls and the men who had slept in them had pressed the grass flat. What he never found, though, was the spot where someone had been shot off his horse, and maybe he wasn't being realistic to expect to find this place even though the Brinkley riders had found it, obviously, and had left their imprints. He abandoned this aspect of his investigation, went back where the group of riders had night camped, picked up their sign, and rode slowly along on the same course.

Once, he saw a horseman top a low land swell and sit Indian-like, motionless and wary, watching each step Cleve took for at least a half mile. Then the stranger turned back and dropped from sight down the back of the low land swell. He could have been one of the men who had shot Barney, in which case Cleve might shortly also encounter hostility. The impression Cleve had got over all that intervening distance was that the watcher on the land swell had been a range man, probably a Brinkley rider.

The horsemen Cleve was shagging went on a direct course into the northeast as though they knew exactly where they were going. If they were the men Cleve suspected they were, it was probable that they knew this entire grassland as well as the men who rode it every day and who owned it. What particularly intrigued Cleve Hampshire was the individual identity of those men, and where they were going. As far as Cleve knew, there were no more towns or villages hereabouts, which left the destination of those riders either some particular campsite they enjoyed, or a ranch, and if they were heading for a ranch . . .

He swung left and right keeping close watch as he rode. He also avoided tree clumps, arroyos, and those rolling ridges of land that increasingly dotted the upper range the closer one got to the distant foothills and their correspondingly more distant, and more impressive, rearward mountains. He came across the stage road and knew he was due northward of Valverde, but how *far* northward he could only guess. Then he saw a pair of riders east of the roadway watching his progress from the heavy dark shade of a thick clump of old trees. He might never have seen them except that a horse threw its head and in all this immensity of silence and stillness any kind of movement was instantly noticeable. He did not even hesitate, but reined southward as soon as he reached the roadway and plodded along back down in the direction of Valverde. He knew all he had to know for the time being, and, if he could dupe those watchers into believing he was just some range man or saddle tramp whose destination had never been anything but the southward roadway, so much the better.

As for the pair of watchers — it must have been from some very similar situation that strangers had emptied Barney Glasser's saddle.

By the time he got back to town and went down the westside alley to the livery barn to hand over his horse for care, there were long shadows in the streaked sky, and Cleve Hampshire was hungry.

He ate a little early, had a beer at the saloon in order to pick up any fresh gossip, found nothing he was interested in, and went along to the rooming-house porch to sit and smoke, and ponder.

Sooner or later Twenty-One McKinnon and Levi Holt were going to pick up something about a stranger being bushwhacked west of the Brinkley home place, and, if Tom Porter wanted the information to be leaked about that stranger carrying a Ranger badge, Levi and Twenty-One were also going to hear that.

What happened was that neither Holt nor McKinnon had heard anything because they arrived in Valverde after nightfall the same day that Cleve had done his backtracking, the same day Barney had been shot. They converged upon the rooming-house porch almost simultaneously, and, when Cleve told them what had happened, neither of them had anything to say for a while, then Twenty-One made a laconic observation. "If those fellers were crossing diagonally across Brinkley, and across the roadway toward the north country range, they had to be heading into the foothills, which is where I been riding after lost horses for the past few days. If they'd shoot Barney, someone they didn't even know, what would they do to a man riding for one of the cow outfits up close to those same damned foothills?"

Levi answered that. "Maybe nothing. Maybe they knew Barney wasn't supposed to be out where they run into him." Levi looked over at Cleve. "Did they go through his pockets afterward?"

"Just shot him and rode away," said Cleve. "At least that's what the local lawman told me this morning."

"Well," stated Levi a little skeptically, "that local lawman, for your information, Cleve, used to have a kind of bad reputation in these parts. That was years back, and folks said he was a bully and a troublemaker. I picked this up from the range boss of the cow outfit I ride for. The range boss has been around here long enough to remember Porter when he was trouble any way a man approached him." Levi looked at the other two men out there alone with him on the porch in the darkness, and said: "I'm not saying this means anything . . . I'm simply telling you what was told me. And I'm thinking maybe we just might run into more darned rattlesnakes than we can shake a stick at."

Cleve acknowledged this possibility with a dry remark. "We didn't take on this assignment expecting it to be a lot different than it's turning out to be. Twenty-One? Can you scout through those foothills in the next few days?"

McKinnon had his long legs upon the porch railing. "Yeah, I expect I can make a scout up through there, and, knowing there might be danger, I'll be forewarned." As though the prospect of also being bushwhacked no longer worried him very much, Twenty-One then said: "You been down to see Barney?"

Cleve hadn't. "Been in the saddle all day. The doctor told Constable Porter that Barney would make it."

Twenty-One was unwilling to accept this. "We can all three of us go down there right now. I know where the doctor's place is. Two of us can stay outside while you sort of ease inside and get it first-hand for Levi and me before we head back."

Cleve shrugged and rose, but motioned for the other two men to precede him, and go down the eastside rear alleyway. They understood and departed. So far there was no particular reason why the three of them should not be seen together, especially at night when no one would give them a second glance, but Cleve still chose for it to be this way and Cleve was head honcho.

The town was quiet except at the saloon opposite the stage station, and its brilliance and noise was subdued in comparison to what it would be at the end of the week as Cleve walked past.

A panhandling drunk stepped from a recessed doorway with his hand rising. The man was almost entirely sobered by what happened. Cleve only saw someone coming at him from the darkness, right hand rising. Cleve came down upon the balls of his feet twisting sideways and drawing at the same time. The panhandler saw the gun, heard the hammer snap back, and couldn't even breathe for several seconds, then he quavered a plea. "Mister, I aint even armed. I don't have no gun at all, mister. Christ Amighty, I was just going to ask for a nickel for a glass of beer."

Cleve hung poised to kill and only gradually loosened his stance, eventually easing off the gun hammer. "You damned idiot," he growled at the panhandler. "I ought to knock your head off." He turned and strolled onward without once glancing back.

The panhandler was as sober as he had been in days. More sober, in fact, as he turned to go toward the saloon. He had seen the constable walk in there a while back, and it was in his mind that any lawman ought to be willing to pay a nickel to know there was a man walking the roadway of his town who could draw a gun faster than lightning.

Cleve did not get over being angry even after he got down to the doctor's place, swung through the picket gate, and went up to knock lightly. When the tall, gaunt older man opened up and peered testily out, Cleve said: "I'd like to see that cowboy you got in here who got shot through the chest this morning."

"Would you now," growled the tall old scarecrow of a man.

"And when is he supposed to get his rest . . . when you other saddle tramps decide not to bother him?"

Cleve reached high with a powerful grip and eased the taller, thinner man back steadily as he walked in out of the night and kicked the door closed after himself. "Mister, I just had a bad scare up the road a piece, and right now I'm just not in any mood for arguments." Cleve released the tall old man and gave him a light shove. "Lead the way."

Dr. Henrickson adjusted his shirt and vest and glared. "For two-bits I'd arrange to have you spend the night in the *calabozo*, mister. Who the hell do you think you are, pushing folks around in their own . . . ?"

"Which door?" asked Cleve. "Doctor, I don't have all night. I didn't mean to push you around, but I had my reasons. Now . . . just lead the way, will you, please?"

Jerome Henrickson was a good judge of men. He finished adjusting his attire as he turned and went stalking, stork-like, through the lighted parlor to a somewhat dingy, long corridor, and entered a lighted room where Barney Glasser's swarthiness was again accentuated by the sheets and other white objects of the room.

The doctor flung back the door and stepped aside for Cleve to enter. Instead, Cleve edged over closer and sort of brushed the doctor ahead of him on into the room before closing the door.

Barney watched from the bed with candid interest.

CHAPTER
SEVEN

Dr. Henrickson was a man who had long been experienced in deductive philosophy. There were very few good doctors who had not been trained in this and who had not in their ensuing years continued to develop it. Henrickson studied the shorter, powerfully put together man who had forced him to go along to the sick man's room with frank and shrewd interest. He seemed to resent Cleve Hampshire less and less, and to become more and more concerned as Cleve and the man flat on his back in bed looked at one another, and as Cleve said — "Are you making it?" — and as Barney Glasser replied dryly: "Yeah, but if the feller had been a little better shot, I wouldn't."

"Where did it happen?" asked Cleve.

"Southwest of the Brinkley Ranch headquarters, about a mile or so just outside a clump of trees. He was in there waiting for me. I saw him, but not in time. Saw early light reflected along his gun barrel, and started to drop down as he fired." Barney paused to gaze enquiringly at the medical practitioner; this got his attention drawn back to Cleve when Hampshire asked another question. "How many of them were in the camp?"

56

"Six," replied Barney. "I scouted them up before daylight and was leaving when this one evidently spotted me and ducked ahead to lay his ambush." Barney smiled. "Funny thing . . . there was never any pain, Cleve. Just felt like I'd had all the wind knocked out of me, and afterward it was kind of hard to take a deep breath." Again Barney glanced in the doctor's direction, but this time the medical man had a comment.

"Luck, young man, pure luck . . . and maybe the fact that you anticipated it and were dropping down." Dr. Henrickson looked quizzically from one of them to the other one. "You are *both* Rangers," he said. "I saw the badge they took off this injured man. Constable Porter has it." His bold, shrewd old eyes lingered longest on Cleve Hampshire. "Both of you are Rangers."

Cleve offered no refutation. "You resent the law, is that it?" he asked, and got a surprised look from the tall older man.

"Resent it? What kind of a stupid thing is that to say to a man who spent four years . . . lacking four days . . . upholding the best of Constitutional law?"

Barney didn't understand. "You were a Ranger?"

Dr. Henrickson snorted. "No. I was a physician and surgeon in the Union Army. *That* was upholding the law in the biggest and best test of the law this nation has ever had. And now you come along and say I'm against the law!"

Cleve's retort was blunt. "I apologize, Doctor. I was plumb wrong."

Henrickson accepted the apology in stride. "But that is still the truth, isn't it? You are both Rangers . . . not just the one in bed."

"Both," conceded Cleve cryptically. "Who do you have in mind telling, Doctor?"

"Who says I have to tell anyone?" demanded the older man. "Sonny, in my trade you carry more secrets and have less reason to divulge any of them than a priest." He gestured. "Go ahead, talk to him and get it over with, because he's got to get his rest."

Cleve looked long at the gaunt big old man, and decided he could safely gamble. He turned toward the bed again. "What did you make out about them?" he asked, referring to the strangers again.

"Not a hell of a lot except that there were six of them, they came up from the southwest, and were heading northeasterly on a diagonal course across the uninhabited part of the range west a few miles from the Brinkley place. I couldn't get in close enough to see the brands on their horses and it was too damned dark when I scouted them up to see men's faces. But I'll guess it's not local range men after all who are doing the raiding and rustling, Cleve. I'll guess it's this bunch . . . and, if you go man-hunting, for gosh sakes don't get within rifle range of them. That bunch shoots first and looks afterward."

"They didn't look," stated Cleve. "They didn't go any closer once they'd dumped you. But it don't make much sense. They didn't go up afterward and see who they'd shot. Why in hell shoot a man at all, when it was too dark for them to make him out properly?"

"Because," put in the doctor, "there was someone in their territory who was not supposed to be there."

Barney was less convinced of this probability than the doctor was. "Hell, Doc, there is always someone out where they aren't supposed to be."

"Not," stated the doctor, "in the territory of men who value life not at all, which evidently is the case with whoever shot you."

Cleve waited until this small argument subsided to add his observation. "For some damned reason you were a danger to them, Barney. It had to be one hell of a peril. Men who are entering a critical territory who don't want to be seen or investigated don't shoot people. There's no better way under the sun to bring out the law."

"If," Barney said, "the law ever went out on things like bushwhacks."

"He'll go," stated Dr. Henrickson. "Grant you he may be a few days getting out to make an investigation, but Tom Porter is conscientious . . . he's just not ambitious or eager."

"How about honest?" asked Cleve.

Dr. Henrickson's shrewd eyes narrowed slightly. "You've been asking questions and listening to tales," he said. "All right, I've heard the same stories and maybe in his youth Tom was obnoxious. But I've known Tom Porter for eleven years now and I've yet to see him do anything bullying or vicious. His biggest vice now is that he is lazy." Henrickson's attitude, changed a little. "My personal feelings toward Tom Porter are simply basic. He's helped me and I've helped him, and otherwise he's a good man to play a little poker with, to have a nightcap with, to swap lies with."

"How about co-operate with a rustling syndicate?" asked Cleve, and saw the look of mild surprise cross Dr. Henrickson's features.

"What syndicate?" asked the doctor. "No, Tom wouldn't do it. What kind of a syndicate are you talking about?"

Cleve pointed. "The kind that got this man shot, Doctor, and that's all you've got to know." Cleve turned toward the bed again. "Barney, lie low, get your rest, and damn you anyway . . . the next time you see sunlight off a gun barrel, drop faster."

Cleve went back to the parlor followed by Dr. Henrickson. At the door as they exchanged a look, Cleve said: "You don't have to tell Tom Porter I was here tonight, or who I am. But if you *do* tell him, Doctor, you'd better make up some beds down here because they're sure as hell going to get filled up." Cleve walked out of the house and closed the door after himself, then turned to glance left and right before walking down the little pathway and out through the picket gate northward in the direction of the rooming house, except that he only got as far as the first wall bench in the utter blackness out front of the general store. Levi and Twenty-One were waiting there.

Levi said — "How does he look?" — and got a curt answer.

"About like you'd look if you'd been shot through the chest."

"How does he feel?" asked McKinnon.

"Good," reported Cleve. "In fact, he's in a lot better condition than I figured he might be in." Cleve reached to start rolling a smoke. The roadway was empty in both directions except for some slight activity up in front of Valverde's most popular saloon, and that was a considerable distance from where the three men were quietly talking in darkness out front of the general store. "The constable is lazy," reported Cleve, "and I'd guess this is general knowledge. Also, according to the doctor, he is honest, but doctors are no different from the rest of us about being mistaken."

"Except that they can bury their mistakes," growled Twenty-One, who evidently was one of those people who had little use for doctors. Twenty-One rose. "I'm going to head back." He looked from Cleve to Levi and back to Cleve again. "As soon as I've got something about someone riding into the northeasterly foothills . . . ," he said, and never completed it as a gunshot erupted down by Henrickson's house, but around back, as though it had been fired in either the rear alley or perhaps in the yard out behind the cottage.

All three Rangers moved simultaneously, and, because Twenty-One McKinnon was the tallest with the least weight and the longest legs, he led the full distance. But Twenty-One did not veer in through the picket gate. He slid to a halt pointing down where someone was running southward, then swore and resumed the foot race, but this time with a drawn Colt in his hand.

Cleve barked to Levi Holt: "Back him up!" Then Cleve alone turned in and strode swiftly to the door, but this time he did not bother to knock; he leaned a powerful shoulder, twisted the knob, and barged straight on into the parlor. Down that dingy corridor there was a blaze of light coming from the open door of Barney Glasser's room. As Cleve started ahead a man's garrulous voice said: "Well, he's still a lousy shot."

Cleve filled the doorway. Dr. Henrickson's back was to him as Henrickson worked over the man in the bed. Cleve said — "What happened?" — and, as though Jerome Henrickson had known he was back there, the doctor replied tartly: "What did it sound like happened? Someone tried to blow your friend's head off through the back yard window, that's what happened."

Cleve walked ahead. Barney was all right, but the pillow and the headboard of the bed were ruined. Barney was sipping something in a shot glass that could have been medicine but that looked suspiciously like whiskey to Cleve Hampshire.

Dr. Henrickson finished gathering the torn pillow slip as he turned to glower. "These pillows filled with genuine goose down are very hard to come by. Anyone can get the ones filled with duck down." He turned carefully to put aside the ruined pillow and to turn back holding a new one. "This one has duck down. If I'd thought something like this might happen, I'd have put the one with duck down under your friend's head in the first place."

Barney grinned. "If that son-of-a-bitch don't get me before I get out of here, Cleve, I'm going to hunt him down if it takes a year."

It was a warm night. Cleve walked to the window. The glass portion had been raised to admit as much cool night air as possible. Cleve leaned and poked his head through, looking out into the black, quiet yard. Two gunshots sounded, one slightly ahead of the other one. This exchange had taken place southward. Cleve pulled back and turned to find both Barney and Dr. Henrickson looking at him. He shrugged, did not speak a word, and stalked back through to the parlor, then out to the sidewalk, and turned briskly southward.

So far, there was not a soul in sight up the north roadway. Prudence sometimes emptied roadways and kept them emptied when men with cocked revolvers were roaming through a town.

Levi called quietly: "Here, Cleve! Over here."

Twenty-One was reloading about fifteen feet from a man lying on his back in the weak and watery star shine. The dead man's Colt was lying nearby and Cleve retrieved it without asking any questions. One empty casing was beneath the firing pin. Cleve shoved the gun into his waistband and leaned. "Grab his arms," he said, "and let's go up the back alley with him to the yard where he tried to bushwhack Barney. I'm beginning to get an idea about this. I want Barney to look at this feller."

Levi and Twenty-One hoisted the corpse at the opposite end from Cleve and dutifully began marching down through to the eastside alley, then they turned up it making a unique three-man procession carrying a limp dead man.

Over on Main Street someone called out that they could not see anyone down the roadway, and a second man called back for them to keep on looking, that someone had to be down there, unless neither one of those people who had fired could hit the broad side of a barn. Gradually, now that enough time had passed for whatever had occurred down below the doctor's place to have fully ended, more and more men ventured forth. But there was nothing down there.

In the morning people would find blood on the plank walk, but by then it would be too late to do much about it.

CHAPTER
EIGHT

Dr. Henrickson looked flabbergasted as three stalwart men pushed their way into his cottage from out back, lugging a very limp, very dead individual with them. He mistakenly thought they had brought him someone to be cared for and would have led them to a separate examination room, but Cleve Hampshire, who knew the way, steered his friends down to the room occupied by Barney Glasser, shoved back the door, and said: "You recognize this feller?"

Barney rolled his head and tried to raise up a little. "Come closer," he ordered.

Cleve, Levi, and Twenty-One hauled their inert burden into better light and Barney said: "By God, yes . . . that's Perry Stockton."

Dr. Henrickson leaned to make a cursory examination while the corpse was being held suspended.

Twenty-One growled: "Doc, he's dead. You see that hole in the middle of his brisket? He's dead. No one gets up and walks away from one like that."

Barney leaned for a still better look. "Is *that* who tried to wing me through the window?" he asked.

Cleve nodded. "Same one. Levi and Twenty-One chased him."

Twenty-One leaned to lower the dead weight to the floor. "He's heavier than he looks," Twenty-One mumbled, then straightened up and smiled. "You look good, Barney. Yeah, this is the feller and he tried to make a battle of it when I ran up behind him. He got off one round on the fly and I stopped to aim." Twenty-One shrugged. "Too late to explain to him that you can't do your best shooting twisting around while you're running."

"That son-of-a-bitch," said Barney Glasser, dark eyes brightening a little more all the while. "Hell, *that's* who it was. I should have guessed when he waylaid me out yonder on Brinkley's range. It was Perry sure as the Lord made green apples."

Cleve, who had figured this out earlier while gazing down at the dead man, had a question. "Why, Barney? What are you to him that the moment he recognized you even in the lousy pre-dawn light, he had to risk his life to kill you. Why?"

"Goes back six years to when I was on the border below Eagle Pass," explained the man in the bed. "He and his brother and a Mex named Valdez had a little horse-stealing business going for them. I got it out of the Mex what they were doing and showed up on our side of the line as they came through on the run. In the fight that followed I killed his brother and took him prisoner when I dropped the horse under him." Barney sighed and leaned back. "By God, I didn't see him with those six men in the pre-dawn morning."

"Well," said Cleve dryly, "he sure as hell saw you. Maybe he figured you were riding for some cow outfit up here, but, whatever else he thought, he sure thought about evening the score."

Twenty-One said: "Let's get out of here before the whole blasted town comes a-looking." Twenty-One smiled tentatively at Dr. Henrickson. "You got any need for a used carcass, Doc?"

Henrickson sniffed. "Just go. All three of you just get out of here."

Cleve hesitated. "What about the body? Doctor, there are still five more of these outlaws, and right now we don't want the town . . . least of all your own constable . . . to know anything they don't have to know."

"I'll look after the corpse for you," said Henrickson. "Now go. How long do you suppose it'll be before half the town is all around looking for you, including Constable Porter? Just go and keep on going!"

Cleve led the way out back. From a dilapidated arbor the three of them stood in blackness watching a small group of noisy townsmen go plodding past, southward, out in the alleyway. The townsmen were armed with rifles, carbines, shotguns, and also with belt guns.

Levi Holt leaned to whisper: "How about that sawbones?"

Cleve reassured them both. He personally had faith in Jerome Henrickson. Right now they did not have much alternative but he was not especially worried. Cleve Hampshire was just as good a judge of men as Jerome Henrickson.

They could leave the arbor after a while and make their furtive way up the alleyway in the opposite direction. When it was possible to leave the alley at the north end of town, they aimed for the rooming house, and over there, when Cleve looked around, he was suddenly quite alone. Somewhere between the alleyway and the front of the rooming house both Levi Holt and Twenty-One McKinnon had vanished. Their patient horses were tied out there somewhere.

Cleve went to the porch, found it empty, rolled a smoke, and sat down to enjoy it. Southward there were men making a search with lanterns, and occasionally a word or two would float up where Cleve was sitting and relaxing. He had faith in the doctor. He had no clear idea as to how Dr. Henrickson would be able to dispose of that corpse, or hide it, but he had faith that Henrickson would manage somehow to keep the presence of that dead outlaw from the general knowledge of the townsmen. As for how Henrickson would handle Tom Porter, that might be something quite different, but even in that matter he had faith in the medical man.

Later, after the search had died down and only a few men were still seeking some trace of the combatants down where those gunshots had been exchanged, Cleve Hampshire retired. He had evolved an idea about the identity of the livestock thieves he wanted to apprehend, and that dead man had provided him with it. The corpse had been an outlaw by the name of Perry Stockton. Outlaws more than law-abiding people were kept track of. Wherever Perry Stockton had had his last run-in with the law, there would be a record not only of the crime Stockton had committed and where it had been committed, but also a record of the men Perry Stockton was riding with, and that was what Cleve wanted to know. He wanted to be able to name the remaining five outlaws who were evidently the night riders who did the actual driving off of all the stolen livestock.

In the morning when he ambled down to the café for breakfast, he encountered Constable Porter at the breakfast counter. The lawman looked up, nodded a trifle stiffly, and went back to his meal as Cleve straddled the bench on Porter's left side, then signaled to the café man that he was ready for breakfast. It did no good to order a particular variation of food at this or most other cow-town restaurants. For breakfast the café man prepared what he was sure his customers would eat.

Cleve turned toward Tom Porter. "I heard shooting around town last night, I think," he said, and watched the other man's color deepen a little before the lawman growled his reply.

"You'd have had to have been deaf as a post not to have heard shooting, mister."

"What was it? What happened?"

"Damned if I know," admitted the lawman. "There is dry blood some ways southward on the plank walk, but there's no body and no one has showed up around town this morning wearin' bandages. And Doc said he wasn't called out to treat anyone."

"A mystery," murmured Cleve as the vinegary-faced café man brought his breakfast platter of fried potatoes, steak, and warm applesauce, plus black coffee.

69

The constable belched softly behind a discreetly upraised hand, then gazed at Cleve Hampshire as though he disapproved of shootings being termed mysteries. "I'll find out what it was all about," he grunted, shoving up to his feet. "There is nothing at all mysterious about gunshots on Main Street in my town."

After Porter had departed, a man wearing a stained, dark apron who had been sitting southward alongside the lawman lifted tawny eyes and gazed sardonically over at Cleve. "I've known him twenty years," said the graying harness maker, or whatever he was, "and all a man's ever had to do to get his dander up is to hint there might be something he don't know about."

Cleve nodded and reached for the coffee cup. "What *was* the shooting about?"

The harness maker shrugged. He wasn't too concerned. "Damned range men mixing it, maybe, or some pepper-bellies full of *pulque* most likely squabbling over a fat *señorita*. What's the difference? There wasn't no corpse down there come sunup, just a little blood, so I'd guess someone got winged and this morning he's at home moaning more about his headache than his perforated ham or his busted darned arm."

Cleve laughed. It was early for the kind of dourness to be manifest that the harness maker seemed inherently to possess, but it tickled him anyway. He finished, paid up, and strolled out front. Valverde had a telegraph office but telegraphers were notoriously nosey. He tried to devise a way of encoding the message he wanted to send so that, if the telegrapher were indeed nosey, he wouldn't be able to bring harm upon the undercover Rangers.

In the end he strolled up to the office, and sent a message to Charley Runnels down at El Paso in which he asked for information concerning Perry Stockton. It might not pass as an innocent query, and then again it might. An examination of the telegrapher's face while he was reading the message to be transmitted showed absolutely no interest at all and to reinforce this attitude, as Cleve counted out silver coins to pay for the transmittal, he said: "Darned weasel was supposed to meet me here last week and I'll give you five-to-one odds he's still down in 'Paso with a snootful, chasing some *señorita*."

The telegrapher smiled, his first change of expression since Cleve had walked in. "There's worse things to be doing," he averred. "And there's sure as hell a lot worse places to be doin' 'em than down in 'Paso."

Cleve passed back out into the sunlight, crossed to the shady side of the roadway, and almost collided with Jerome Henrickson who was backing out of a store, still talking to the proprietor about croup medicine. Cleve waited until the doctor turned and saw him, then he walked a short distance from the doorway with Henrickson as he said: "How's the patient this morning?"

Instead of a direct answer Henrickson said: "You know how much the cabinet maker is going to charge me to repair the headboard of the bed?"

"No."

"Three dollars! Why, damnation when I was your age a man could buy a whole blessed bed for three dollars."

"You're forgetting the goose-down pillow," murmured Cleve.

Henrickson looked around and down, evidently suspecting he was being teased. Which he was. "I'll add the cost of that," he exclaimed, "to the other costs . . . which means for embalming that man who got killed last night, and also for patching up your lung-shot friend. By the way, I turned over to your friend the effects I removed from the pockets of that corpse. All right?"

Cleve nodded. "Fine. Doctor, eventually someone is going to come around asking about that corpse. No, I don't mean today or tomorrow, but sooner or later, and excepting Constable Porter I'd like to know who he is. Can you manage that?"

"Manage it? Of course I can manage it. But who is going to tell anyone, even Tom Porter, there *is* a corpse?"

"No one." Cleve smiled. "Certainly not my friends and certainly not I, but you see, that son-of-a-bitch came here with five other outlaws, and . . ."

"*Five?*"

"It'll be all right, Doctor. Yes, five other outlaws, and, when he doesn't return to wherever those men are camped, my guess is that maybe one or two of them will show up in town asking around, and if they hear there was shooting last night . . . being the kind of men they are . . . they're going to put two and two together, and hunt up the local medic and ask. You see?"

Dr. Henrickson's long stride slowed considerably as he began to grasp the implications of his co-operation with the Rangers. "I've done it again," he groaned. "I've stuck my confounded nose where it had no business, and in an effort to support the processes of law and order, I've shoved my neck into someone's noose."

They were out front of the gunsmith's shop when Henrickson said this, and, as Cleve slowed as though to take leave of his older and taller companion, he said: "Doctor, your help will make a lot of difference."

Henrickson sniffed. "That'll look very nice on my headstone," he said, and kept right on walking.

CHAPTER
NINE

For Cleve Hampshire the immediate concern was neither that dead outlaw named Stockton nor the other five outlaws, it was the individual he was confident existed, probably right under his nose in town, who would coordinate all the conditions that would make possible another successful raid on someone's horse or cattle herd.

He knew Charley Runnels would take his telegram over to Captain Tomlinson and between them they would guess what he wanted, and would in due course supply it, but in the meanwhile it was very probable someone's range was going to be swept clean, and, if this happened, all hell would probably bust loose. Maybe some of the big cow outfits had agreed to say nothing about being raided in order to facilitate the investigation currently under way, but it was asking an awful lot to expect them to go right on being meekly quiet for some indefinite period while they were raided again, and perhaps again and again.

There was a ray of hope. If those rustlers in their foothill camp got tired of waiting for their companion, Perry Stockton, to return, and went looking only to discover that Perry Stockton had completely disappeared — especially after a gunfight in town — they would probably delay any other plans they had for an excellent reason: prudence. Until they knew more of the Stockton affair, they would probably not raid someone's range.

Cleve decided he had to count on this, and, while it seemed entirely reasonable, he had been an officer of the border country law long enough in his lifetime to realize that expecting outlaws to do the reasonable thing was seldom a rewarding pastime.

He had to kill time and that always played havoc with an active man's nerves, but in this instance killing time was different than it was for Barney Glasser. Cleve was ambulatory, and, since he suspected at least one more of those rustlers would appear in town, he made a particular point each day of working out a routine that took him from the café down to the livery barn, back to the general store, then later in the day on up to the stockmen's favorite saloon.

Not that he expected to be able to recognize one of those outlaws on sight, but if a stranger arrived at the general store, for instance, and purchased a quantity of camp supplies, or if he left his ridden down horse with a strange brand on it, at the livery barn, or if he visited the saloon and bought a couple of bottles to take away with him, there was a possibility that it might pay Cleve to tag along after him when he departed from town.

The trouble was that none of these things occurred while Cleve was in any of the three major business establishments in Valverde, but he did have one interesting encounter. He was smoking a cigar out front of the café after supper one evening when Tom Porter strolled up and said: "In a town this size things come to a man's attention that might go unnoticed in a bigger place. Such as you bein' interested in that Ranger who got shot through the lights."

Cleve gazed at the lawman impassively. "Meaning?" he said.

"How many more badges like that are around my town?" replied Porter.

Cleve continued to gaze at the heavy-set man, then he laughed. "You're accusing me of being a Texas Ranger?"

"No," drawled the constable. "You're a mule trader. You told me that yourself." Porter bobbed his head and walked into the café, leaving Cleve out there smoking and speculating. There was no such thing as a complete secret, especially in Cleve Hampshire's line of work. Eventually Tom Porter and a lot of other people around Valverde would know he was indeed a badge-carrying Ranger. The ideal situation was, of course, to prevent this knowledge from becoming general information until he was ready for this to be obtained.

That night, when he crossed the road and strolled thoughtfully to the rooming-house porch and sat up there in the darkness as he'd been doing every evening since his arrival in Valverde, he was visited by Twenty-One McKinnon, and the lanky man had a report to make about a camp of strangers in the northeasterly foothills.

McKinnon, who was anything but a novice, had not gone out purposefully manhunting. He had fabricated a plausible reason for being in the foothills by first making certain that the saddle stock he was sent by his employer to locate had been chased back up through the lower country, and even then, as he deliberately and in plain sight for the first couple of miles tracked the lost animals, his ultimate design was to reach the high ridges and to remain on the near side of them where he would able to see all around with a minimal chance of being seen.

"They got a camp east of the stage road about a mile and a half," he told Cleve, "near a spring that comes out of some rocks in a clump of trees, and I'd guess that must be where they hide out each time they arrive in the Valverde country because there are some fairly permanent signs of use up there."

"Anywhere near the regular range riders' trails, by any chance?" asked Cleve.

"Nope. In fact, I didn't go down on to the range and come around front, then look up through the trees toward that place, but I'd say it's just about invisible from out on the grassland. Back where I was, up a slope a quarter mile or so behind them, you could see fairly well, but otherwise there wouldn't be any way to get near. They got good visibility in all directions. Even back where I was, there aren't too many trees, so, if they suspected anything, they'd even have a pretty fair sighting back in that direction, too."

"You saw all of them?"

77

"Four," said Twenty-One. "Maybe there was another one out lookin' after the livestock or up in the underbrush, but I only saw the four of them." Twenty-One lit a smoke and leaned his long back against a porch upright. "They seemed to me to be waiting," he said. "Maybe the moon isn't right or something."

The idea behind a period of waiting struck Cleve. "Or maybe they don't move until someone from down here rides out there and draws them a diagram, Twenty-One."

McKinnon was willing to believe this. "All right. And what you want is for me to get back up into those hills and keep a close watch. Right?"

"Yeah, and the minute Levi shows up, I'll send him up there, too, so you be on the watch. Don't let him ride into them."

Twenty-One said: "What do I need Levi for? I can keep watch by myself."

Cleve yawned and rose. "I know you can, but suppose the man who is organizing their strikes rides out there, and rides back. Who is going to keep watch and at the same time get word back down here to me?"

Twenty-One dumped his cigarette, stamped it out upon the porch planking, and looked around at the quiet week-night town. "I'll watch for him," he stated, and moved off the porch without more conversation. He had a long ride ahead of him and he had been in the saddle since before sunup. No matter how sinewy and durable a man was, there were limits to his endurance.

Cleve retired, thinking that finally they were going to come up with something worthwhile after all this time, and the following morning shortly after breakfast, when he was handed a slip of paper by the local telegrapher, it seemed that indeed things were beginning to unravel.

The initials at the bottom of the telegram were simply *C.T.* for Captain Tomlinson, and the information in the message supplied two names. Not five or six, just two, but Cleve was perfectly willing to accept this. If he could pinpoint at least two of the outlaws Perry Stockton had been riding with, that would be a good start.

Later, about noon when he encountered Tom Porter again, the lawman said he'd been down visiting with Barney Glasser. He also said Barney had broken into subdued laughter when Porter had suggested that he was part of a group of Rangers in the Valverde territory.

Cleve was interested. "What did he say?" he asked, and Constable Porter looked disgusted.

"Nothing. He rolled over and closed his eyes and old Henrickson run me out." Porter did not gaze at Cleve as though his earlier hint that Hampshire himself might also be a Texas Ranger were still in his mind. In fact, Cleve got the impression that the lawman would not like to have that brought up, which was perfectly agreeable with Cleve.

"What else did he say?" asked the Ranger. "I mean who shot him?"

Tom Porter scowled. "You know what he had the gall to tell me? That someone might have been out hunting

79

back there on Brinkley's range, and winged him by mistake."

"What's so impossible about that?" demanded Cleve.

"You know darned well a man sitting atop a horse don't look at all like a deer nor an elk nor whatever else a man would be hunting over there for, and, in case you didn't know, Mister Brinkley don't allow hunting on his range at no time of the year. Not even by the fellers who ride for him. No, sir, don't you believe that Glasser feller was shot by accident. He was just making smoke, coming at me with anything that silly."

Cleve was willing to agree. "All right. Then who *did* try to kill Glasser?"

Porter sighed. "Someone," he mumbled. "Right now that's all I know. But that shooting in town the other night . . . that likely was tied in some way."

"How?" challenged Cleve, who knew precisely what the tie-in had been.

Porter still mumbled. "I don't know . . . yet. But I'll find out. This much I do know . . . some Mex beer makers were over at their crocks that night and saw two men chasing another man, and saw the feller being chased turn and shoot, and *saw* a lanky feller return the fire and down the feller who was being chased."

Cleve's brows steadily climbed. "Witnesses? Well, what else did they see?"

Porter rolled up his eyes. "They ran," he groaned. "I went all over hell asking questions, and couldn't so much as find one person other than those two who even saw that much. But someone got hit, I'm sure of that."

"Then where is he?" asked Cleve.

"Maybe up in the hills somewhere at a camp nursing a hole through his carcass somewhere. Maybe right here in town lying quietly by," stated the lawman. "That's what I've been doing the last couple of days . . . looking for him."

"If you can find him," said Cleve Hampshire, "you sure as hell might get some answers, at least about Glasser being winged."

There was nothing left to be said, so Tom Porter sauntered off across the road in the direction of his jailhouse office, and, as Cleve Hampshire stood gazing after him, it crossed Cleve's mind that the harness maker or whatever he was that Cleve had met one morning at the café, who had said Porter was lazy, hadn't been too far wrong. Any other active lawman wouldn't head for his cool and peaceful office at a time like this, he'd be out conducting an investigation. But as far as Cleve was concerned, the constable of Valverde could spend all his time over there keeping cool.

Cleve sauntered to the saloon for a beer and saw two dusty, lean, quiet men already at the bar, discussing the town with the bar man. As soon as Cleve entered and the bar man walked down to take his order, the pair of dusty men turned slightly to assess the newest customer, then impassively turned back to their beer again.

Otherwise the saloon only had three old men at a window-side table playing pinochle, and one townsman at the free-lunch counter organizing an impossible sandwich.

Cleve's interest was in the pair of strangers, and, when he was half convinced that they could be a pair of those upcountry outlaws, one of them tossed down a small silver coin and called over to the bar man. "See you in a day or two, Pete, when we've got another excuse to hit town."

Cleve watched the riders depart by lifting his eyes to the backbar mirror, and, when the bar man came down, he said: "Range men?"

The bar man casually replied. "Yeah. Ride for an old buzzard named McGregor who's got a place about six, seven miles northwest."

Cleve sighed. One more disappointment at a time when he felt he deserved better than that from his private fate. He drank the beer and ordered up another one, and over at the pinochle table one of the old men hurled down his cards and swore with all the splendid hair-raising eloquence of either an old-time freighter or an old-time blacksmith.

CHAPTER
TEN

Levi Holt arrived out of the westerly night and came around to the rooming-house porch carrying both spurs in one hand so as not to make a sound. He was so successful in fact that, until he straddled the railing and Cleve caught murky movement from the corner of his eye, Levi's arrival had gone entirely undetected.

Cleve wasted no time. He explained what Twenty-One had discovered in the northeastern foothills and told Levi exactly what he expected from them both. Levi was willing to leave immediately, this same night, but first he had to quit his job and this he did not think could be done until morning. After that, though, he promised to head into the foothills.

Cleve could have warned him against being detected by the encamped men beyond the first tier of upended country, but he refrained. Levi Holt was no more a novice than Cleve or Twenty-One McKinnon were.

They had a little more conversation before Levi left as silently as he had arrived, and during the course of it Levi mentioned that an old cowman named McGregor, who ranched a few miles north of the outfit that had hired Levi, had been a week now making a marketable gather.

Levi mentioned this for two reasons. One of them was that old McGregor had only two range riders on a range that covered no less than twelve miles, and also because, to Levi's knowledge, McGregor was the first cowman in the Valverde country to start making a gather. It was too early; cattlemen usually did not start rounding up for a drive until every last blade of green grass was gone, meaning that they preferably kept their critters just as long as it was possible for the animals to pile on one more pound of saleable weight.

Cleve's interest was understandable. If one cowman offered a temptation for rustlers over the other local cowmen, he would deserve the attention of the undercover Rangers.

"Tell Twenty-One," he ordered. "Then the pair of you keep close watch and, if those outlaws up in the foothills head for McGregor's range, one of you get back down here and bring me word and we'll all three of us meet over there, the feller who remains in the foothills to shag after the renegades, me and whoever comes down here, to ride over there from here. But it'd better be early in the day. McGregor's ranch is a long ride from here."

Holt left and Cleve did as he ordinarily did — he had his last smoke of the day out there on the empty, dark front porch fitting the little bits and pieces together as he gazed down the darkened long southward roadway toward the lower end of town.

There was a light at Dr. Henrickson's place, but Cleve had noticed that there usually was a light down there at night, and there were of course the pair of smoking old carriage lanterns spiked to the front of the livery barn's front wall on either side of the doorless wide front opening. Otherwise, excepting a saloon light or two, and a lamp burning from the cubbyhole office of the stage line supervisor, Valverde looked to be fairly well bedded down.

Cleve finished his smoke, saw a horseman emerge from a side street midway down, and, as he straightened back from killing the cigarette, he watched as that horseman crossed the road toward the westside alleyway.

For no special reason except that he knew he could get away with it and because by nature he was frankly curious, Cleve stepped over the porch railing and headed briskly down the side of the big old rooming house to a place near someone's dusty woodpile where he had a view of the north-south alleyway.

That rider came slogging along on a good walking horse. The animal had his head down, his reins swinging, his big body moving in easy and rhythmic unison as man and animal went northward.

Cleve leaned and watched, and recognized the rider as a man named Harry Turnbow who owned and operated Valverde's large and thriving general store. Cleve had been waited on a few times by Turnbow, and, while he had not thought much about the storekeeper one way or another, there had been one inescapable impression. Harry Turnbow was a man whose sense of profit and whose motivation toward as much profit as he could legally get were powerful enough to be exuded noticeably even in the presence of a man such as Cleve Hampshire who had felt no interest in the man at all.

Now, leaning in the woodpile watching, Cleve was two-thirds of the opinion that, if Harry Turnbow were riding out tonight, heading beyond town obviously, which meant he would most likely be unable to return to town for some hours still to come, there would be an excellent and profitable reason.

Turnbow was past, up near the farthest end of town, when Cleve began to have an inkling. It did not have one single basis in fact. Cleve was disgusted with himself for having such an idea. Nevertheless, he stepped briskly clear of the woodpile and trotted southward down the same alleyway to the livery barn.

The night hawk was snoring on a pile of sweat-stiff horse blankets, which facilitated what Cleve Hampshire had in mind, and it also helped that the night hawk was one of those individuals who could sleep through a distant cannonade.

Cleve got his horse rigged out, and rode up the alley on Turnbow's tail without causing even one break in the rhythmic snoring of the slumbering night man. Fortunately for the night hawk Cleve was not a horse thief. Beyond town Cleve had to go almost completely by sound, although once, when Harry Turnbow crested upon a wide, low land swell and had to ride without an adequately shielding background for roughly a quarter mile, Cleve had him in sight that full distance, and it was under these particular circumstances that Cleve decided with misgivings that Harry Turnbow was not going up on to the northeasterly range after all, as Cleve had initially thought would prove to be the case, and which in fact Cleve had hoped against hope would indeed prove to be the case.

He had just about decided Harry Turnbow had to be the local mystery man who was setting up those very successful rustler sorties. What doubts he entertained were based upon a practical realization that simply because a man left town late at night, riding northward, did not have to mean anything sinister at all. But he hoped very hard it did mean something sinister.

He was unfamiliar with the countryside beyond town except in a very general way. He knew, for example, that the stage road ran almost due northward and due southward down through town. He also knew from what little he had seen above town for a fair distance that there were no residences within sight of the road. Otherwise, though, his visits to friends in the Valverde countryside had been largely confined to the lower end of town.

But Harry Turnbow clearly knew the countryside over which he was riding. He made no particular haste, although once or twice he did in fact gallop where the land was safely level, and regardless of his gait he pressed steadily along in the same general northwesterly direction, but on such a generally circuitous course that, although Cleve was certain Turnbow had a valid destination, it was difficult to guess in advance what it was, when a man who was following carefully through the star-bright night dared not get close enough to see his prey.

Cleve was as vulnerable to detection far back, as the man he was following was vulnerable up ahead — by sound. Turnbow made no attempt to ride quietly but Cleve had to make every such attempt in order not to arouse the wonder, and then the suspicion, of the storekeeper.

Finally, a considerable distance ahead up where there existed a gentle wide fold in the land, Cleve caught sight of yellow-orange lamplight. He had no idea what was up there — a cow camp or a residence — but he was certain of one thing, neither he nor Harry Turnbow had covered enough miles yet to be anywhere near either the Brinkley home place nor the ranch of the cowman named McGregor.

He still was not ready to yield. Turnbow *had* left town well past the hour when most folks had retired, and he *had* made a point of not riding up Main Street out of town but had used the back alley where he would be the least likely to be seen. Tenuous as these things were, Cleve had ridden several miles out of town in the darkness straining every resource not to be detected strictly on the strength of these suspicions, and now as the man up ahead, moving like a dim wraith toward that lamp glow several miles onward, persevered, so did Cleve Hampshire.

It did not take long. Turnbow lifted his horse over into an easy lope and covered more than a mile before hauling back down to a walk, and for the first time Cleve's suspicions received support when the storekeeper halted and sat his saddle out in the night, for all the world like a bronco Indian strong heart, gazing steadily at the low, log house up ahead.

Cleve dismounted, looked for a place where he could safely tie his horse, then went ahead on foot. He saw Turnbow ease on up another dozen or so yards, then halt again, and this time the storekeeper swung to earth, stepped to his animal's head, and whistled.

Cleve reached down to ease off the tie thong of his holstered Colt. Up at the cabin a door opened and swiftly closed, permitting one brilliant flash of lamp light to come and go. Cleve stepped ahead a foot at a time until he could clearly and distinctly make out Harry Turnbow standing there with his frock coat and his flat-topped hat. It was impossible to be certain at that distance in the darkness, but Cleve did not believe the storekeeper had a gun belted around his middle beneath the coat.

A second shadow moved darkly ahead. Cleve's interest was intent. If this were another of Turnbow's rendezvousing horse and cattle thieves . . .

"Are you alone?" Turnbow softly inquired, and the reply that came back through the warm, pleasant night was offered in a voice pitched a notch or two higher.

"Yes. Earl won't be back until tomorrow night . . . Oh, Harry!"

Cleve straightened up very slowly as that second figure, the one with the throaty, higher voice suddenly ran over and hurled herself into Turnbow's arms. The two people clung, then after a while turned in the direction of the lighted log house in the swale of the softly limned night.

Cleve did not move for a long while. Not in fact until those nocturnal lovers entered the log house, and, within moments of this event, the lamps were turned so low it was difficult to make out any light up there at all.

Then, finally, Cleve reached down to re-secure the tie-down on his holstered Colt, and to turn back woodenly, reach the tethered horse, and swing up as he turned back in the direction of town. There were plenty of times in a man's lifetime when he did things he felt chagrined about, things he chose never to mention, and tonight Cleve Hampshire had done such a thing.

It did not help his disposition any that by the time he finally got back to town and put up his horse, then shuffled up to the rooming house to retire, it was almost time to get up again. In fact, he got a total of three hours sleep, and the last half hour of that was stolen from the daylight hours shortly after sunup.

He ate a late breakfast and for that reason did not encounter any of the diners he usually met down at the little hole-in-the-wall café in the morning. He had no regrets at all. He was still monumentally disgusted with himself.

Later, when he had to go around to the general store to replace his dwindling supply of smoking tobacco and was personally served by Harry Turnbow, he had difficulty smiling back when Turnbow smiled. When Turnbow said — "There you are, friend, that'll be five cents." — Cleve put down the coin and picked up his tobacco sack and turned to walk out of the store without even a nod. If Harry Turnbow noticed, he probably decided the burly, weathered man who had just replenished his supply of smoking material just naturally had a vile disposition. This morning, anyway, Turnbow would have been quite correct.

Cleve's disposition did not improve until near midday, and by then his disapproval of Turnbow had crystallized into something less condemnatory toward the storekeeper, whose keeper Cleve definitely was not, and into something more like abysmal disgust toward himself.

CHAPTER
ELEVEN

He had kept away from Barney Glasser for a good reason — he did not wish Constable Porter to wonder any more than he already had wondered about Hampshire's interest in the wounded Texas Ranger, and, as things turned out, he did not even have to seek out Dr. Henrickson to be informed concerning Barney's progress. He met Tom Porter over in front of the harness shop the morning after he had wasted half the night shagging Harry Turnbow, and the constable reported that Barney was doing very well, that in fact he wanted to leave his bed and Dr. Henrickson was indignant enough about this to have hidden the Ranger's clothing.

Another time Porter would probably have been amused. He did not lack a sense of humor. But this time his smile failed to manifest as he said: "That damned Ranger knows who shot him sure as I'm a foot tall, and, by God, he won't even give me the time of day. And there's not a lousy thing I can do about it. You can't haul a hurt feller out of bed and pitch him into a jail cell, and you can't browbeat anything out of him."

"Why is it all that important to know?" asked Cleve.

"Because *someone* darned well got shot down there in that runnin' fight those two Mex beer makers saw, that's why. I want to know who it was shot that man and if it was another Ranger. In case you didn't realize it, shooting a Ranger is one hell of a good way to get yourself killed."

"Give Glasser time," Cleve said a little indifferently, as though he could not appreciate the urgency about all this. "Maybe when he's good and ready he'll . . ."

"You miss the point mule trader!" exclaimed Constable Porter. "Whoever got shot down there wasn't just accidentally shot. I want to know *why* he was shot as well as who shot him. That's what folks pay me to do."

Cleve responded in a placating manner. "Well, I'd sure help if I could, Constable."

Porter came right back. "You can. You've been around town a couple of weeks now. I've seen you over at the store and down at the livery barn. You move around a lot and you're bound to hear talk. You can keep your ears open, and, if you hear anything that might have some bearing on just what the hell might be going on around this town, you can hightail it over to the jailhouse and let me know."

Cleve regarded the lawman thoughtfully. "Be a sort of spy?" he murmured, and at once the constable did his utmost to make it sound more respectable than that by saying: "Friend, there isn't no let-up in the everlastin' war between right and wrong, and folks on the side of *right* don't spy, they serve what all us decent folks believe in." Porter looked as though, having delivered himself of this philosophical utterance, he expected Cleve to agree, so Cleve obliged him.

"All right, anything I hear that I figure you'd ought to know, Constable, I'll see that you hear about it." Cleve smiled and shuffled off in the direction of the livery barn. It had occurred to him — with a sinking sensation — that someone down there might have noticed that his horse had been ridden the night before, and they might also have felt curious enough about this to report it to the local law.

As it turned out, the day man had not crossed paths with the night man, and therefore no confidences had been exchanged. When Cleve got down to the cool and pleasant livery-barn runway, the day man was cuffing off his horse briskly and the horse was standing drowsy-eyed, enjoying every brush stroke.

Cleve flipped the day man a silver coin and strolled out back where the public corrals were. Someone had arrived in Valverde not too long before, driving a wagon. His teams were eating meadow hay in several of the cribbed old patched-together public corrals, and, when Cleve wandered over to look, he saw another horse in one of the livery man's pens which looked vaguely familiar. It was the good walking, husky, quiet horse the philandering storekeeper had ridden to that tryst upcountry last night. Cleve turned and retraced his steps to the roadway, coming out under a huge old tree between the livery barn and the blacksmith's sooty place of business.

Up the road Jerome Henrickson was talking with a rather heavy woman, and, when he saw Cleve emerge into tree shade from out back, Henrickson terminated his discussion quickly, smiled at the woman, and turned to hike diagonally across toward the same tree shade.

"How long," he asked, before he was even close enough to preface his remarks with the traditional "good morning", "is it going to take you to get things straightened out around here? After all, there is a definite limit on how long I can keep that corpse above ground. This being summertime and all."

Cleve knew Henrickson too well to try an evasive reply. Maybe it would have been better to have said Cleve knew Henrickson's type of individual too well to attempt being evasive. He tried a shot in the dark. "Couple more days . . . if all goes well." Then he used his most engaging smile. He might just as well have made an attempt at charming a stone wall.

"Two more days, then I've got to sink him," said the doctor, "and in order to do that in our local bone grounds, I've got to get a clearance from Constable Porter . . . and where does that leave me? How do I explain keeping that corpse secreted for so long?"

Cleve blew out a ragged breath. "I thought I had something last night," he confided. "It turned out to be the wrong man, and it also turned out to be the wrong kind of a rendezvous."

The gaunt old medical practitioner considered this ambiguous remark, studied the face of the man who had made it, then threw up his hands. "The only thing I'm interested in at this point, Ranger, is that corpse. I did what I had to do in order to support the law. Now, by God, the law had better do what *it's* got to do to support *me*."

"Have faith," muttered Cleve, then switched the topic. "How is Barney?"

"Troublesome," stated Dr. Henrickson. "He wants to be up and around. One of the bad features about dealing with people like Glasser is that they are too darned dumb to realize that simply because they are not in particular pain, they aren't also in good fettle." Henrickson considered, then also said: "Two more days, then I'll expect you to do something about Glasser, too."

Cleve tried that charming smile again. This time the big old gaunt medical practitioner simply turned on his heel and went stalking back across the roadway in the direction of his fenced-in combination clinic and residence.

Cleve turned, and fifty yards up the northward plank walk a range rider was leaning indolently against a porch upright out front of the harness works, smoking. He looked trail-wise, bronzed from long exposure, and as solemn as a judge. He was not looking in Cleve Hampshire's direction, but since he was Levi Holt, it was a reasonable assumption to presume that he was not standing out there like that for any other reason than to be noticed in broad daylight.

Cleve walked up as far as the apothecary's shop, one door south of the saddle and harness works, and passed between both buildings down through a dogtrot on his way to the rear alley.

Out there he only had to wait a couple of minutes. Levi still had the cigarette in his lips as he stepped through, saw Cleve, and walked on up to say: "I was on my way northwest after quitting, and come on to two riders splitting a gather up in the brakes near the foothills."

Cleve looked surprised. "So you rode all the way down here, first?"

Levi nodded. "Yup. Those two riders work for McGregor, and those cattle they were dividing up wore the old man's brand, and it was just short of sunrise when they were making the split, at a time when no one's out and moving much . . . and when they saw me far out, they just dropped out of sight back into the foothills. Otherwise . . . yeah, I rode down here to tell you because I just love to ride in the chill of pre-dawn."

Cleve said: "Had your breakfast?"

"No. I quit the ranch before breakfast this morning. Are you inviting me to the café?"

Cleve fished forth a silver cartwheel and passed it over. "Yeah, breakfast on me . . . without me . . . and afterward head up there where Twenty-One should be. If those McGregor men are somehow or other part of the rustling organization, and are making that split to get things going a little better and faster, why then I'd sort of guess those men Twenty-One is watching should be striking camp and heading west through the foothills to take delivery. Does that sound about right to you?"

Levi refused to commit himself. He clutched the silver dollar and squinted out past Cleve across the empty vastness of grass country, and shrugged high, thin shoulders. "Are you goin' to head north?" he asked, and, when Cleve agreed to do this, Levi turned and walked up through the dogtrot again on his way over to the café. Holt was an individual who did not function at peak personality on an empty gut.

Cleve headed for the livery barn, got his horse rigged out, and under the interested gaze of both the liveryman and his day hostler, rode out the rear of the barn and northward up the alleyway.

What he had hoped to do, had in fact actually expected to do, was locate the local chieftain of the rustling syndicate, first, and after he had done that he had expected to begin rounding up the lesser men, the actual riders who picked up the herds and drove them out of the country, but the way this thing was turning out it appeared he was going to locate the actual riders first, and then, maybe, he might get lucky and locate the chieftain.

There were dangerous disadvantages. If the man at the top were captured first and it was done swiftly and efficiently, there was little chance the actual workers on down the line would realize what was happening until it was too late for them to come to his aid. This way, Cleve, with two other lawmen, were well on their way to bearding a band of outlaw livestock thieves who not only outnumbered them, but who would most certainly be as deadly as a herd of rattlesnakes.

He considered the beautiful, vast rangeland on all sides as he rode northward, and decided that a man played the cards that fell to his hand, and he did it the best way he could, and if that wasn't good enough, well, damn it, no one could do any better.

He did not see a single soul, not even over on the stage road, but then it was either too early for most travelers, or it was too late for the dawn stage.

When he was passing around and through a low series of serrated little barrancas he remembered something and topped out on one of them to look northwesterly. Sure enough, he could see that log residence off in the distance where Harry Turnbow had kept his tryst the previous night. He probably should have noticed that place before; he wasn't entirely alien to the north countryside, but aside from the fact that the house blended so perfectly with its surroundings that unless a person looked directly at it, or already knew it was back there, he probably would not even see the house, even though it was near enough the road to be noticed.

Beyond, bearing more to the northeasterly with some idea of at least detecting high dust where a band of horsemen would be passing overland in and out among the foothills, Cleve missed no movement, but, excepting horses, cattle, and a couple of small bunches of antelope, all he saw was the azure sky with its turquoise edges, the clear-cut lifts and rises of this endless cow country, and one mangy old dog coyote trying his utmost to catch a young digger squirrel who could not only duck back quicker than the old coyote could turn, but who was fleeing for his life and had that much more reason to be impossible for the dog coyote to catch.

The coyote was so intent upon breakfast he did not even catch sight of the horse and rider until he ran almost directly across in front of them and the horse snorted. Then the coyote glanced up, gave a little yip of astonishment and fright, turned on all the speed still left in him, and shot past the digger squirrel in a burst of desperate speed.

The squirrel crouched in pure amazement as his deadly enemy overtook and passed him and did not even look back, then the squirrel reared up, also saw the man and the horse, and with one high dive disappeared down a nearby hole.

CHAPTER
TWELVE

Cleve saw the dust in the northwest long before he saw anything else, and he had to assume those riders for McGregor were probably pushing their split-off toward the other rustlers because it was too much dust, and it was coming from the wrong direction, to be part of the telltale sign of the rustlers over along the northeasterly foothills. He assumed that he had been seen. He was still out upon the open rangeland and anyone driving cattle, even doing it legitimately, would be alert and watchful. If they were thieves, they would be even more wary and watchful.

He was heading due northward, parallel of the more distant easterly stage road, which was on an intersecting course with that oncoming dust, which was traveling slowly from west to east. It would — it *should* — look very natural if he simply kept to his present course, did not increase his gait, and encountered the drive up ahead as though the meeting were a pure coincidence. It was the only reasonable course left open to him now that he had seen the dust and was positive the drovers had also seen him.

His biggest worry was not two range men stealing their employer's cattle. His biggest worry was where, exactly, the other riders, four or five in number, would appear to take delivery — providing of course that this actually *was* a rustling operation. If those other men saw Cleve Hampshire, they just might decide even a harmless witness, which they would probably assume that he was, could be a lot more dangerous to them alive than dead.

Twice he stood in the stirrups and looked back. Both times the land southward was as empty as the land also was to the east and west. If Levi were on his way upcountry by now, he was certainly not anywhere within sighting distance.

The dust seemed to settle a little where the foothills deepened and broadened. Cleve's surmise was that the rustlers had halted their gather back in a place where there was sufficient grass to keep the critters placated for a while. *Why* they had done this could have two meanings: one, the rustlers might want to settle with Hampshire before pushing onward, and, two, perhaps that was the place where they were to hold the split-off until the other thieves arrived and took delivery. Either way, as Cleve pretended to be riding blithely up into that place where the dust was fading, he was heading into some kind of trouble and he knew it as well as he knew his own name. Even if the McGregor riders assumed he was just another traveler, he was still riding into something that was potentially very deadly.

The sun was high, the day was hot, his horse sweated without having been lifted out of his fast walk more than a couple of times, and Cleve was mopping his neck and face with a big blue bandanna when a pair of lean horsemen appeared, one on each side of a narrow pathway between a split hillock. He recognized them both even before he lowered the handkerchief. They were the two men he had seen one time in the saloon, and who he had thought might be strangers in the country, but had turned out to be riders for someone named McGregor, according to the bar man. He was careful about lowering his right hand with the blue handkerchief in it, and he smiled as he said: "Howdy, gents. It's hotter'n a June bride on a feather mattress, and right about now I sure could use a drink from someone's canteen." He reined to a halt and sat there while the sinewy, faded, hard-eyed pair of men studied him, then one of them reached back to unhook a canteen and pass it over as he said: "If you're travelin' through, you sure ain't makin' a point of stayin' on the road, friend. Why should that be, I wonder?"

Cleve drank, stoppered the canteen, and passed it back with a great sigh and a sentence of appreciation before he made an attempt to answer the range man's question. "Well, friend, over on the stage road you meet folks, and sometimes you get caught in wagon dust, and there isn't any shade." He shrugged, glanced around, looked from one range man to the other, then also said: "And I'd just as soon be solitary. That's my nature . . . to be sort of by myself." He grinned, looked past where some cattle were visible, and jutted his jaw in that direction. "You boys making a gather out of these here brakes?"

The cowboy who had up to now said nothing nodded his head. "Yeah, picking up all we can find. We ride for an old gaffer named McGregor, westerly a few miles. It's hard work for darned little reward."

Cleve was sympathetic. "Yeah, friend, I know how that goes. I used to ride a little, then I got into the mule trading business and . . ."

"Mule trading!"

Cleve looked up guilelessly. "Yeah, mule trading. I know this isn't the country for it, but just about every other part of Texas I been in, folks use mules, and mule trading beats range riding all to hell as a way to make a living." He grinned. "Except hereabouts, which is why I'm heading on out. Well, gents, I'm right obliged to you for the water. Maybe you could tell *me* . . . is there water holes and springs and suchlike on up across these mountains?"

One of the wolf-like leaned-down range men raised a gloved hand. "Stay closer to the roadway," he said, "and about four miles on up through the pass you'll come to a water box fed by a hollowed out sapling that comes directly from a spring on up in the mountains. Best darned drinkin' water in all west Texas."

Cleve looked relieved. "Gents, I'm sure obliged," he said, and lifted his rein hand just as a man's high cry from off through the considerable westerly distance echoed faintly down through the hot, heatwave atmosphere. Both the range riders drew straight up in their saddles, twisting to peer in the direction of that shout. Cleve waited a moment, until he could decently ride on, then he muttered his gratitude again and pushed on up through the low little uneven passageway and emerged onto a wide, sloping little meadow where

104

the cattle were spreading out as they grazed along. He made a particular point of easing far around to the left, rather than the right, which would have been easterly in the direction of that high shout, and he neither looked back nor slackened his gait. He wanted to be well out of this area by the time those McGregor cowhands decided they might not have done the wise thing by allowing a stranger to pass through.

What that shout had meant was anyone's guess. Cleve was at a loss to explain it, unless someone was heading toward that grassy meadow as a rendezvous, and wanted to let those McGregor riders know they were approaching.

He got well around on the west side of the cattle and set his course dead ahead for a spit of unkempt old bull pines, beyond which the broken country seemed to become more upended, more rough and wild just before the fluting upthrust of genuine mountains took over and soared in stair-stepped heights up to their forest rims and top outs.

Cleve's destination was not the mountains. He did not in fact want to have to depart from the foothills because the surest way to watch all that transpired down in that hidden broad meadow where the cattle grazed was by remaining at an elevation that was sufficiently low — but not too low — so that the visibility would not be impaired by that wavy, blurry heat haze that seemed to curse the hot daylight hours at this time of year.

By the time he got in among the old bull pines and could pause to look back, there was no sign of those two lanky, faded cowboys. The cattle were evidently content to remain without spreading too much in their grassy secret place. They had probably been driven since well ahead of sunrise, as Levi had reported, in which case, by now, they would be very hungry, and that too was probably part of the rustler's strategy. After all, only thoroughly knowledgeable cattlemen ever made thoroughly successful livestock thieves.

He saw a pair of riders coming into the meadow from the east and at first decided they had to be those same two range men who had intercepted him, but then he saw that pair turn out into the open meadow from down near the low pathway where they had stopped Cleve, and that of course made it clear that the riders approaching from the east were different men altogether. He was watching very intently.

Finally, when those four riders aimed for a place in hillock shade to rendezvous, Cleve swung down from the saddle and turned back to tether his animal, then to walk off a short distance, a half dozen or so yards, where he had the same excellent visibility, and to resume his intent vigil. Apparently one of those men who had just arrived in the meadow must have been the source of that earlier shout. Now, watching as the four of them swung down and stood loose and easy as they conversed, it dawned upon Cleve that the pair of newcomers were possibly the advance riders of that band of outlaws McKinnon was supposed to have kept in sight since the day before. They would be part of the same crew Levi Holt would be heading upcountry to locate, and also to keep watch over.

What Cleve wondered, now, was where the other outlaws were — unless of course he was as terribly wrong again as he had been during the Henry Turnbow interlude — and he absolutely refused to think about this possibility. He couldn't be that wrong again, not this time; the odds were just not that great, but very clearly those two McGregor cowboys, who had waylaid Cleve, had not acted that way because it was customary to ambush someone from both sides of a pass through the foothills, and also, as Levi Holt had already reported, those two lone wolves hadn't rounded up that split-off from the McGregor gather and pushed them eastward far from McGregor range just because they enjoyed driving cattle.

No, he wasn't wrong this time. He was certain of it as he stood beside a big old pine tree watching as those four horsemen passed around a canteen, then made a few arm gestures during the course of their discussion, and finally turned to look out where the greasy, fat, slick redbacks were grazing. Cleve could almost hear the haggling, clearly those McGregor riders had done this before, had worked for an outfit, and had systematically rustled from it. Without a doubt, this sort of thing had to pay very well because it was deadly hazardous.

One thing lingered in the back of Cleve Hampshire's mind. This split-off was not a big bunch of cattle. There were no more than a hundred and fifty head in the herd. That was not the kind of rustling Captain Tomlinson had talked about. Cleve's impression was that this rustling syndicate stole upward of five hundred head at a time.

It crossed his mind that since there were five of those renegades — had been six until Stockton had been killed — and there were only two of them down there now talking to the McGregor range men, the other three outlaws might be somewhere else doing this identical thing with another pair of dishonest range riders — making another contact and taking delivery of another hundred and fifty head of slick cattle.

That way, of course, they could, over a period of a day or two, pick up five hundred head without much difficulty, and there might even be a special advantage to doing it this way. The cowboys themselves who were charged with making up someone's gather would indeed have completed the gather and would have taken the split-off to some secret rendezvous like this one, would have handed it over to the thieves, would have been paid by the rustlers, and would then have returned to their home range pretending still to be making up a gather, which would allow the rustlers all the time they needed to get out of the country.

Cleve sighed and waggled his head and left off watching those four men, who were now heading for their horses again, to turn and gaze around. Three totally silent, motionless men on horseback were back behind him on a carpet of thick pine needles, gazing stonily at his back with six-guns in their fists! He lost his breath for several seconds. How those men had got back there without being heard, how they had come upon him like this so obviously accidentally, and why his own horse hadn't even nickered at the strange horses, all added up to something deadly for Cleve Hampshire. There was no way under the sun he could go on pretending he was just a traveling mule trader. Not now, not after those three men had seen him watching everything out across the meadow with such clear and obvious interest.

One man quietly said: "Reach down, left-handed, and dump that six-gun." Cleve obeyed because there was nothing else for him to do. "Now walk over to your horse, get on him, and rein down into the meadow," ordered the same outlaw, "and, if you give us half a chance, we're going to back-shoot you."

Again Cleve obeyed because there was no other choice available to him.

CHAPTER
THIRTEEN

All five of those outlaws were in the meadow with the pair of McGregor riders, when one of the McGregor riders said: "Damn, he just seemed as harmless as some darned old down-at-the-heel horse trader or something."

They had emptied Cleve's pockets and the last thing lying atop his other effects was that nickel-plated circlet with the Texas Ranger star inside it, with the word *Ranger* engraved across the star.

"Harmless as a lousy sidewinder," snarled a very dark man with high, flat cheek bones and the slightly slanted eyes of a half-breed Indian. "I knew it. I been figuring it'd happen sooner or later around here, and that's what I told Harry. We got to change . . . we got to make these damned range men deliver the critters down closer to where we get rid of them."

A tobacco-chewing lanky man spat, shifted his cud, and with a lot less agitation said: "All right, Fred, maybe you was right. Only that don't cut no ice right this minute, does it? We got us a damned Texas Ranger who was back up there watchin' every lousy thing we done down here. He's got enough to get us all hanged."

"Oh, hell," growled the Indian-looking half-breed. "He's as good as dead. It ain't this one I'm sweatin' over. Is there any more of 'em?" As though to lend emphasis to this remark, the man twisted his thick, powerful torso from the waist and looked far out and around. The others did the same, then one of the McGregor cowboys removed his hat, mopped sweat off a white forehead, dropped the hat down again, and said: "Sid and I got to leave. We can't make it back on time unless we pull out right now. Otherwise, if we come in too late, McGregor's going to wonder where in hell we been all this time."

One of the outlaws gazed sulphurously at the speaker. "Sure," he growled. "You like the pay, you just don't like seein' a Ranger get shot, and buried under a mound of stones."

The half-breed, who was apparently the leader of those five renegades, made a little gesture of dismissal. "Go on," he told the McGregor cowboy. "You got paid . . . we got the cattle. That's all you was supposed to do anyway. Go on . . . and, if I was in your boots, I'd never so much as open my mouth even to each other about what happened down here today. Go on, head for home if you've a mind to."

The pair of cowboys required no additional encouragement. Neither of them would turn to look at Cleve Hampshire, not even when he called softly to them: "Thanks again for the water."

One of the rustlers gouged Cleve with an elbow and snarled at him: "Don't be cute. Just stand still and be quiet."

The half-breed turned muddy black eyes. "How'd you happen on to this place?" he asked.

Cleve said: "Dust. I saw it coming over from the northwest range."

This direct and honest answer impressed the half-breed. "All right. How'd you happen to be on our trail, then?"

Cleve answered just as forthrightly again. "Been an awful lot of complaints come down to El Paso from the Valverde country over the past year or so. I got sent up here to see if it was as bad as some of those complaints swore it was." Cleve did not take his eyes off the half-breed. "It was just as bad, and no matter what happens to me, mister, whether I ever show up again or not, the El Paso division will send a crew up here."

A couple of those strangers seemed fascinated at having captured a Texas Ranger, but the half-breed and another pair of the outlaws were a lot less impressed; they were older men, and clearly they were also hardened renegades. But it was one of the younger outlaws who said: "Fred, damned coincidence that Perry disappeared and we turn up a Texas Ranger at about the same time?"

They all looked at Cleve with fresh interest. The half-breed called Fred had another question then. "There was a shootin' in town the other night. We had a friend down there in Valverde that night and he never come back. Ranger, you lie to me and I'll stake you out, spread-eagled, and skin off your eyelids and leave you in the sun. What happened to the feller who rode with us and went down there to town?"

Cleve's eyes did not waver. "If I knew what happened and told you, it wouldn't keep me alive one minute more," he said evenly.

112

They stared at him. Courage was something all men, red or white, outlaws or not outlaws, respected and even at times admired in an enemy or in a friend. That lanky, tobacco-chewing renegade with the lowered head and piercing gun-metal eyes laconically said: "Ranger, you're most likely right enough about that, but there is something you might like to figure on . . . we ain't in the murder business. We're in the rustlin' business. Meet us halfway and see what can happen . . . what happened to the feller who rode with us and disappeared down in Valverde?"

Cleve could prolong this discussion, and hope hard, and that was just about all he could do. He dared not even risk a look northward or eastward where succor might come from — if it was going to come at all.

"Your friend is dead," he said quietly.

Two of the outlaws made little sounds of resignation or acceptance. Fred inclined his head as though he, too, had already come to believe this was what happened to Stockton.

"Your friend shot a man named Glasser who was riding for the Brinkley cow outfit over on the west range," stated Cleve, still not dropping his gaze from the half-breed's coarse features. "Only he didn't kill Glasser, he only shot him through the lights, and the Brinkley outfit took Glasser to town to the doctor's place. Your friend, somehow or other, learned about this and went down there in the night and tried to shoot Glasser through his bedroom window. He missed, so they say, but a couple of townsmen took after your friend, and in a runnin' fight down Main

Street they killed him." Cleve waited, and, when nothing was said for a moment or two, he asked a question: "You mean to stand there like you didn't know where that friend of yours went?"

The tobacco chewer replied laconically and impersonally. "All he said was that he'd seen a man he owed a killing to. Perry wasn't a feller you pushed, if he didn't want to talk about something." The man spat aside, drifted his gun-metal gaze around among the others, then fixed it upon the half-breed. "We goin' to stand around here in the hot sun all day?"

Fred ignored the clear implication that they should commit a murder, then get on about their cattle stealing business.

Cleve had decided to exaggerate very little, once he heard one of those men mention someone named "Harry". If it were indeed Harry Turnbow the outlaw had referred to, then everything Cleve told these men had better be either very close to the truth, or the actual truth itself because there was no doubt about it, that half-breed looked quite willing to do exactly as he had threatened to do — stake a man out and flesh away his eyelids.

Fred turned to the laconic tobacco chewer. "You and Steve head on over to the Brinkley rendezvous. Don't pay to keep 'em waitin' too long. Give 'em the money and turn the split-off up in this direction." He turned to one of the younger men. "Find yourself a top out and set up there . . . but not on your damned horse for everyone to see like you did the last time . . . and keep close watch." He gestured. "Ride on out. We'll keep this

114

gather right here in this meadow where it can't be seen until you fellers get up pretty close, then we'll come down and lend a hand, bunch 'em together, and, come nightfall, start the drive across to the eastward range before heading southward. You understand?"

No one answered. In fact, Cleve got the impression that Fred had not said a thing the others had not already known. It was very probable that they *did* all understand what was expected of them. These men were not novices, if one could make a judgment based upon appearances. Only two of them seemed the least bit uncertain, and those were the pair of younger men.

One of these men now said: "Makes a man damned uneasy driving like this in broad daylight."

Fred groaned. "I told you. Damn it all, I been tellin' you for the past two weeks . . . everything is taken care of. You could almost ride right down there and gather up the critters under the noses of Brinkley's men. Harry and Brinkley's range boss taken care of everything. Damn it, just do it, will you?"

The tobacco chewer jerked his head at the pair of younger outlaws and led them over to the horses where Cleve and the others could hear him grumbling warningly to them as they snugged up cinches and got ready to ride.

It was hotter now in the meadow than it had been up until now. Fred and the remaining two outlaws took their prisoner over into the lee shade of a knoll. Fred sent the other two men after their horses, which were out a fair distance, and Cleve was convinced that this was a ruse to get rid of the last of the men who might be witnesses to a murder. He walked as close as he dared to the half-breed. The second the half-breed moved his right hand in the direction of his hip holster Cleve intended to hurl himself forward and, whether he failed or not — and he probably would fail — at least he would not die just standing there.

The half-breed was evidently in no hurry. He rolled a smoke, offered the makings to Cleve who declined with a wag of his head, then the half-breed lit up and stood gazing from black eyes across the intervening distance. He was clearly an individual who took no careless chances. Perhaps this was why he was still around, still operating outside the law when a great many men younger than he was had long since been planted in cemeteries.

He was also a businessman, apparently, because he said: "Ranger, you know the west Texas territory very well?" When Cleve nodded, Fred then said: "Ranger, we got a good organization. No one's going to bust it, including the lousy Texas law . . . you could make five times as much in one year with us as you could ever make with the Rangers . . . you know what your choices are?"

Cleve knew. "Sure, accept the offer, or get shot right here."

Fred trickled smoke and stood stonily eyeing the other man without making any attempt to speak again.

"Anyone would accept," stated Cleve. "Even if he had no intention of working for you any longer than it would take to get near a town where he could make a run for it. What the hell kind of a choice do you call that, anyway?"

The half-breed almost smiled. "The only one you got, Ranger. As for runnin' off . . . the first time I hand you three, maybe four hundred dollars for two or three days of work, Ranger, you wouldn't feel so much like runnin'. No man does. Look, I got to kill you or take you in, and I got to do one or the other before those other two fellers return. I'm not goin' to stand here and argue. It's your choice."

Cleve said: "How much for two or three days work?"

"Three or maybe four hundred dollars," reiterated the half-breed, exhaling gray smoke. "You wouldn't do it every three or four days, naturally. Only when we get something organized like we got this job going today. But as often as we can clean out a country, you'd work, and I'd guess that'd ought to maybe be as often as a couple of times a month."

Cleve was truly impressed. Not that he had any intention of riding with the rustlers, but he was truly impressed because up until now he'd had no inkling of just how much money the outlaws who rode for the rustling syndicate actually made.

"A couple of times a month," he exclaimed in genuine astonishment, "and three or four hundred dollars each of those times? Are you telling the truth? Six to eight hundred dollars a *month?*"

Fred fidgeted a little. "Well, maybe not always. Sometimes your share would only be maybe a hundred or two hundred dollars a trip, depending on how many cattle we got away with and how much we got for them

117

down south near the border where we deliver 'em. But even so . . . hell . . . the worst you'd do with us would be two to four hundred dollars a month. That'd be the *worst*, and I know how much they pay you Rangers. You'd be tripling your pay every month with us, and only working maybe six or eight, or ten or twelve days out of each month."

Cleve changed his mind about that offer of tobacco and papers. The half-breed fished them forth and handed them over, then stood and watched with frank interest as Cleve Hampshire thoughtfully rolled a smoke.

Whoever that damned fool was who said crime didn't pay, didn't know his behind from a round rock!

CHAPTER
FOURTEEN

One rider was coming back with two led horses, Cleve Hampshire's horse and the horse of the brigand chieftain. The other three men were already angling off in the direction of the Brinkley cow outfit's range.

Cleve lit up, thanked Fred for the makings, and eyed the half-breed steadily. "You wouldn't want to explain to me how all this works," he said.

"No," agreed Fred. "Why should I?"

"Mister, until an hour ago I never saw you before in my life," explained Cleve, "and you tell me I can make all that cash money riding with you . . . and I'm expected to believe every word you say." Cleve smiled without humor. "Change places and tell me . . . would you believe me if I told you a cock-and-bull story?"

The half-breed replied wryly: "No, maybe not, but, Ranger, your choices aren't so good you can be skeptical. If I was in your boots and had a choice of gettin' myself shot or makin' some money, I wouldn't have no trouble at all making up my mind which I'd go for." He glanced out where the oncoming horseman was approaching. "And, Ranger, you only got about one more minute to make your choice."

Cleve was not thinking in terms of Twenty-One or Levi now. Even if they had caught up, were somewhere over yonder in the foothills with their carbines, they would be far out of gun range of Cleve and the half-breed outlaw, with no chance of creeping closer before Fred drew and fired at Cleve. It was exactly as the half-breed had said it was.

Cleve blew smoke. "All right, mister, where do we ride?"

The half-breed did not look or act very elated at this successful recruitment, he merely loosened his stance slightly and swung to glance downcountry where those three rustlers were already growing small in the distance, and, when the man on horseback came on up with his led stock and halted, gazing from one of them to the other, Fred said: "We'll just keep the cattle from drifting down out of here, Whit, and kill time until the Brinkley split-off gets far enough northward for us to see it." He casually jutted his jaw in Cleve Hampshire's direction. "He'll be ridin' with us."

The mounted man said nothing. He tossed the reins of their horses to them, glanced impassively at Cleve, then started to rein back around as though to ride out and begin the big circling ride it would occasionally require to keep the stolen McGregor cattle bunched in the big hidden meadow.

The half-breed called to him: "Climb a knoll now and then!" That was all Fred said. It was all he had to say; they were outlaws, hunted men, and like all renegades they could never stop keeping a good vigil even in territory where they felt the safest.

120

Cleve finished the smoke, stamped it out, and lifted searching eyes to the broken serrated low and rather distant foothills. Twenty-One was out there, somewhere, and Levi was also out there by now, and, while those two were Cleve's best allies, right at this time they also constituted his biggest peril. All they had to do was be found out there, the way Cleve had been found, and the badges they were also carrying would put an end to them as well as also to Cleve.

The half-breed leader of the outlaw riders was not a man to be talked out of very much. After that quiet man had ridden off to keep an eye upon the grazing cattle, Fred took down a canteen from his saddle, drank, offered the thing to Cleve, then hung it back when Cleve declined. "By tomorrow evenin'," he told Cleve, "we'll be south of Valverde about fifteen miles, providin' we don't have a bunch of sore-footed cattle to slow us down. They'll take delivery down there, pay us, and that'll be that." Fred kept studying Cleve. "You're not curious?"

"You know better," stated Cleve. "You're darned right I'm curious. But I'm just not going to start right off asking a lot of questions. In time I expect I'll see how it all works."

Fred nodded approval of all this, then demonstrated his own variety of curiosity by saying: "When we first talked, you said there'd been a heap of complaints to El Paso about rustlin' up here around Valverde."

"That's right," conceded Cleve. "For about a year the cow outfits around Valverde have been complaining about being raided."

"And it took the Rangers this long to do something about it?" asked Fred.

Cleve grinned. "No, not exactly, but we get dozens of complaints like that every month, and about half of them are from cow outfits who've lost bunches of strays or who've neglected to make a correct tally, and, when the counts don't add up, they start seeing rustlers behind every buckbrush."

Fred accepted this. "Then what finally decided the Rangers to sendin' you up here now?"

Cleve was on thin ice. "Well," he replied, "partly because we kept getting the same complaints from the same outfits up here, and partly because it was about time for us to make a sashay around through the Valverde country."

"And if you don't show up again, or don't send them back no report?" asked the half-breed.

Cleve shrugged. "In a month they'll figure the outlaws salted me down and send in another Ranger. Maybe that time they'll send in a crew of Rangers."

This was what Fred had been probing for. He said: "All right, then we quit raiding the Valverde country for a while."

"For a year," suggested Cleve, and the half-breed did not offer any protest.

"For a year then," he agreed. "We got plenty more country to operate out of."

Cleve said: "Through Harry? Hell, Valverde is his territory. What good could he do in a place like . . . say . . . Fort Worth or Dallas?"

Fred's answer to that was dry. "You don't know Turnbow. He's got more contacts than a man can shake a stick at. He's one hell of an organizer, and maybe when a man's willing to spread his money around as Harry is . . ." The half-breed turned to look far out, then he looked back again. "How did you happen to mention Turnbow?" he asked softly.

Cleve shot back a direct answer. "I didn't, you did. When we first met over here, you said something about having warned Harry that this territory was getting too hot."

"There are a hundred Harrys around," stated Fred.

"Not in the Valverde country," stated Cleve. "There is only one that I know of who would be big enough and experienced enough, and he'd be the storekeeper in town." Cleve faintly frowned. "What difference does it make?"

Fred spoke forthrightly: "Well, if you suspected Turnbow while you was making your investigation, and you'd sent in a report to El Paso about him . . ."

"Naw, hell," stated Cleve. "I haven't sent in any report." He remembered the telegram to Charley Runnels, and was very glad he'd sent it to Charley instead of to Captain Tomlinson — just in case someone in town might have been suspicious enough of Cleve to look at the message. If anyone had, apparently they had said nothing to the half-breed outlaw chieftain because Fred changed the subject, acting as though this fresher topic more nearly held his interest.

"We got to be out of the Valverde territory tonight, no matter what. I've had a feelin' even before you

123

showed up. I go a lot on my hunches and I've had this feeling for the last couple of weeks that we'd ought to peel out of here and work somewhere else for a while."

"You got good hunches," stated Cleve, turning to look out where the grazing cattle, filled up now on good grass, were beginning to turn logy, to lie down to chew their cuds and perhaps also to sleep during the hot part of the day. "Any interest at all by the Rangers ought to be a warning to you, Fred, and, if they send one out to look around, you can darned well figure you're just a little bit short of being caught."

Fred rolled a smoke, saw the man who was riding around the stolen cattle, and turned to mount up as he said: "Come along, we might as well do our share." Then, as he turned to step up across leather, he said: "You don't expect full pay for this job, do you . . . because all you done so far was come in after all the other work had been done."

Cleve offered no argument. "Whatever you say. You're the boss."

They left shade and passed over into direct heat and sunlight. It was a sufficient reminder to them both that not only was the day advancing, but so also were the seasons. From time to time Cleve glanced over in the direction he was certain McKinnon and Holt would be hiding and watching. He saw nothing nor did he actually expect to see anything.

When they finally got around to where the other outlaw was sitting on a big stone, smoking, holding the reins of his drowsing horse, the man on the rock nodded and said: "Couldn't be more peaceful if a man was in heaven."

It certainly seemed that way. There was not a discordant sight or sound in any direction, and because it was the time of day for cattle in summertime to bed down in shade and chew cuds or drowse, there was no particular movement to be observed, either.

Fred left them and rode out to a knoll where he dismounted and walked to the top for a long look around. The outlaw, sitting on the rock in meager shade, watched all this and eventually said: "They're goin' to have to get up awful early in the morning to get ahead of that feller, Ranger."

There was admiration in the outlaw's voice. Cleve looked from Fred upon his distant knoll to the man on the stone whose name was Whit. In that list of men Perry Stockton had ridden with furnished Cleve by Captain Tomlinson over Charley Runnel's signature was one Whitman Mayo, wanted for murder in Indian Territory, wanted for bank robbery and murder in east Texas, and wanted for highway robbery in Colorado.

There had been no description of Whit Mayo, but there did not have to be. Not many men with a name like that were riding with Perry Stockton when Stockton had last been seen heading for west Texas.

Cleve was not especially impressed. Whit did not look like a murderer, but then most actual murderers probably did not look like murderers if one went according to the popular conception of what a villainous murderer looked like. Cleve raised his head a little — and saw a hatless head with sandy hair

125

sweat-plastered to a pale forehead less than a hundred and fifty yards distant, rearward, where a man was squatting Indian-like behind some jumbled boulders. He felt like sighing. Twenty-One had made it after all. Now all he had to do was look elsewhere and see Levi Holt.

He looked, but there was no sign of Levi or anyone else, and, when he would have made a more intent study of the rearward broken country that flanked the stolen herd and the men who were watching it, his attention was distracted by the seated outlaw crushing out his cigarette upon the rock and saying: "Yonder's dust. I'd guess that'll be the Brinkley split-off. I'll be damned if I ever imagined stealin' livestock could be this easy and safe . . . in broad daylight, raising a dust just like it was all plumb legitimate and all."

Cleve turned slowly, found the faint discoloration against the southwesterly horizon that was Whit Mayo's dust banner, and, while he watched it move ahead toward them, at least toward the same foothills where they were waiting, he decided that McKinnon might as well apprehend Whitman Mayo, which would then leave Fred alone with Cleve. With the odds evened up, Cleve had no doubts at all of his ability to clean out the half-breed, and this was probably the proper time to start the cleaning up, not later when all the outlaw crew was reunited and it was time to start the drive.

Cleve Hampshire had no intention of allowing the drive of all those stolen cattle to get under way, and, that being the case, then there probably could be no better time to begin cleaning out the renegades. He

126

turned very casually, while Whit was still intently gazing out where the half-breed atop his little knoll was also watching that oncoming dust cloud, and made a lazy little hand gesture as he moved to lift his hat and resettle it atop his head. McKinnon's partially exposed face over in the shimmery rocks slowly raised and slowly sank in a nod of understanding.

Cleve turned back to watching the dust.

CHAPTER
FIFTEEN

All three of the watchers, including Fred, watched intently as that spiraling, faint stand of dun dust moved slowly but very steadily in the direction of the foothills.

There was a lot of daylight left and by the time the stolen herds were intermingled back in the secret meadow it would be about time to begin the eastward drive that would take the stolen cattle along in front of the mountains where their rising dust would be unnoticeable against that tawnier backdrop.

With all the time they had, with darkness on the way before the drive was far enough eastward to be swung south toward the border country, and with the full night ahead of them, and no one to realize what had happened until the following day, there was just one reason why this grand theft might not work, and that one reason squeezed sweat off his face with a wrinkled sleeve, resettled his hat, and watched the half-breed come down off his knoll, swing up across leather, and turn back in the direction of Cleve and the solemn cow thief sitting in thin shade nearby.

The cow thief said: "I think after this raid, I'll head on over to Hortonville. That's where I come from . . . I still got kin over there. They ain't seen me in something like six, seven years."

Cleve, alternately watching the half-breed and the much more distant dust banner, said nothing. He knew Hortonville. It was one of those central Texas towns that had in its favor wind, a leached-out barren countryside, ugly little unimaginative buildings, and taciturn, evasive people. He was not at all surprised to learn that Hortonville was where Whitman Mayo had come from.

Fred rode on up and stepped to earth trailing a bridle rein. Beyond, where the McGregor cattle were perfectly content to lie and loaf, there was a little more shade from the accumulation of summertime heat that seemed to be thrown back into the foothills by the more distant mountains, making the area where the men and cattle were less hospitable as the hours passed. It usually was like this in midsummer against almost any mountains, almost anywhere, and once the build-up of reflected heat began dissipating as the sun sank beyond the highest peaks, the foothills cooled out fairly rapidly.

Fred shook off the sweat and sank to his haunches between Whitman Mayo and Cleve Hampshire as he fished around for the makings and created his cigarette almost without glancing downward. "Couldn't see much," he reported, "except that it don't look like the boys are fetchin' up the Brinkley split-off directly into this here meadow."

That made Whit Mayo scowl. "Why not?" he asked. "They know darned well everything's got to fit in or the whole damned thing is in danger. We got to meet and mingle the gathers and get to movin'. Can't horse around up here and maybe be spied out by some passin' range rider."

Fred was unperturbed as he inhaled and exhaled. "We got all night and half tomorrow," he stated in a reproving tone. "And if they ain't comin' directly to us, believe me, they got a good reason."

Cleve twisted casually and speared the area where he had seen Twenty-One with a quick look, but there was nothing back there but a jumble of big, old, gray boulders worn as smooth as a spanked baby's bottom. He faced forward as Whit Mayo suddenly straightened a little on the rock where he was sitting in weak shade, and for a moment or two sat perfectly still and erect before saying: "Hey, there's a rider coming."

Fred and Cleve turned instantly. It became very clear almost at once that neither Fred nor Whit were the slightest bit sympathetic toward the idea of someone riding up into the foothills at this time.

The rider was actually a couple of miles distant, but he was galloping his horse through the shimmery heat, which in itself suggested urgency, and he was heading directly for the general area where the McGregor herd was hidden. Whoever he was, Cleve got the definite impression that his appearance was no coincidence.

Fred slowly rose and tipped down his hat brim as he stared. Finally he said: "Get mounted, Whit, and slip over eastward. You can tell about where he's going to cut up past the first knobs, and, if you hurry, I think you can get behind him."

"And do what?" asked Mayo, turning immediately toward his drowsing saddle animal.

"Depends on who he is," stated the half-breed. "If it's just some damned fool" — Fred shrugged — "knock him over the head and leave him tied and disarmed." For a while the half-breed added nothing to this; he stood perfectly still, doing his utmost to make out the details of that oncoming rider. Finally the horseman pulled down to a fast walk and arrived within the vicinity of the nearest broken segments of the foothills. That was when Fred said: "Hold off a minute, Whit."

They all remained motionless, including Mayo who was sitting his saddle now.

"Well god-dammit!" exclaimed the half-breed in a surge of genuine surprise. "That there is Harry."

Fred did not give a reason for his astonishment but Cleve could guess the cause of it; the storekeeper probably never came out to watch the actual cattle stealing operation. Cleve's impression of Turnbow was that the storekeeper was a schemer, a plotter, planner, and deviser. He might ride through the empty night to a clandestine lover's rendezvous, but he was not the kind of a man who would knowingly ride into any other kind of risk, and this worried Cleve.

It seemed gradually also to worry the half-breed as he peered and pursed his thin lips and finally said: "Whit, hustle on around. I'm sure it's Harry, but all the same you make certain, and, if it is, fetch him on over. I'd say something has went plumb sour. Otherwise, he sure as hell wouldn't be comin' out here this time of day in such a lousy hurry."

Mayo reined away and Cleve watched his departure thoughtfully. Man to man, he was sure he could handle the half-breed, but first he had to be certain they were alone.

Fred moved slightly away in order to be able to watch Mayo's oblique progress, which was hidden by foothills from the oncoming horseman. It was an impromptu movement, Cleve was certain of that, but it also put more distance between them at roughly the time Cleve wanted them not to be that far apart.

Cleve turned again to glance in the direction where he had glimpsed McKinnon, and as before there was nothing to be seen back there but the raw countryside. He was straightening around when a man's faint high call rang across the leaden distance, but not from Turnbow's direction, from the opposite direction, over in the general area of that oncoming dust cloud. Cleve was distracted and so was the half-breed. As both of them turned, a rider appeared off in that westerly territory also riding a little faster than was advisable in this kind of heat, and this of course implied more urgency.

Fred looked at Cleve. "Something's went wrong," he muttered, and reached down to loosen the tie-down on his Colt. "I can feel it."

Cleve was of the opinion that a man did not have to possess a great amount of perspicacity, or whatever it took, to figure out something was wrong, but he was just as baffled as the half-breed was, and this probably was what now saved his life.

The half-breed turned on Cleve with a snarl. "Damn you, Ranger, you wasn't alone out here. And you started something before you come out here sure as hell."

Cleve, already baffled, was taken aback by the sudden violence of the half-breed's accusation. He stared, then he exclaimed loudly: "What the hell are you talking about? You're not making any sense at all, but I'll tell you one thing . . . the longer we just stand around here, like sitting ducks, the worse off our situation is going to be." He gestured in the direction of the rider approaching from the west. "That feller's got to be coming from the men with the Brinkley Ranch split-off, and ridin' that hard in this heat means something has gone wrong with that gather." He dropped his arm and glared at the outlaw leader. "Well . . . you're the head Indian . . . what do we do, just stand here until it's too late to run for it?"

Fred wavered, probably because, without a doubt, Cleve not only sounded very convincing, he looked and acted it. The reason he could act so convincingly was because he was not acting. Whatever was happening, whatever it was that was approaching meant trouble, and regardless of whether it was trouble for the rustlers or whether it was the thieves themselves who had discovered something and were now trying desperately to warn their half-breed leader, Cleve Hampshire was squarely in the middle. No matter who won, he lost.

That man approaching from the west passed around behind an upended small brake out a mile or so to the west, and to the east Harry Turnbow, urging his horse over into a trot now, came from around a knoll and almost rode into Whitman Mayo as the rustler from Hortonville jumped his horse out of shelter and confronted the rider from Valverde. Turnbow's horse shied violently at this sudden appearance of another horse and rider. He almost slid from beneath his rider.

Cleve saw those two men gesticulate as they spoke back and forth very swiftly, then he also saw Whit twist in the saddle and stare back in the direction where Cleve and the half-breed were. He decided that he only had as long as it would take for Whit and Turnbow to race back toward the place where he and the half-breed were to make his move, and whatever Turnbow had said to Whitman Mayo had impressed the outlaw, otherwise Whit would not have twisted like that to stare.

Fred swore and said: "It's Lon." Fred was pointing with his left hand. The rider coming from the west was visible again when he emerged from around the upended little barranca.

Behind them, the loafing cattle seemed to pick up some kind of bad sensation from the very air. Neither of the oncoming messengers, Turnbow or the man called Lon, was close enough even to shout yet, but those cattle were lumbering up to their feet as though they had detected something unfavorable.

Lon, Cleve decided, was the name of that laconic, tall lean man who chewed tobacco, the one who had ridden off with the two younger outlaws to the rendezvous with the Brinkley gather.

Suddenly the half-breed said: "I'll tell you what's wrong, damn it all." He raised his left hand to point again. "That's not a herd of cattle off there to the west heading toward the foothills. That's a bunch of horsemen. They're movin' too fast to be cattle."

Cleve looked, and half decided the half-breed was right. But if it *was* horsemen, then who were they, and, if they happened to be a party of cowmen, who had tipped them off so they could be on hand when the outlaws struck?

Finally it dawned on Cleve that his particular peril was increasing just about as fast as was the particular peril of Fred and the other outlaws. Those oncoming cattlemen would not know Cleve Hampshire from Adam's off ox. He did not even have his badge now; it was still lying where he had been searched and disarmed. He did not even have a gun!

Again that oncoming man heading from the west called out, but this time, seeing the two men over near the rocks watching, he gestured frantically with one hand, making motions that looked as though he were trying to signal them to get astride and run for it.

The half-breed though had been imperturbable up to now, and, although he certainly realized that serious trouble was practically breathing down his neck, he remained standing, motionless and watchful. The only indication that he might suddenly break and run for it was in the way he gently tugged the reins to his horse through bent fingers as he steadily eyed the approaching horseman from the west.

Cleve had just about decided it was time for him to jump the half-breed when Fred twisted to look back where Whit and Turnbow were also rushing forward. Fred was facing Cleve across a distance that precluded an actual frontal confrontation, so Cleve hung there scarcely breathing, deciding that now he had gone right down to the wire, now he did not have more than a couple of minutes left before all three of the oncoming riders would be within killing range of him, and, once they got that close, it would be too late for him to attack the half-breed with any hope of doing it without also being killed.

CHAPTER
SIXTEEN

Several things happened almost simultaneously. Turnbow suddenly stood in his stirrups and yelled something while gesturing as he and Mayo loped forward. Turnbow's words were not quite distinguishable but his gestures seemed to indicate some great agitation, and Whit Mayo was also beginning to gesture.

Cleve knew they were gesturing about him. He turned to see if the half-breed had figured this out, and, as he did so, the man approaching from the left raised his handgun. Cleve saw the reflection of bitter yellow sunlight off gray steel out beyond the half-breed, and dropped instantly, just as Lon tugged the trigger. The gunshot sounded flat and heavy in that bad atmosphere, but it was definitely a gunshot and Fred spun seconds after Cleve had dropped. As though this were a signal, Whit Mayo also drew his six-gun. Cleve could see him holding it aloft, waiting for his chance also to fire, and squawked to the half-breed: "They're trying for your bounty sure as hell!"

Under calmer circumstances it probably would not have fooled the half-breed at all, but right now, and for the next ten or twenty seconds, Fred did not seem able actually to understand what he should do, except that he crouched a little as Lon came onward, still holding his gun hand up and ready.

Whit Mayo was evidently a very cool killer. He made no premature attempt to fire at Cleve as Lon had done, but the moment Whit knew he was within six-gun range, he yanked his horse back to a sliding halt, raised his rein arm, the left one, and gently placed his six-gun barrel across it and took careful aim.

Cleve knew he was looking death in the face. He started to spring up and hurl himself away, but a carbine made its sharper, more incisive sound from Cleve's left somewhere, and the half-breed leader of the rustlers looked shocked at finding a gunman back yonder in among those jumbled gray boulders.

Whit Mayo must also have been shocked. He did not have time to cock his Colt and squeeze off the shot. He sagged slightly in the saddle and turned his head slowly in the direction of the Winchester shot, then he turned loose all over and dropped like a sack of wet grain. His horse side-stepped almost nonchalantly, at least it looked that way, as Whit hit the ground and half rolled beneath the animal.

Harry Turnbow was yanking back, was desperately trying to halt the onward rush of his mount toward Fred and Cleve, but Harry was staring glassily over toward those jumbled gray boulders. He had seen the Winchester; he knew he was well within killing range of it, and he had just seen the mounted man at his side get shot out of the saddle by that same gun.

Cleve heard the rider coming from behind and twisted to locate him. Lon was clearly visible. It was almost as though he had been frozen in time the way he was glaring wildly at Cleve and swinging his six-gun forward and downward. As long as Cleve lived, he would always remember the expression on the man, and the straining, sweaty look of the horse as they both bore down upon him.

He rolled, called to Fred, and gestured to divert the half-breed. When Fred drew and swung to look westerly, Cleve hit him below the knees with his hurtling body. At that exact moment Lon fired. Cleve heard the bullet strike hard into the nearby earth.

Again that Winchester made its distinctive high and snarling sound, but this time, although the aim had been good, McKinnon's target had still been moving and the slug sang past. But close enough to force Lon to wince as he tried one more wild shot at the clawing, rolling, cursing men on the ground. Lon missed again.

The Winchester did not sound again, but from over where Harry Turnbow was fighting to turn back and flee, a contingent of riders appeared as though up out of the ground; they came down from the northward brakes and inward from the easterly countryside, strung out. It looked to be at least seven or eight of them. Turnbow was cut off. He reined to a halt and dropped his rein hand to the saddle horn and simply stared in bewilderment.

Cleve had no time to notice. All he instinctively sensed was that whatever had gone wrong had now arrived in the secret meadow as Lon's sweaty mount plunged past and its rider, twisting in mid-jump to fire, had to hold off because the half-breed was fighting back and locking himself in wild close combat with the Texas Ranger.

Cleve had not underestimated the half-breed, but neither had he expected him to be as experienced at hand fighting as he proved. Very few range men were good fist fighters, and Indians were almost never adequate fist fighters, but somewhere along the checkered career of this particular half-breed someone had taught him how to battle.

He couldn't quite break free of Cleve to stand up and slug it out with the lawman, but he strained his utmost to get clear while at the same time swinging his arms like flails, able to use them both while Cleve, because he was desperately clinging to his armed adversary, could only employ his right hand and arm.

He slugged hard and concentrated upon the half-breed's midsection. If he allowed the outlaw to break free, Fred could kill Cleve with his handgun. As long as they were locked together, Fred could not draw the weapon, but he tried, and each time Cleve hammered him in the belly again, forcing the half-breed to abandon his reach for the gun and throw his right arm across in front of his stomach to block the next strike.

Lon was turning back, leaning far from the saddle and straining to force his excited horse to make as short a turn as possible, when someone over near those jumbled, gray boulders called to him clearly and distinctly — and calmly.

"Hey, cowboy!"

Lon instinctively swung his head.

McKinnon fired from a standing position. Lon was knocked back against the high cantle of his Texas saddle. He looked more astonished than pained, and raised his six-gun. He fired, and gray slag broke free from the stones in front of Twenty-One and made McKinnon jump aside and wince.

Cleve was swinging the half-breed by his shirt front, was momentarily looking over the half-breed's bowed, hatless head, and saw the bullet drive deadly stone chips into McKinnon's face. Cleve aimed his best punch from high up, staggered the half-breed with it when he hit him just behind the ear, and, as Fred sagged, Cleve wrenched away the half-breed's six-gun, spun it in his hand for grip and heft and sighting, squeezed gently as his thumb pad fell away from the hammer, and the gun exploded thunderously, giving Cleve a solid backlash of power that threw his hand up.

This time Lon did not look around. He tilted and kept right on tilting over the cantle of his saddle, over the sweaty rump of his startled horse, and made a complete somersault before striking the ground, belly down. The gun in his fist flew a hundred feet and slid in the dust.

In the west several racing horsemen, who Cleve had not noticed until now, shouted ahead and brandished weapons as though they were hurrying to the aid of the outlaw chieftain and Lon. Cleve turned to look over a shoulder and saw them coming. Farther back he also saw more riders. It looked as though there might be six or eight of them out there dancing in the heat waves as though they were phantoms, the hoofs and legs of their horses several feet off the ground and the men themselves shimmery and vague in the gray dust they were stirring to life.

Someone fired a weapon and Cleve dropped to the ground, uncertain of the source and the destination of that bullet. If it had been aimed at him, it must have gone wide, because he did not hear it strike close by nor did he hear the sound of it cutting through the air near at hand.

Fred rolled on the ground, pushing up onto all fours and turning to look around. He was dazed; more than that, he was unarmed and at the mercy of the sweaty, torn, and rumpled man nearby who had his gun cocked and held, rock-like. Fred stared from black eyes at Cleve Hampshire, then he did an odd thing. He slowly let himself flat down on his stomach and did not move again.

Those distant half dozen or so riders, approaching from the west, responded to someone's unheard order and spread out until they were loping ahead toward the battleground with as much as ten or fifteen yards between each horseman.

Eastward, over where those other range men had halted, also strung out, Harry Turnbow was about to be swept up and taken prisoner. Cleve could see these things. He also saw Twenty-One McKinnon over among the gray stones wiping at bleeding scratches on his face where those shards of sharp granite had struck him.

A riderless horse cut across in front of Cleve, heading southward. He stepped upon a trailing rein and snorted loudly as the bit in his mouth was yanked with cruel force, almost halting the animal. Cleve could probably have caught that horse. Instead, he wished the confounded thing would get past his line of sight where those oncoming riders were pressing steadily inward. He was certain they were local cowmen; how they happened to have arrived in the secret meadow at this specific time he had no idea, nor did he especially care; what had him worried was the excellent possibility that one of those oncoming cowmen, either behind him or in front of him, would decide that Cleve Hampshire had also to be an outlaw, and shoot at him.

There were two renegades coming in from the west. Cleve did not fear them particularly; they would be considering anyone up where their half-breed leader was lying as another renegade, but behind them, spread out and gradually slowing their pace as they closed the big surround, were the other cattlemen.

Cleve worked his way, lizard-like, until he was close enough to use the half-breed's prone carcass as a shield, then he shoved the cocked six-gun dead ahead within inches of Fred's face. All the half-breed did was slowly turn away. Whatever had happened to Fred, he was now completely out of it, baffled, stunned, totally bewildered or whatever it was that troubled him. Fred was no longer capable of functioning. Perhaps it was the result of the savage beating he had taken from the Ranger.

One of those two oncoming outlaws yelled ahead. Cleve gestured with the upraised six-gun. He could have shot the man out of his saddle with ease, but neither of those two had guns raised. They clearly were of the opinion that Cleve was one of their group. Perhaps they assumed he was Whitman Mayo. They certainly could not see him well enough where he was two-thirds hidden by the half-breed to make a positive identification.

He yelled at them. "Get down! Get off those damned horses and get over here!"

They heard him and left their animals on the run. One of them lost his footing and went end over end, but he bounded back upright and raced beside his companion up to where Cleve was lying.

Cleve aimed the cocked Colt. "Hold it! Right where you are, hold it and *don't touch a gun!*"

The outlaws were those two younger men, the pair that had seemed reluctant earlier when it had appeared that Cleve was to be shot to death. They had gone with the dead outlaw called Lon to take delivery of the Brinkley split-off. Now, they stared from ashen faces at the steady cocked Colt in the hand of the dirty, ragged man lying across the motionless half-breed. There was no way to misinterpret the expression on the face of Cleve Hampshire — he was primed to kill at the slightest excuse. Neither of those two men moved a muscle, although their sweaty shirt fronts heaved from hard breathing.

Out a half mile to the east Harry Turnbow had been swept along in the slow advance of the strung-out ranchers and their riders. To the west those other men, strung out also but much farther, began to curve inward as the silence and the dust began to settle on all sides.

Cleve wondered about McKinnon but did not look over there. He said — "Throw down those belt guns." — to the young men in front of him. As they silently obeyed, he gathered both legs, then, using the yielding flesh of the half-breed as his lever, Cleve got upright and gestured. "Move around to the left. Keep moving." He stepped away, with the unarmed rustlers in sight, and growled at the half-breed: "On your feet, Fred."

The half-breed twisted to glance up. He saw the pistol barrel, the drawn back hammer of his own gun, and pushed slowly against the ground with both palms.

To the west a familiar voice sang out: "Hey, Cleve, you all right?"

Cleve did not look around nor make any attempt to reply, but now he knew where Levi Holt was — leading those ranchers who had come upcountry from the direction of the Brinkley range, and that explained something else — how did those cowmen from down there happen to be in behind the rustlers heading for the foothills at the same time as the outlaws were heading up in that direction.

Levi had also been busy, apparently.

CHAPTER
SEVENTEEN

Cleve was angry. More correctly he was fiercely indignant, and yet as the ranchers converged and swung down around him to stand, staring, it was hard for Cleve to decide whom he should be angry with.

A graying man strolled over and smiled. "I'm Curt Brinkley," he announced, and, turning slightly, Curt Brinkley motioned for several of his riders to haul those two unarmed rustlers away, then he turned back facing the half-breed. "This one," he said thoughtfully, "must be their leader."

Cleve eased off the hammer of the half-breed's six-gun, dropped the gun into his own hip holster, and said: "How did you know that?"

Brinkley answered casually: "My range boss told me they were headed up by a half-breed."

"Your range boss?" inquired Cleve, dimly remembering someone mentioning that Brinkley's foreman was the man responsible for delivering the rustled cattle to the outlaws.

Brinkley continued to smile pleasantly as he explained. "Yeah. He spent a lot more money in El Paso the last time we took cattle down there than he could have earned from me . . . I watched him and kept what I saw to myself until this time, when we made an early gather, then I set up the riding crew also to watching. We saw him take a split-off and head into the foothills with it damned early this morning."

"And you followed," said Cleve, turning as someone tapped his shoulder.

McKinnon's face looked as though it had been fed through a meat grinder an inch at a time, but he was grinning. "Got pretty hot out here for a while," Twenty-One laconically observed.

Cleve turned, searched out Levi Holt, and said: "Where in hell did you go? You were supposed to tie up with Twenty-One."

"Saw all these cowmen riding along in the wake of that split-off and figured, since you and Twenty-One was already up here, someone had better warn those cowmen not to shoot any Texas Rangers because it was against the law." Levi did not smile but several of the range riders did. "Where those other fellers came from is a mystery to me," he concluded, jutting his jaw in the direction of the range men who had come in from the north and east, the men who had scooped up Harry Turnbow as they had completed the surround of the embattled outlaws.

A grizzled, lined, and pale-eyed older man who stood slouched and as lean and slab-sided as someone thirty years younger answered Levi's remark with a choppy little hand gesture that included the men standing around him on the east side of the crowded little area. "We just naturally followed him," the older man said, curtly nodding in McKinnon's direction. "When I

147

hired him on, I figured he might be an outlaw, and, when he didn't come back after a few nightly rides into town until real late, I figured he was palavering with some of his outlaw partners, and set up a watch on him. When he snuck off and commenced trailing these other fellers . . . well, hell . . . me and my other riders figured we was sure enough on the trail of one of those bastards who've been raiding up through all the Valverde country this past year or so."

McKinnon eyed the old man and his riders but said nothing. Cleve's shirt was clinging to him and his throat was hot and dry as the excitement gradually began to leave him. All his indignation did not depart; some of it lingered because, as he now saw this situation, it was not the fault of the cowmen; they had been entirely justified in reacting as they had. It had to be the fault of Captain Tomlinson down in El Paso not to realize how ready and eager these Valverde cowmen were to take matters into their own hands. Tomlinson's oversight, if that was what it really was, had come very close to getting Cleve Hampshire killed.

The trouble with dispassionate indignation, of course, was that by the time a man got back down to El Paso where he could tell someone what he thought of them, all the irritability would have atrophied.

A cowboy sauntered over and offered Cleve his canteen. The water was cold because the outer sides of the canteen had been covered with blanketing material that was kept wetted down from time to time. Water had never tasted so good. Cleve offered the canteen to Twenty-One who also drank deeply.

Elsewhere, several range riders got astride to catch the loose saddle stock of the outlaws, and a couple of the other range riders dragged the dead renegades over out of the direct sunlight.

One of those younger rustlers bitterly glowered at the half-breed, and, when he had an opportunity to do so, he said: "You was so damned smart and all, always sayin' you could sense trouble!"

Cleve turned. Harry Turnbow was limp; his features were slack and shiny with greasy sweat. He did not resemble the storekeeper down at Valverde at all, right at this moment. "What happens to your rustling syndicate now?" Cleve asked

Turnbow feebly said: "I don't know what you're talking about."

Levi Holt walked over with Cleve's gun and badge, the personal effects the outlaws had taken from him when they had first captured him. Turnbow saw the badge and looked up at the man who pocketed it.

Cleve shed the half-breed's six-gun and replaced it in the holster with his own weapon, then he said: "Harry, before we go back to town we're going to need the name of every crooked cattle buyer you've ever delivered cattle to, and the name of every man who's ever sold out to you, like Brinkley's range boss did and like those two riders for McGregor did . . . And the reason we're going to need that before we take you back to town is because . . ."

"I'll give it to you," said the storekeeper swiftly, unwilling to hear Cleve's grim conclusion.

Levi Holt scratched the top of his head and lowered his hat, then said: "Those fellers who work for McGregor?"

Cleve and McKinnon nodded at Levi.

Curt Brinkley sighed, shook his head, swore a little, and said: "Three, four of you fellers ride up to the old man's place and bring those two back." He was addressing his own range men, and three of them turned without a word and loped off northwesterly as Cleve looked around, saw a cowboy holding the reins to Cleve's horse, and walked over to retrieve his animal and to lead it back in front of Brinkley and Twenty-One McKinnon.

"Get all the names out of Turnbow," he told McKinnon. "Lock the bastard up and see that Cap Tomlinson gets the names . . . Levi, you and Twenty-One might as well head on back to town and hang around down there until the loose ends are knotted."

Levi nodded. "All right. You'll be along directly?"

"No," replied Cleve, stepping up across his saddle. "I'm going antelope hunting, and, when you see Cap, you can tell him that's where *I've* gone, and where *he* can go is to hell!"

Cleve jerked his horse around, spurred it up into a slow little lazy lope, and did not even look back at the knot of men standing back there staring after him.

FIGHTING MARSHAL

CHAPTER
ONE

Cole Travis stayed with the main trail and it presently took him to one of the many clear meadows that broke a forest's solid gloominess. He saw some deer on this meadow. They fled at sight of him and Cole Travis passed on across to fade out into the trees again. Then he drew rein, sat entirely still for a time, and then dismounted where a little crease in the hills held a snow-water creek. It was hot beyond both forest and hills, where the plains lay, but in here it was fragrantly shadowed and cool. He loosened the cinch of his A-fork Texas saddle, removed the bridle, hung it upon his saddle horn, and let the horse walk over and drink. Then Cole Travis began to work up a cigarette.

The timber in here was ragged old first-growth pine and fir, huge at the butt and rising upward to a great height where interlaced top-covering limbs made a solid shelter from sunlight. It was breathlessly still here, and the resin scent was very strong. The stillness had a great depth to it; Cole Travis could hear his own breathing; he could distinctly hear the cadenced swallows of his animal at the creek. That stillness lay hard upon everything.

He did not know this land although years earlier he'd ridden through it outbound, and since those other days his life had been a series of hills like these, and deserts, and grasslands, and towns, and the prospect of being a stranger did not trouble him, for in the first place he was not really a stranger here, and in the second place being a stranger had never bothered him. His home for the past ten years had been wherever night had overtaken him, his hearth the little stone circle of a rider's cook fire. Cole Travis was range born and range bred. He had never asked more of life than to be left in his natural environment. He asked no more now.

He smoked and twisted to look on southward where the running land sloped gently away toward a low down pass he could not see and that was locally called Gunsight Pass. None of this was at all fresh in his memory, yet he knew it was there, and farther downcountry, beyond the last spit of trees where the hills sucked back to form a rich, secret valley, was a town. The town was named Gunsight — after the pass — and this he also knew.

The years had a way of doing things to a man — changing the chemistry of his body, shearing the fuzziness from his thinking, firming up his ideals and his actions until he was mature, and after that they seemed to stand clear to see what this composite would do, only dropping by the way as he progressed down them to become older, inexorably older, but otherwise unchanged after maturity came.

The horse finished drinking. It began nipping creekside grass, the sound of its grinding teeth a solid sound. Cole Travis finished his cigarette, killed it, and let the silence, the agelessness of this place, go deep into him. It made his muscles turn loose, his mind become drowsy, and, since it was morning and he was in no hurry anyway, he eased down with his back to the rough red bark of a giant tree, thumbed his hat forward to shield his eyes, and slept.

Later he came wide awake without moving, heeding that breath-gone thunder of a startled heart, knowing something had awakened him like this, tense and set to whirl upright, and waiting for it to come again. It did — the ring of a shod horse's hoof upon granite. Cole Travis gauged the distance and direction, then he pushed back his hat and sprang up, waiting. The rider was coming straight toward him. He did not believe, in all this great forest, this was a coincidence. He stepped along to where he might see that meadow, and caught sight of the rider pausing in the far fringe of trees. He watched the rider's shape bend in the saddle, then straighten back for a searching pair of eyes to probe the onward forest where he stood. Leather rustled, that far horse struck out into the meadow, and ploddingly crossed it. He moved easily aside, let the rider come into his private sanctuary, then stepped out, saying: "Hello."

The rider halted. It was a girl. Her hair was the color of fresh-cured meadow hay and her eyes were dark, brown actually, but in here seeming almost black. She was attired in a long split skirt of rusty hue and a light shirt. As she looked directly down at him, Travis saw the fresh-cream smoothness of her face and throat; they were in his eyes quite flawless. Even now as she sat there studying him, on her guard against him, skeptical of him, of his presence here, she looked strikingly handsome. She was not a tall girl; he could see that, but she was abundantly curved and molded and her mouth, like those liquid-dark eyes, showed temper, showed fire.

She said at once: "Who are you? What are you doing here?"

Travis recognized her hostility but could imagine no reason for it, so he was faintly annoyed. "Why?" he asked. "What does it matter who I am or what I'm doing here? Does this forest belong to you?"

"Where you're standing belongs to me, yes. I don't encourage trespassers."

"Well, now, lady," said Travis, a range man to whom the laws of trespass meant as little as they did to other range men, "I never knowingly go where I'm not wanted. But it's the rule to put up signs. That's what the clodhoppers and homesteaders do. Otherwise, how's a man to know . . . ?"

"I'm telling you now," answered the beautiful girl, her sulphur gaze hardening against Travis. "And I want to know who you are and what you're doing here."

Travis kept his steady blue eyes upon the girl. It became obvious that his mild annoyance had now become something else. He did not speak for some time, then he said in a very quiet tone: "Miss, it never hurt anyone to be a little civil. I don't mind telling you who I am or what I'm doing here. But not until you show some manners."

They exchanged a hot and hostile stare. The girl said nothing, so Travis turned upon his heel, went along to where his horse stood, bridled the beast, and snugged up the cinch without looking around, then rose up to settle over leather. That was when he looked around. She was white with anger. This made her eyes even darker. In spite of what lay now between them, though, her beauty sang across the little distance that separated her from Travis. He felt disappointment, and a vague and troubling kind of regret. Then, when she remained obdurately silent, he made a stiff little nod, turned, and eased his horse out, riding easterly through tall trees and gloomy shadows until she was lost to his rearward sight.

Travis kept his easterly course until the land began to buckle, to pitch upward toward an unseen height. Then he angled southward so as to avoid this and came to an angling buck run that cut along a wind-scoured ridge where nothing grew, and dropped straight down a stone face toward a broad and hidden little meadow below. Down there he saw sunshine burning away the last stubborn streaks of predawn. He thought that meadow might be a good place for a man to make his camp and eased off until his animal went gingerly to the buck run and began feeling its way out, over, and downward, following this scuffed pathway. Travis's cantle tilted upward as his animal tilted downward. Once, watching the onward trail, he thought he sighted a shod horse track freshly made, then he passed over this spot and was not sure because in the increasing dust he found no more such signs.

The land here was deceptive; he had left behind a lift of hills much higher than he'd thought. Either that or this hidden meadow was much lower than the countryside around about, for it took some time to reach those lower levels. But it was eventually done, and Travis heard the tinkle of water somewhere in among a little willow thicket, and, when the saddle cantle no longer gouged his back, his mount was once more upon an even keel, Travis made for that brush patch.

He found the spring and its southerly twisting concourse in among a greenery world of lace-work willows and rank, stirrup-high grass and mountain flowers. He also found something else — a little hand axe driven hard into the bole of a cotton-wood tree. He dismounted, glided over by the old cottonwood, and stood gazing at that little axe. Who, he wondered with an increasing degree of interest, had left his axe here, why? His horse dragged its reins, passed along some ten or fifteen feet, and dropped its head. It had taken one large mouthful of grass, then froze with the grass stems protruding from each side of its mouth. Travis saw this. He followed out the animal's line of vision but saw nothing right away, did not in fact see the other horse until seconds ahead of the quiet, stony voice that spoke out roughly from hiding to say: "Drop the gun, mister. Drop it easy now."

Travis was slow to obey and the earlier annoyance he'd felt returned. Standing unarmed, he began a very slow, twisting turn. The unseen man made no objection; he rose up from some brush and willows as

Travis came fully around. He was young, younger even than Cole Travis, and his whiskery face looked grim, looked desperate. He was Travis's height and build — leaned down from hard living, and angular with the sturdiness of a range bred man; he held his cocked gun low and steady. "Go over to your horse," he said to Travis, "pull out that carbine and throw it down, too."

Travis obeyed. He hesitated though, estimating his chances of springing away so that, while he had the carbine in hand, he might also put the horse between them. In the end he decided against this, not out of fear because he doubted if the younger man could hit him with the first shot, but out of curiosity. This obviously hiding man did not have that dissolute and vicious look that went with genuine outlaws. He let the carbine fall into the grass and straightened up.

"Maybe," he said sarcastically, "I ought to shed my spurs, too, feller. For all you know they might also be loaded."

"Very funny," replied his captor, assessing Travis. "If you're no better at shooting than you are at making jokes, why then I'd better let you pick up your guns, mister."

Travis and the younger, equally as spare and tall man keenly considered one another. The younger man's face, when he shifted a little so that sunshine struck him, had the indelible sharp, almost feral expression, one sometimes saw in hunted men. Casually then, the younger man put up his gun. "All right," he said, "you found me. What're you goin' to do about it?"

Travis said nothing. He blinked, then put a slowly rummaging glance about him for signs of this man's camp, and didn't speak until he'd finished this. "I'm not going to do anything about it," he eventually said. "Why should I?"

Now it was the young man's turn to look doubtful. "You're part of the Stuart Ranch crew, aren't you?" he asked.

Travis was piecing loose ends together. He said: "Is there a girl with honey blonde hair and brown eyes on this Stuart Ranch?"

"Barbara Stuart," stated the young man.

"And is she kind of hostile?"

The young man's lips curved a little. "Kind of hostile, mister? Why no . . . she's *plumb* hostile."

"I met her an hour or so back," said Travis. He stooped, plucked a grass stalk, carefully examined it, then put it between his teeth. "Suppose you tell me what this is all about," he said to the younger man. "I don't know her, I don't know you, but I'll be damned if I don't have a suspicion I just rode into the middle of a nest of rattlers."

The younger man relaxed. He continued studying Travis for a moment longer, then he said: "You had breakfast yet?"

"Nope."

"Come on then, for neither have I and I'm hungry." Without another word the young man turned and began pushing his way through the thicket. Travis watched this a moment, then shrugged and went along, too.

The young man came upon a new trail through crushed grass and paced steadily along it without once looking back. He stopped where a curl of the creek had cut a wide, deep, and glass-clear pool. There, Travis saw the camp — the rumpled bedroll, the cook fire stone ring with its little dry oak fire sending forth no smoke at all, and other signs that whoever this man was, he'd been hiding in here for many days.

"Coffee's done," the young man said, gesturing toward a rusty can. "Use that cup. The meat'll be fried before you know it."

Travis got the coffee and threw aside his hat as he dropped down in dappled shade to gaze at the rippling little pool, at the man things hanging from limbs roundabout, and on over where his host was slicing dark red venison from a haunch.

"My name is Cole Travis," he said. "I was bound for Gunsight. I was waterin' my horse and this Barbara Stuart came on. She'd been trackin' me . . . I saw that the way she rode. She was pretty grim and short, too, when she ordered me off her land. Care to explain what you can figure from this?"

"Sure," said the younger man without looking away from that cooking meat. "My name's Bart Hayden. I'm hidin' in here because my horse hurt a leg comin' down that damned buck run you passed over to get down in here. I got to stay here until he can walk again."

"A feller could walk out o' here," said Travis. "Gunsight isn't more than eight, ten miles from here."

"I'd never get to Gunsight," said Bart Hayden, holding up a piece of meat to drip grease. "They know

161

I'm in these hills some place and they're making a methodical hunt for me. Even if I tried walkin' out at night . . . as soon as I hit open country they'd see me . . . they're watching for that, Mister Travis. They'd kill me on sight."

"Who would?" queried Travis, putting aside his empty coffee tin. "What's this all about?"

"The Stuart Ranch riders . . . they're after me like they'd be after a calf-killin' cougar."

"Why?"

"Because Miss Barbara wants it like that. I don't expect she ever wanted anyone dead as bad as she wants me dead." The younger man slid that dripped-out piece of venison steak onto a dented tin plate and held it out.

Travis took it, fished for his boot knife, and waited to cut into this breakfast. "Why again?" he asked.

"Well," said Bart Hayden with some reluctance, "you see, Mister Travis, I killed her paw. He drew on me an' I protected myself, an' when the smoke lifted he was down dead with my slug through his head."

"Fair fight, Mister Hayden?"

"Plumb fair, Mister Travis. He called me . . . I tried to talk my way clear . . . he was a big man hereabouts, real big, an' I sure Lord knew what'd likely happen if I shot him. I talked myself blue in the face. But he wouldn't listen. He went for his gun and that was that."

"Not quite," murmured Travis, beginning to eat. "Now you're spread-eagled in this damned cañon with a lame horse and, if this Stuart outfit's as fired-up as you say, why then, Mister Hayden, I'd say you're in

162

about as bad a fix as a man can get into, because if they're really lookin', they're goin' to find you in here, sure as God made green grass. They'll kill you here, too. I thought anybody had more sense than to go down into a box cañon when they're bein' chased."

CHAPTER
TWO

Bart Hayden doused his cook fire with dirt and eased back on his haunches to eat from the fry pan. After a time he said, from a curious face: "What brings you into these hills, Mister Travis?"

"I'm bound for Gunsight, Mister Hayden."

Travis finished eating, cleaned the tin plate with creekside sand, and put it aside. He wished for a smoke but did not think it wise right then to make one. If, as Hayden had said, Stuart Ranch riders were scouring these hills, they'd smell tobacco smoke providing they were close to this secret place, and Travis had no wish to divulge Hayden's hide-out, or become involved in a shooting war, either.

"That was a good breakfast," he said mildly. "I'm obliged."

Hayden looked up. "It'd have gone better with sourdough bread or biscuits. But I didn't have much time when I lit out from the Stuart Ranch and there aren't any stores right handy to this place." He did not look amused as he said this.

"You seem to be makin' out pretty well," murmured Travis. "You killed a deer."

"With a snare ... was afraid to risk shooting. Venison's fine when you're hungry but I've always held it's best fit for dogs and Indians. I'm a meat-and-potato man myself. Cow meat." Hayden wiped his whiskery mouth with the back of one hand. He then turned to cleaning his utensils and putting them out of the way. "You got a smoke?" he asked, and caught the sack Travis tossed across.

"They can smell that a mile off, Mister Hayden."

"I can't help that. I plumb ran out of tobacco three days ago, an' I guess, when a man's as bad off as a hunted dog, he'll take risks just to reassure himself he's still a man."

Travis watched Hayden make the cigarette and light it. He saw how the hunted man sucked back that initial big lungful, then let it slowly out. "Funny," he said to Hayden. "Trouble's got a way of winding around a man and squeezing everything out of him, making him almost as you said ... an animal. He thinks that if he ever finds a good hide-out like this one, he'll ask for nothing more. But it doesn't work like that, does it?"

"What do you mean, Mister Travis?"

"You. You're so sick of talkin' to yourself and doin' without you're willin' to risk your neck just to be able to rear up on your hind legs again like a man."

Hayden thought about this. He nodded, saying nothing, and smoked on.

"The next step, the way you're feeling right now, is to say 'to hell with it' and just up and walk out of here."

"I haven't gotten there yet," muttered Bart Hayden.

"But you're close to it."

The younger man stared at Travis. "You seem to know how a hunted man figures, Mister Travis," he said in a hard way, but added no more to it.

Travis raised his shoulders and let them fall. "I've been around over thirty years," he explained quietly. "A man finds himself in all kinds of situations in a length of time like that. Mister Hayden . . . ?"

"Yes."

"Tell me the whys and wherefores of that killing."

Hayden smoked and considered Travis from eyes drawn out narrow. "Not a lot to tell," he ultimately said. "I worked for Mister Stuart. Signed on early this spring."

"What brought it on . . . that gunfight?"

"Well, he sent me to look for a particular band of stray heifers. I knew the bunch all right . . . I also knew about where they'd be. Only I didn't find them, not a hide nor a hair. So I come on back to the ranch and there he was, waitin' for me in the big meadow north of the home place, all fired up about something and beet red in the face. He jumped me before I ever got my horse stopped. Said a lot of things . . . called me names no man'd take . . . then he did it."

"Went for his gun?"

"Yeah. I saw he was goin' to, Mister Travis, and started talkin' like a scairt kid tryin' to head it off. But as I already told you . . . he just plain wouldn't listen." Hayden pushed the cigarette into the ground where he was squatting. He continued to stare at it as he resumed speaking, his voice turning dull and morose. "Hell, I didn't want to draw on him. He was an old man, an' fat, an' rusty with guns." Hayden's troubled eyes lifted, shot their solemn gaze outward. "But I had to. He didn't leave me any way out. Even then, though, I let him draw. He even fired well ahead of me."

"Then you drew and fired?"

Hayden nodded. "Yeah." He took up a twig, looked at it, and flung it away.

Silence settled in the hidden camp. Travis turned, looked at the pool, and rolled his brows inward. There were some parts missing here, he thought. Still not looking around he said: "Why? Why did he do that?"

"I don't know, Mister Travis."

Travis turned. He assessed the young man across from him with a critical attention. "Guess," he said. "Had Stuart ever been good with a gun?"

Hayden shook his head. "He was a cowman, not a gunfighter."

"Was he a hot-headed man . . . fiery or belligerent?"

"Not that I ever saw, but I hadn't been around him a whole lot. Like I said, I just signed on this spring. And his foreman run things. I didn't have too much to do with Mister Stuart personally."

Now Cole Travis's face grew wintry with impatience and he said harshly: "Damn it all, Hayden, a rich old cowman doesn't just up and for no reason call out a cowboy ridin' for him an' try to kill him. There's got to be more to it than this. A whole lot more."

"I know that," mumbled Hayden, his expression changing toward hopelessness. "I keep thinkin' of that every time I get the urge to try walkin' out o' here despite those sentinel riders Miz Barbara's got posted on the hilltops." Hayden took up Travis's sack of tobacco and went to work manufacturing another cigarette. "Suppose I got clear of those damned sentinels, Mister Travis? Suppose I got plumb down to Gunsight . . . who would ever believe me when I told them exactly how that fight came about? Hell, they'd drag me out to the nearest tree and string me high enough for the birds to make nests in my hair." He finished with the cigarette and lit it. "They'd believe my story about as much as you do," he concluded, watching Travis's face. "And that's not believing it at all."

Travis motioned for the sack. Hayden tossed it over and Travis too bent to making a smoke. When this undertaking was completed, he said: "There's more. Whether you know what it is or not . . . there's more."

"Then *you* tell *me*," said the dour-looking fugitive.

But Travis rose up off the ground and turned his gaze southward where he could see another buck run scrambling along the shale side of a hill and fading out in yonder bitter-brush. "That pathway take me to Gunsight?" he asked.

Bart Hayden stood up. "Sooner or later, if you keep bearin' south, it'll take you maybe to some other trail lower down . . . then you'll see Gunsight Valley. After that, all you'll have to do is follow your nose." Hayden shifted his stance. He looked troubled now, in a different way. He muttered: "I reckon, if I let you ride out o' here, I'm as good as sealin' my own grave, too."

Travis looked at him. "How long do you reckon you can stay in here . . . how long could you keep watch over me?"

168

"That's just it," the fugitive candidly answered, and looked resigned and dispirited.

Travis considered Bart Hayden and thought he was neither better nor worse than average. He was too young yet to have tossed the coin of life and made his start toward the good or the bad. He said: "Listen, Hayden, you're safe here as far as I'm concerned, only I'm plumb curious about something."

Hayden, understanding this readily enough, shrugged. "It don't really matter," he said. "I killed him and they'll kill me. That's what matters." Then he said: "I could take your horse and leave you mine."

But Travis wagged his head over this. "It'd never work. Where would you strike out for? You said they'd know about you down in Gunsight and be waitin' for you."

"I could maybe head out over the hills northward."

"Naw. They'd find me on your lame horse. They'd simply backtrack me to this place, pick up your trail, and . . ."

"I reckon so," murmured the fugitive, and made a crooked little hopeless grin. "Reckon I'll just live on, down in this cañon, an', if they don't find me, I'll be here a hundred years from now."

Travis went back along the crushed grass pathway to his horse, picked up and dusted off his guns, put them away, and swung over leather.

Bart Hayden stood back where the pathway lay in deeper, speckled shadows, stonily watching all this. "Good luck," he said to Travis. "If anyone stops you before you're clear of the hills, why, I'd admire it if you'd sort of lie a little."

169

Travis inclined his head. "I'll lie a little. I'll also give you some advice. Don't move from here, but quit spendin' so much time down in the cañon loafin'. Get up high some place and keep a sharp watch because I've a notion, since Miss Barbara bumped into me, there'll be others coming over this way, too."

Travis then reined away and went slowly southward. The brush got thicker, almost impenetrable, at once. He cursed and battled his way through it for more than a solid hour. When he found a trail skirting upward around a hill base above this spiny tangle, he had his first glimpse of the southward flow of land; it was nearly free of underbrush but those giant trees kept him from being able to see Gunsight. Not that he cared, the day was still young and he had no other destination anyway.

Another hour later he passed on out of the trees to halt poised upon a gentle land swell looking down upon the village of Gunsight in its lovely valley, and here, for the first time since boyhood, Cole Travis felt a sensation that had, evidently, always been there deep inside him, but that, until this moment, had never before rose up so solidly and fiercely in him. It was a welter of bitterness, of bad memories, of savage antagonism, and through it ran the solid desire to hurt the people down there. To bring them pain, to grind them down in fear, to match their brutality to a fatherless boy with a variety of brutality they could not face, to give them misery for misery and pay them back with usury for every mean and bitter thing they had done to him so many, many years before. And if

Gunsight still abided by its same selfish, cruel rules, he would abide by those same rules and serve them up exactly what they had served him up.

His hands lying lightly upon the saddle horn were quaking. He fought to control this savagery, subconsciously surprised at its fierceness and beginning to think that it had, quite unknowingly, grown in him unconsciously over the lean, the hard, and the good years since he'd fled from Gunsight Valley with the scald of hot tears his only companions.

He eased off on the reins. His animal began a phlegmatic onward and downward descent. Yonder roofs shone dully under dazzling sunshine and far out and around were other roofs, of ranches and homes and big log barns. But Travis's dry stare was for the town alone; it had in it a lot of pride, a lot of manhood; he was back here now to spoil these things for the town of Gunsight. When those people asked mercy, he would give them none even as they had given him none. These were his acid thoughts.

He had no inkling of anything else until the sharp unpleasant sound of a ridden horse broke the stillness coming onward from behind and off to one side of him. Then he remembered about the Stuart Ranch sentries and all his hot and fierce resentment closed down upon this hurrying horseman. He turned the slightest bit, sighted the rushing rider with his naked carbine in hand upraised, and in one blur of movement drew and fired. That cowboy went over backward and struck down hard upon the summer-dried ground. His horse gave a loud snort and went speeding away. The cowboy's carbine lay broken over a large stone.

Travis turned his horse easily and walked him until he was over that sprawled form. The bullet had plowed a ragged gouge along the downed man's ribs and he was breathing with difficulty. Travis put up his gun, crossed both hands, and sat there. When the rider groaned and moved and groaned again, opening his eyes with their shock-dilated pupils, Travis said: "Can you hear me, mister?"

The cowboy fixed his eyes upon the wintry blue eyes overhead. He did not attempt to speak, only locked his lips against another moan.

"You better tear up your shirt and stop that bleeding," said Travis impersonally. "Then you go on back to Miss Stuart and you tell her the man she stopped this morning is named Cole Travis. And you tell her the next time she sends someone down on me from behind, she'd better make damned sure it's an army corps, because she doesn't have a damned cowboy working for her that can do that alone . . . and live."

The rider's face was gray as pain began building up in him. He put an exploring hand timidly to his side. "How bad . . . ?" he whispered.

"Maybe a broken rib . . . maybe two of 'em. You'll live," growled Travis. "Did you hear what I told you?"

"Yes. I heard."

"And you'll tell her?"

"Yes, sir, I'll tell her."

Travis turned and continued on downcountry. He did not look back.

172

CHAPTER
THREE

The town of Gunsight faced the northward hills, but it also faced the westerly flow of rangeland and all around it, far out, were stiff-standing mountains whose great shadows in wintertime protected the town and the valley somewhat from an otherwise fierce coldness. A double row of wooden buildings stood neatly upon either side of Main Street. This was the business section. Where Main Street doubled around were residences. They faced westward, mostly, and otherwise there was a scattering of smaller shacks and cabins cast down at random, which constituted the environs of Gunsight.

It was mid-afternoon when Travis rode in, put his horse up, and hiked over to the hotel to buy a bath, a room, and a Cheyenne newspaper that was two weeks old. He took this along the pleasant roadway as far as a circular wooden bench made at the base of a cottonwood tree, and sank down there in warm shade, spread out the paper, and, from over its top, studied the village.

He did not recall Gunsight too well, but what he now saw of it seemed distantly familiar and unchanged. The town marshal's office was southward just beyond the heart of town. Across from this building was the land and abstract office. Across from this place stood Flannery's Saloon. There was a big, two-storeyed building north of Flannery's that was Gunsight's main general store. The name of this mercantile establishment was Wilson's. He remembered those two names: Wilson's and Flannery's. He also remembered the cemetery.

He watched people moving along the sidewalks. None of the faces actually was familiar, yet he felt that he'd known some of them. Still, the hot and distorted memories of a thirteen-year-old kid were not, he knew, to be entirely trusted by a man of thirty-three, so he left off straining to recognize those passers-by and eventually read his newspaper.

Afterward, with water-blue dusk coming, he walked the town, familiarized himself with its byways, its stores and homes, its back alleys and its dogtrots. Then he passed along loosely to the hotel dining room and took a wall table well away from the prominently lighted part of this large room, and ordered supper. He was in no hurry; he expected trouble but he did not anticipate it until the following morning. He thought, though, when this trouble came, it would be a spectacular kind of trouble. It would wrench Gunsight out of the solid complacency he'd noted this day.

Then, as he finished eating, rolled a smoke, and lit up, he remembered Bart Hayden. He watched people come and go from the dining room, well-fed looking, clean and secure and comfortable, and could not avoid contrasting them to the fugitive cowboy hiding in the breaks of that lost cañon depth. Very gradually an idea began to form in Travis's mind. He got up, eventually, flung down a coin, and made his way back out to the sidewalk. There, he teetered undecidedly, then paced away with heavy steps eastbound through town toward a little fenced-in plot no more than two acres in size that lay beyond the farthest outskirts upon a little gentle hill. Here he passed through a gate, here, too, his memory was sharpest and did not fail him. The grave was where he knew it would be; there was an accumulation of old grass upon it, showing neglect for this place, showing indifference. He stood at the foot gazing upon a head board that was badly checked and so bleached out that the name was scarcely distinguishable. It did not matter about that, right then anyway. Travis knew the spot. He knelt and began systematically rooting out those weeds, those tangles of dead grass and thistles, and afterward he set the head board straight again so that a rising pewter moon touched upon its smooth face picking out some letters: *Martin Travis*. There was a date for birth and a date for death, and once there had been a little obituary thing that Cole could not recall at all, but these things were entirely obliterated now. Details, he thought as he got upright from cleaning the grave's earth, the details of death are not important — only death is important. Death and life. He hooked his thumbs, standing there with his pain, his loss, and his bitterness. Death and life — one went with the other. You couldn't breathe deeply of the one without inhaling a little of the decay of the other, and, if you were a sensitive man as his father had been, shame and desolation and bewildered anguish brought you closer to the one than to the other.

He remembered only vague fragments of those far-away times. His mother had been a beautiful woman. He remembered that. She had run away with a traveling man. Why, he had never known. His father had been a carpenter, a quiet man, industrious, gentle with a good smile and a rich laugh. But he hadn't laughed those last two years; he'd spent them at Flannery's drinking himself steadily to death. Afterward the son of the town drunk had been a butt for cruel jokes until he'd run away.

Now he was back and those intervening years had made him very different, very deadly and iron-like in his set ways. Twenty years was enough time for a frontier boy to become a frontier man.

He turned, with the high-riding moon passing silently overhead, and started down from that little gentle hill back toward town. He did not observe the gnome of a little old man seated beside another grave whose sharply inquisitive eyes watched his every move, and who, after Travis had passed along, got up and hiked over to the grave of Martin Travis to stare curiously at its freshly smooth top soil and squint closely at its reset head board. The little old man reared back to run an arthritic hand along his scraggly jaw in deep thought. It took a while for him to remember this grave's occupant, but he eventually did because, like all old men, twenty years was as yesterday to him. Then he thought to other things, to the taffy-haired beautiful woman with the red ripe mouth who had been Mary

Travis and who had run off with a peddler, and how he, along with everyone else in Gunsight, had snickered over that.

Then he recalled the lad of that union. Even recalled his name: Cole Travis. He dwelt on this memory particularly because, while he'd not seen that brooding man's face, he had knowledge that in all those intervening years no one else had once come to care for this grave, which meant that Cole Travis had returned to Gunsight Valley.

The little old man stood for a long time putting all this together; it was hard work for a mind that had a tendency to wander, but he accomplished it. He also made some shrewd deductions as well, for there had once been a time in his own life when the blood ran hot and the testiness of a yeasty nature never let him forget a slight. He came to a sound conclusion, using this form of reasoning: Cole Travis was not back to renew old acquaintances in a town that had scorned his father, maliciously gossiped about his mother, and had poked contemptuous fun at their son, because he had no friends here. None that the little old man could recall at any rate. So he had to be back here to even some old scores, extract retribution for some old wounds, and this delighted the little old man, who was also scorned in Gunsight Valley simply because he was a futile little old man.

But there was a flaw in all this contemplative deduction. Travis did have one friend in Gunsight. He went to her home after he left the cemetery. She was an old woman now, but still sturdy and self-reliant. She no longer took in washing, but she still did sewing and occasionally a little housecleaning and cooking for a few of the old families in town. Her name was Aletha Brand. She'd been widowed on the Plains crossing and had raised a son who'd been a few years older than Travis. Her son now was, although Travis did not yet know this, the town marshal of Gunsight. He no longer lived at home though, so, when Travis passed over the rickety porch to knock, Aletha Brand was quite alone. She stood in the doorway staring at Travis as though at a ghost. She didn't move or speak even after he'd said his name and had smiled down into her face. Then she'd made a little whimpering moan and had reached for him as though he were still a shock-headed tall and thin waif with that look of bewilderment in his eyes she'd last seen so long before.

She led him by the hand into her little parlor and took away his hat. She had some cookies she'd made for neighborhood children that she brought to him. She examined him critically from several angles and dabbed at her eyes, saying unsteadily: "My, how you've grown, Cole. You're a man now."

He put a warm glance upon her; there was a tightness in his throat, in his chest. She'd been a mother to him; she'd mended his clothing and had fed him. She'd fought for him, too; he remembered those times now when, raw red hands upon her hips, jaw outthrust, and eyes flashing, she'd denounced others for their jibes and their snickering cruelty.

"Fred will be so happy you're back, son," she said. "He's town marshal now. We've often talked about you."

Travis had a cookie halfway to his mouth. It hung there forgotten. "Town marshal?" he said.

Aletha beamed with her pride. "He was elected two years back. Can you imagine that . . . my son town marshal?"

Travis had a clear recollection of Aletha's boy. Fred had been like his own brother; he'd never been condescending like other boys had been despite the six years between their ages. In fact, it had been Fred Brand who had brought Cole to his mother after Martin Travis's death.

The cookie would not go down. Travis replaced it gently upon the plate at his side. He'd shot a Stuart Ranch rider. That trouble he was looking forward to would come — and because Fred Brand was now town marshal, he'd be right in the middle of it. Travis carefully considered what he must do as Aletha's voice ran on, telling him of those who he would know who had died, or had gotten married, or had moved on, gone into business, gone to ranching.

Somehow, some way, he had to keep Fred out of this. He had no idea at all how to accomplish this. In fact, as he thought about it, the likelihood became gradually fixed in his mind that there just was no way to do this at all, not with Fred Brand being Gunsight's lawman, for what he had done to that Stuart Ranch cowboy was clearly the law's business. More so, in fact, than it was even the business of Barbara Stuart.

Aletha made a pot of coffee. She chattered and she flitted around him, and, when, an hour later, he arose to leave, she said: "Now, Cole, I want you to promise me to go and see Fred right away . . . tonight."

"But he'll likely be abed, and tomorrow will be . . ."

"No, no, he won't, son, and there's nobody he'd rather see than you, so I want you to promise me you'll go see him right away. He's got a room at the hotel now, Cole." She reached out impulsively and put a hand upward along Travis's cheek, her eyes softening toward him. "Ah, son," she said through a misty gaze, "you'll never know the prayers I've said at night for you."

Then she withdrew the hand and half turned away making her tone brisk and light and strong again. "They were answered, Cole. An honest prayer is always answered."

He left her, moved down into the moonlighted side street, walking heavily back toward Gunsight's center. His thoughts were even more bitter now than they'd been earlier at his father's grave. He came back around to the sidewalk, stepped upon it, and paced slowly toward the hotel. With Fred Brand being town marshal the awkwardness, the near impossibility of the things he meant to do to this town firmed up, step by step, until he stopped outside the hotel and leaned there upon an overhang upright, feeling cheated and empty and futile.

Across the way tinny music came from a saloon. Southward somewhere, and behind Main Street, a little feist yapped furiously, probably at a raccoon bent on raiding someone's hen roost, and overhead that lop-sided old moon went serenely on its way.

Two cowboys swung along past the hotel, speaking quietly to one another, and a woman hurried past behind Travis holding a shawl tightly at her throat. A little old man came shuffling out of nighttime shadows to pause and peer and come to a shuffling stop down a little distance from where Travis leaned. He groped around for a wall bench, found it, and eased gingerly down to sit there, vacantly smiling in the direction of the tall and brooding-faced young man onward from him whose face was hat brim-shadowed and whose hip-holstered six-gun was iridescently reflecting moonlight from a smooth, ivory grip.

CHAPTER
FOUR

Travis did not enter the hotel. He went over to the livery barn, got his own animal, and hired a second one, saddled, which he led out of town at a plodding walk traveling north. Around him full darkness relieved by that raffish old moon lent the countryside a melancholy, haunted appearance. Once, shortly before he entered the hills, he encountered a rodent-hunting owl skimming noiselessly on silent wings, and a mile deeper into the hills he came upon a mother coyote and three sly-eyed pups. They scrambled into the sage and sat saucily looking out, in plain sight and unafraid. Later, where the bitterbrush began again, so dense and tortuous, he rode up along that buck run around the fat shoulder of a hill until he could see into Hayden's moonlighted cañon. He pushed onward making no attempt to hide his coming.

Where the willow thicket lay, silver light came up from creek water. Here, Travis dismounted, tied both animals, and turned to move onward. He found his way blocked by a blurred shadow with a steady carbine held low and cocked. "It's me," he said. "Point that thing some other way." The gun swung clear, its holder mincing forward into moonlight.

"I didn't expect this," said Hayden. "I figured the best I could hope for was that you'd keep quiet about meeting me."

"Gather your stuff," said Travis. "I didn't see any of her sentinels on the way in, so maybe they're not out at night any more."

Hayden eased off his cocking mechanism, grounded the gun, and steadily regarded Travis. "You know why they're not out tonight, don't you? Because you shot one o' them."

Travis peered across at the younger man. "How did you know that?"

"I went out a ways after you left, takin' your advice to keep a look-out. I heard the shot and later I saw two other Stuart riders carryin' that feller off."

"That doesn't mean I shot him, does it?" demanded Travis.

"It doesn't mean that, no. But you did, didn't you?"

"Yes. Now get your stuff and let's get out of here."

Hayden did not move. He said slowly: "I been wonderin' about you. Why did you shoot that feller? Who are you? What's on your mind?"

Travis's gaze hardened against the younger man. "If you want to save your bacon, get your stuff and let's ride. What you've been wonderin' about me is none of your business. I happened to stumble onto you is all, Hayden, and because I don't like raw deals, I came back tonight to help you get clear. Other than that, our trails fork. You go your way and I'll go mine."

"As long as that's how it'll be," murmured Bart Hayden, a trifle edgily, "I'll go along."

Travis glared. "How else could it be?" he demanded. "We've got nothing in common. We don't even know each other."

Hayden said nothing, just nodded his head, then snapped upright and faded out through the willows. Travis heard him throwing his effects together. As he listened to these faint sounds, he puzzled over Hayden's altered attitude. It was not the shooting of that Stuart Ranch rider that had been entirely responsible for Bart Hayden's change, he was sure of that. Then what was it? He was waiting, still standing near the tied horses, when Hayden returned with a lumpy bedroll and his carbine.

"What's troubling you?" Travis asked. "I want to know the answer to that before we ride out of here."

Hayden stopped, balanced his load, and looked squarely at Travis. "It's a feeling I got," he answered back. "I think you mean to use me some way. How, I got no idea, Mister Travis, but I got that feelin' and I don't aim to be used by you or anyone else."

"Use you . . . how?"

Hayden raised his shoulders and let them fall. "All I can say is that ever since I first saw you, I read something in your face, Mister Travis, an' it sure Lord means trouble. You're a smart feller . . . you got something on your mind. I didn't get the impression that you'd go around riskin' your hide for the fun of it, an' that makes me think now that you didn't come back to help me get away just because you think I'm gettin' a raw deal." Hayden cocked his head a little and asked a question: "When you were in town, did you ask around about the killin' of old Rock Stuart?"

Travis shook his head.

"Then you still don't know whether I lied to you or not about it bein' a fair fight instead o' murder . . . yet here you are fixin' to help me get away. You see what I mean about bein' suspicious, Mister Travis?"

Cole stood there with indignation becoming a solid part of his thoughts. But he was a basically honest man and because he had planned to use Bart Hayden, he knew how false that indignation was. Still, it piqued him to be read so easily by a man who was little more than a boy. He turned, flicked loose two sets of reins, tossed one set to Hayden, and prepared to mount his own animal. As he rose up, it came to him that nothing, so far, had gone as he'd planned — nothing at all. Not even the idea he'd had for Bart Hayden — which had simply been to throw Gunsight into turmoil by riding boldly into town with Hayden, importing the best attorney he could find, and fighting the town, the Stuart Ranch, and anyone else who favored lynching Hayden, to a grim finish. In a sentence, using young Bart Hayden to humble Gunsight.

He had proposed to do this without first apprising Hayden, but now, as he turned his animal to begin the outward trip beyond the silent hills, he knew he would have to reveal what motivated him to the younger man, and this reflection brought up a flinty stubbornness in Cole Travis. He was not a man accustomed to explaining himself to anyone. He rode ahead, led out and around the bitterbrush thicket, and did not halt until, miles along where soft moonlight touched downward through high pine limbs, Gunsight Valley lay onward in its nighttime setting of haunting beauty.

He sat easy, letting Hayden come up beside him. The younger man said nothing for a while, only sat there looking out beyond the final trees, taking in the hushed length and breadth of that yonder valley.

"You know," murmured Hayden. "I once thought I'd like to put down roots here. It's good country . . ."

"Yeah," answered Travis. "Good country. How about the people?"

Hayden swung his head, saw Travis's lean, stony profile, and said: "It's here, isn't it? Whatever you got gnawing inside you, is right here, isn't it?"

Travis broke off his onward looking. He bent an assessing gaze upon this young cowboy. Within him stirred a grudging respect. "You know," he replied in a wondering tone, "I don't figure you out, Hayden. Damned if I do. Most of the things you're seen in me are true enough. But you're the first man I ever knew who saw them so quickly, so factually. You don't strike me as an ordinary cowboy at all."

Hayden smiled; it was a smile that made him look even younger, and it erased all the brooding solemnity from his eyes, his lips, his tanned cheeks. "Did you ever figure it might be you . . . not me? That when a man wants something so bad, it plumb dominates his life, it shows in his face until even a blind man could see it?"

"What shows in my face, Hayden?"

"Wrath. You're up to here with it, Mister Travis. You're schemin' ways to do something, and it's prompted by some awful anger inside you. You hate something or somebody so bad, you can't scarcely think o' anythin' else."

Travis looked steadily over at Hayden. "It shows that much?" he asked.

Bart Hayden nodded. "It scairt me a little, Mister Travis. That's why I said the things to you back at the camp that I said. I've seen men like that before. Not many, but some. I know what it does to 'em, too."

"What . . . what does it do to 'em?"

Bart resettled himself in the saddle. He ran a hand down the livery animal's neck. He seemed embarrassed. "If I ride off now, Mister Travis, how're you goin' to explain about this horse bein' missin'?"

"I'll pay the livery man for it. Never mind that damned horse. I asked you a question."

"I know," breathed the cowboy. "I don't like to answer it, rightly, though."

"Answer anyway."

Hayden took a breath. He said: "That kind of anger gets men killed, and it's usually the men who got that kind o' anger in 'em, not their enemies, who get killed."

Travis sat on, looking far out. For a long time he made no sound or movement. Then he lifted a hand and carelessly gestured with it. "Ride on," he growled. "Go on, Hayden . . . don't worry about that livery critter. He's not worth much anyway. Just head out around Gunsight and keep on going. By dawn you'll be near those yonder foothills. Hole up through the day and light out again tomorrow night. You got any money?"

"Enough, Mister Travis."

"Then get going. The whole night's ahead of you."

Hayden put a soft glance about Travis and said his name. "I'm obliged to you. I want you to know that."

"Forget that. Just watch that gun of yours in the future."

"Mister Travis, I pass you my solemn word about that shooting. On my mother's grave."

Travis winced. He said: "Dammit all . . . *get going!*" He afterward spurred down away from the northward hills and did not look back. Once, well along toward town, he thought he heard hoof beats easterly, passing out and around Gunsight, southbound. But he was not sure. He made that last final mile with a smoky gaze fixed ahead where Gunsight's few lights still shone this late in the night. He went along to the livery barn, left his horse, and said he wanted to see the stable owner in the morning. Then he started toward the hotel, veered off at signs of life in an all-night restaurant, and went there instead. He ate some apple pie, drank coffee, and rolled a cigarette. There were only three other men in the café and two of these were struggling to get black coffee down the gullet of the third man, who consistently flung around, flopping first one way then another, and all the time keeping up a fierce denunciation of his comrades. The two perspiring riders eventually poured coffee into their friend, got him upright, and by supporting him one on each side started doorward. The café man watched this spectacle with an acid expression upon his face until the cowboys were gone, then he turned with a prodigious sigh, and said to Travis: "Damned fool. I figured with old Rock

Stuart gone, we wouldn't have so many of them fellers around."

Travis looked up, put his steady stare upon the café man as something quickened to life within him. "What do you mean?" he asked.

The café man looked back and blinked. Then he made a little apologetic gesture, saying: "Oh, hell, forget it. I mistook you for a local feller. My mistake, stranger. Forget it."

Travis rose up. His brows darkened toward the café man. "What did you mean about Rock Stuart?" he demanded.

The café man looked startled. He became uneasy, too. "Nothing," he muttered. "Really nothin' at all. Only, well, Rock used to get tanked to the gills like that, and he was troublesome when he done it, just like that young feller was."

Travis remained a moment balancing upon the counter, staring hard at the café man. Then he straightened up, tossed down a coin, and left the restaurant.

Outside, late night had its obscuring blackness between Gunsight and the mountains; it lay everywhere thick and hushed and solidly gloomy. The moon was far down the sky moving steadily away. Travis looked at it, thinking that within another two nights it would be completely full and round. Then he started for the hotel, thinking that a troublesome drunk was never a reasonable person, and wondering why this simple solution to the killing of cowman Rock Stuart had not occurred to him before. As he turned in and crossed the lobby toward the stairs, he wondered also why Bart

Hayden hadn't considered the possibility of Stuart being fighting drunk when they'd tangled. Hayden had said he hadn't known Stuart very well. Still, you didn't have to know a man well to see that he was drunk.

Travis entered his room, closed and locked the door, and threw his hat at the dresser. It still didn't make a lot of sense though. Hayden had said Stuart was waiting for him out on the range, that he'd at once provoked a fight.

Travis sat down to kick off his boots. *Hell,* he growled to himself, *no man, not even a belligerent drunk, went riding out to waylay another man and force a gunfight with him without a reason. Particularly if, as Hayden had sworn, he didn't know the other man except perhaps to nod to. No, there was a whole of a lot more to the killing of Rock Stuart than appeared on the surface.*

Travis shucked his shell belt and lay back upon the hotel bed. He was tired, yes, but not sleepy. That senseless riddle continued to ricochet inside his skull. How come, too, so observant a man as Hayden hadn't seen that Stuart was drunk — if, indeed, he had been drunk? Hayden had proven himself entirely observant, to Travis's satisfaction. The answer to that one came, though, just before Travis drifted off. Hayden had said Stuart had jumped him at once, upon sight, and had forced the fight right then, so, whether Hayden had recognized Stuart's drunken state or not, nothing could have been altered by this.

Travis said a tart word and fell asleep.

CHAPTER
FIVE

Travis never did go in search of Town Marshal Fred Brand. He was eating breakfast at the same café he'd seen the drunk cowboy in the night before, when Brand strode in, also for breakfast. He looked around, nodded, and began to lower himself at the counter. Then he turned, put another longer look upon Travis, and said: "Well, I'll be damned."

Travis was amused by this, and the look of purest astonishment. He smiled. "Hello, Fred."

"Cole!"

Brand went along the counter to Travis's side. He pushed out a big hand. When Travis shook, Fred Brand's grip was very solid. They sat together like this, talking, smiling at one another, until the café man came pattering forward for their orders. And afterward, too, as they ate, eating and gulping black coffee, their conversation continued. It was a good reunion, and Travis was warmed by it. He told Marshal Brand of visiting his mother the evening before. He also told him he had not recognized many faces in town. He did not tell him why he'd returned, or that he'd shot a Stuart Ranch rider, or that he'd helped the fugitive Bart Hayden get out of the country.

Their breakfast took a long time. Other diners came and went but they sat on over coffee and smokes. There were many new people in the Gunsight country, Brand told Travis. Some of them were ranchers but mostly they were townsmen. Of the ranchers the Stuarts were the biggest now; they had come to Colorado ten years earlier. They had prospered greatly and now owned six of the old-time outfits, all adjoining.

"And Flannery?" Travis asked quietly, watching Fred Brand's face.

The lawman emptied his cup and put it aside. He said, watching Travis's expression: "Dead. Old Flannery died six years back."

Travis's little smile died. "The sign over his saloon is the same," he said.

"Sure. His nephew inherited the place, Cole. But he's not the old man's type at all." Brand knew how Travis's thoughts were running. It had been the other Flannery who'd refused to throw Martin Travis out of his saloon or limit his drunkenness. As long as he'd had money, Flannery continued to pour rot-gut whiskey into him. Fred Brand knew exactly how Cole Travis felt, for in those other days he'd felt the same way as he'd watched Cole's father drink himself to death.

"Well," said Cole softly, "that's too bad. I'd hoped he'd still be around."

Now the marshal's pleasant look atrophied, too. He sat there gazing at rising smoke from his cigarette. Finally he said: "Cole, that was a long time ago. You didn't come back just over those things that happened, I hope." He looked around, studying Travis's face.

Cole did not respond to this. He said: "What about old Wilson at the general store. How's he doing? Still shortchanging drunks?"

Brand said: "Dead, too. He died nine years back. Listen, Cole, you know how long it's been? Twenty years. Nothing is the same any more. You and I aren't the same. That was another time altogether. Cole? Forget it. For your own sake, forget it. It's too late to do anything about it . . . time has evened up the score for you."

Travis finished his coffee and stood up. "Some things a man never forgets," he murmured, and left the café.

Behind him Town Marshal Brand sat on, lost in brooding thought. It had not escaped him how Cole Travis wore his gun — low, with the specially made holster molded so that the butt was slightly turned out, clear of hip and trouser. He had seen that the leather was flesh side out, which was a gunman trait. With the hair side, or smooth-grained side of the leather inward, usually waxed, too, the six-gun could be drawn fastest. These were the noticeable things about gunfighters and Fred Brand had observed them, along with the quiet, bold look on Travis's face. He called for a fresh cup of coffee and made another cigarette and sat there worrying.

Travis passed over to the livery barn, found the proprietor in a little cubicle office, and asked how much that horse and saddle were worth he'd let Hayden go south upon. The livery man pursed his lips, squinted his eyes, considered an exorbitant figure, then looked Travis up and down and brought his thoughts down to earth, saying: "Seventy-five dollars, mister, for the whole shebang . . . horse, bridle, saddle, an' blanket."

Travis counted out the money and tossed it down without speaking.

The livery man recounted it and said: "Thanks. He wasn't a bad horse . . . had some age on him but sound enough."

Travis left the barn striding forward into morning sunlight. Around him Gunsight was livening up. Roadway traffic was steadily increasing, women with shopping baskets were passing into the general store, and on a back street, somewhere, a smith was hard at his anvil. Travis struck out for a wall bench in front of the hotel. There, he dropped down, pushed back his hat, pulled a knife from one pocket, and began quietly to whittle upon a pine sliver provided by the bench. He did not concentrate upon this, but appeared to be more interested in the northerly approaches to town.

A little old man came up, stopped, and beamed a sly silly smile at Travis. "'Morning," he said. "Fine day, ain't it?"

Travis became quite still. The old man's expression was knowing and raffish. He said — "Yeah . . . fine morning." — and sat on, watching the old man.

"I know who you are, young feller. I knew that last night. Expect I'm about the only one hereabouts who does, though. What d'you think o' that?"

Travis closed his knife with a *snap*. He pocketed it and dropped the sliver. His gaze was steadily unblinking as he said: "All right, old-timer, you know who I am. What of it?"

"Martin Travis's boy. I even recollect your name," said the old man, with triumph. "It's Cole. Cole Travis."

"Go on."

"Well, I used to know your pa right well. That was a long time ago, though." The wet and faded old eyes lost some of their slyness. They began to grow distant and a little uneasy under Travis's constant regard. "Well . . ."

"Yeah? Keep talkin' old-timer."

Now the oldster's uneasiness became fear. It showed in those shifting eyes and the quavering lips. "Your pa an' me used to have a drink now and then, young feller."

"I can imagine. Anything else?"

The old man blurted out: "I seen you at his grave last night, boy. I knew him right well. He wouldn't approve of what you're here for, Cole, and that's gospel."

"What am I here for?" Travis asked, but the old man fled away, all his manhood dissolving under that pitiless stare, went scuttling along as far as the nearest dogtrot between two buildings and plunged in there to go rattling along to the far end where a littered alleyway was. There, he stopped briefly to lean upon a building with the wild pumping of his heart, loud and erratic, then he resumed his way to a tar-paper shack on the far end of town, entered there, and did not appear for the balance of that morning.

Travis sat on.

It was near 10:00 before he sighted a dust banner coming on from the foothill north. He kept his eyes upon this indication of riding men until, where they passed over to the stage road and the dust diminished, he was able to count their numbers. He had no illusions about who these men were, Stuart Ranch riders — six of them, all loping along in a tight and resolute group.

Travis got up, entered the hotel, went unhurriedly to his room, rummaged among his effects for the two parts of a sawed-off shotgun, calmly assembled this weapon, then descended to the lobby again with the weapon lying carelessly in the crook of one arm. The desk clerk saw him thus armed and froze until Travis passed back out to the sidewalk. Then he made a little sound deep in his throat and went flinging out of the hotel by the back alley.

A number of other townsmen also saw Cole Travis take his seat upon the wall bench in front of the hotel, riot gun in hand, and they, too, looked startled, then left his vicinity without hesitation.

Travis felt fine. He had been in this situation before, he knew the ropes, the way things would go, one way or the other, the shoot-out or the backing down. He sat easy with his eyes upon the turning of the roadway where those Stuart Ranch men would appear. He knew how they would be — arrogant in their numbers — until they met him head-on with that brutally lethal sawed-off scatter-gun, until they saw that he would not run from them.

They came around the far corner in a steady onward walk still riding bunched up. He spied their leader easily — he was a large, thick-chested man with sunk-set eyes and a mighty jaw. He came on, sweeping Gunsight's thoroughfare with his steely stare. He did not at once spy Travis sitting there in pleasant shade, not until he was close and a rider at his side bent to murmur something. Then the big man's head snapped up and around, his flinging glance touched down and he drew rein directly in front of the hotel, the other five men closing on him in a bunch. The Stuart Ranch foreman sat there, solid of shoulder, his brittle glare taking in Travis, the shotgun in his hands, and the quite empty sidewalk around him.

"Are you Cole Travis?" he asked.

Travis nodded. "I am. And who are you?"

"Jack Wheeler, foreman of the Stuart Ranch," said the big man, all in one breath. "Why did you shoot my rider yesterday?"

"I expect you know the answer to that," said Travis. "Because he jumped me from behind with a gun in his hand."

"No," said Wheeler, very soft. "That's not the way I got it."

"Mister Wheeler," answered back Travis, "I don't give a damn how you got it. That's how it happened."

Wheeler sat there believing nothing Travis said and considering that shotgun. "That weapon won't save you," he said, then paused as an idea came to him. He looked up and down the empty roadway. "Put it aside, Travis. I'll get down and we'll settle this man to man."

"Sure," replied Cole dryly, "with six-to-one odds. I think I'll just hang onto my shotgun." Travis looked at the other riders. They were considering him, also, without moving in their saddles. A sawed-off shotgun at close range was a mighty prompter of respect. He could see the will to fight in all those faces, but he could also see fear of his sturdy weapon. He said: "Wheeler, if you'd come alone, I'd have obliged you. But then you appear to me to be a man who doesn't do much alone."

"What does that mean?" demanded the Stuart Ranch foreman.

"Take it any way you like," said Travis, seeing in Wheeler's eyes the growing thought of action. "But if I were in your boots, I'd do a heap of thinkin' before I did anything rash." Travis thumbed back both hammers of the shotgun, one at a time; these twin discords of sound were harshly loud in the silence.

A man down the road yelled, long and full, and immediately thereafter they could all hear the quick pound of running feet. Travis did not move, neither did Jack Wheeler. They remained like dogs with their hackles up, each wondering when the opening would come, the battle commence. That cry came again, this time much closer. Travis recognized Fred Brand's voice. He said to Jack Wheeler: "I guess you've made your decision," — meaning there would now be no fight.

Wheeler's reply was quiet. "For the time being, Travis. I don't like the odds."

"Two to one?" Travis smiled with only his lips. "Six of you and one of me . . . and two shotgun barrels full choked with lead chunks. What do you need, Wheeler . . . an army?"

Brand came up and halted. His face was red from exertion. Behind him, far back, the hotel clerk stood watching, poised for flight. Brand said: "What the hell are you trying to do, Wheeler?"

The Stuart Ranch foreman looked at Brand. "That man shot one of my riders yesterday, without any reason, Marshal."

Fred Brand twisted, put a puzzled look upon Travis, and said: "Is that true, Cole?"

"Not exactly. I shot him, sure, but only after he came racing down at me from behind with a carbine in his fist."

Brand screwed up his face, appearing uncertain. Finally he growled at Wheeler, saying: "I'll look into this, Jack. Meanwhile you fellers had better leave town."

Wheeler's eyes widened. "Hell," he protested. "We're to fetch back some supplies from town, Fred."

Brand remained obdurate. "Some other time!" he exclaimed. "Today . . . I don't want Stuart riders around until I get to the bottom of this shooting. Now go on, Jack . . . do like I say."

Wheeler scowled, he rolled his eyes toward Travis, and there was no doubt about the meaning of his expression. He reined around and started back the way he'd come. Around him the cowboys followed after, also quiet, also grim and thoughtful.

Brand remained in the roadway until the last of those horsemen passed from sight, then he turned to look thoughtfully at Travis. Finally he passed over into the shade of the hotel overhang and said: "Where'd you get that shotgun, Cole?"

"From my bedroll. I always carry it with me, Fred."

"That's a gunfighter's weapon."

"It may be," responded Travis, dropping his eyes long enough to ease off the gun's hammers. "But I'll tell you one thing . . . if I hadn't had it a few minutes ago, you wouldn't be standing here talking to me now. I never saw that Jack Wheeler before in my life, Fred, but he's trouble four ways from the middle."

"How about that shooting, Cole?"

"It happened exactly as I told you in front of Wheeler. That damn' fool Stuart Ranch cowboy came down on me from behind as I rode out of the northward hills. He had his carbine out and ready for use. I'd never seen that man before, but his meaning was plumb clear, so I shot him before he shot me."

"He wouldn't have shot you, Cole. He was one of the riders Barbara Stuart put through the hills to find a man who shot and killed her father. Maybe he thought you were that man. As soon as he'd seen you weren't, he'd have left you alone."

"Maybe," said Travis, getting up from the bench. "Maybe not. Fred, someone raising a gun against you doesn't inspire you to talk. You know how that works."

Marshal Brand regarded Travis steadily and thoughtfully. He seemed to be balancing something in his mind, something he thought was probably quite true, but that he did not wish to frame into spoken words. Finally he exhaled a big breath. "Put that thing away," he ordered, bobbing his head toward the riot gun. "Don't bring it out again as long as you're in town, Cole." He then turned upon his heel and walked away.

Travis stood there watching Brand move off. He felt the widening of that inevitable gulf that he'd anticipated between them, and the thought of it made him a little sad, a little melancholy.

CHAPTER
SIX

Word of Travis's near clash with Jack Wheeler and the Stuart Ranch riders spread like lightning. A number of men, having seen Travis and Fred Brand in conversation afterward, went to the town marshal for information about this lean and smoky-eyed stranger.

Travis felt the changed atmosphere around him, and it meant nothing particular to him, yet he was gratified that Gunsight was beginning to break out of its lethargy. He spent the early afternoon at Flannery's Saloon playing cards. He refused four offers of a drink and sat, back to the wall, eyes occasionally watching the door. He won $11 and lost $7. The other players changed from time to time; when new ones sat down to beam upon Travis and ask cautious questions, he chilled them with his grave look and deep silence. In this manner the afternoon wore along, then, shortly before the reddening sun dropped away, a man burst into the saloon with a cry, calling out that Bart Hayden, the killer of Rock Stuart, had been brought to town by a brace of cowboys from miles south of Gunsight, near the distant foothills. In the instant turmoil brought on by this announcement, Travis sat utterly still. Men rushed from the saloon breaking into spontaneous cries

201

and shouts, until Travis, too, finally walked out to the edge of the sidewalk to witness what next ensued.

He did not see Hayden or the men who had brought him in; they were inside Fred Brand's jailhouse. But he did see something that made his heart skip a beat — that livery horse he'd given Hayden, had paid the liveryman for, and which he was now instantly aware would link him with Hayden's race for freedom, as soon as the livery man came along and saw that outfit.

He watched townsmen and range men congregating here and there in little excited groups along both sides of the road. Their purpose was clear enough. Sooner or later someone would appear among them with a rope — then the crowd would batter at Brand's office.

Travis stepped down into the roadway. He passed obliquely across to the marshal's office, conscious that, of a sudden, many eyes were upon him, and there he rolled fisted knuckles over a massive oaken door. Fred Brand swung this panel inward and glared out; he looked harassed and defiant.

"Let me in," said Travis, pushing past.

Seated across the room was Bart Hayden. He looked very white and very haggard. Near him sat two cowboys, their faces alert and interested.

"What do you want?" demanded Fred Brand of Travis. "Whatever it is, Cole, it can wait. I've got real trouble on my hands now." He thrust forth a rigid arm indicating Bart Hayden. "That's the man who killed Rock Stuart. There's been lynch talk ever since they brought old Stuart into town." His arm dropped.

"Look out in the roadway . . . they're beginning to gang up already."

Travis saw the mute look of recognition on Hayden's face at sight of him. He ignored this to ask of Hayden's captors where they had taken him.

"Fixin' to escape out of the valley," answered one of these men. "We was lookin' for stray cattle when we spied him. When we rode up, he tried to run. From that, we figured he must be a wanted man . . . so we got around him, and ambushed him." This cowboy made a slow smile at Travis. "Understand the Stuart outfit's got a big reward for his capture," he said.

Travis looked stonily at these two men. "Nice work," he told them. "You don't often see men who'd sell another man's life for cash any more. You boys ought to be real proud of yourselves." He turned, saw Brand's rising look of disapproval, and went on speaking. "I gave him that horse and outfit, Fred."

Brand's face changed instantly. "You what?"

"I found him in a cañon yesterday, took that horse back to him, and helped him get away last night after dark."

Marshal Brand stood staring at Travis.

From over where he sat, Hayden murmured: "You didn't have to say that, Mister Travis. I'd never have told."

"You wouldn't have had to, Bart. Someone here in Gunsight would have recognized the livery outfit sooner or later."

"Cole," said Fred Brand flatly, "what in hell is the matter with you? First you shoot a Stuart rider. Then

203

you help a known fugitive escape the law. Next you beard the whole dog-gone' Stuart outfit with a shotgun. What the devil are you . . . ?" Brand did not complete his question. He let it dwindle off in a falling voice until he stood there quite silent, gazing hard upon Travis. Then, after a time, he said: "So *that's* how it is with you. You've got a hate for the whole town . . . the whole valley."

Travis said: "Fred, who saw this man kill Stuart? No one at all, that's who. So how do you even know he did it . . . let alone that it wasn't a fair fight?"

"I never said it wasn't a fair fight, Cole. All I ever wanted was for this man to be locked up and tried. That's my job and that's the law. But now you had to butt in."

"Yeah," growled Travis. "I butted in, and, after meeting Jack Wheeler today, I'm glad I did. Hayden'll get about as fair a trial with Wheeler and his crowd around as Sitting Bull got."

"What's it to you, Cole? You don't even know these people."

"I know them all right," Travis ground out. "I know them better than Hayden does, or you do, or anyone else. And I'll tell you something else, too, Fred . . . they won't lynch Hayden! Not while I'm above ground, they won't."

Fred Brand made an angry gesture. His face darkened with angry color. "Cole, dog-gone it," he remonstrated, "what's bothering you is long past. Twenty years past. These are not the same people."

"This is the same town," shot back Travis. "Don't you ever forget it because I haven't. Look out in the road, Fred . . . they're talking neck-tie party right now, out there. Don't preach to me about twenty years ago. I tell you these are the same people and this is the same town, and God's my witness that I'm going to teach them a lesson they'll *never* forget!"

Brand stood stockstill bracing into Travis's terrible anger. After Travis ceased speaking, the silence in that thick-walled room grew and ran on and became almost unbearable. Bart Hayden was staring at Travis with a new expression; his two captors were sitting there unmoving, also staring. Finally Brand said to these last two men: "You can go on now. I'll see to it that Barbara Stuart knows who brought Hayden in. I don't know anything about a reward, but if there is one, you'll get it."

The cowboys stood up. One of them looked as though he might speak. Travis was watching this man. In the end the two range riders departed without saying anything. Then Fred Brand barred the door behind them and sank down at his desk. He said wearily: "You know where those two will go, don't you, Cole?"

"Sure. To the Stuart outfit."

"Yeah. And they'll come boilin' into town tonight."

Travis put a wintry smile upon Brand. "I'll be waiting," he said. "Only in the dark I don't reckon Wheeler'll fight fair, so I'll be watching behind me, too . . . with my shotgun."

"Cole, I told you not to carry that thing in this town."

Travis exchanged a long, wordless stare with Fred Brand. He turned upon his heel and crossed to the door. There, he looked back at both Hayden and Brand. To the prisoner he said: "Was Rock Stuart drunk when he cussed you and went for his gun?"

Hayden made a little reflective scowl, then he shrugged. "I don't know whether he was or not, Mister Travis. It was sundown an' we were about fifty feet apart. And like I already told you, I didn't know him real well. All I can say is that he sure Lord was fired up. He was set to gunfight me an' I couldn't talk him out of it."

Travis looked over at Brand. "You goin' to sleep here tonight?" he asked, his tone changing, becoming quieter now.

Brand nodded. Then he said: "Cole, when Miss Barbara hears you helped Hayden get clear, she'll swear out a warrant against you."

"All right, Fred. When she does that, you come for me. I'll be waiting."

"Cole . . . ," said the marshal, looking up into Travis's face in a pained way.

Travis understood Brand's thoughts. He shook his head slowly down at the town marshal. "We'd never fight, Fred. Not you and me. I'll go with you."

He left the jailhouse, walked out to the very edge of the roadway in front of it, and turned a thoughtful look up and down both sides of town where those little groups of men still stood, saw white faces turn to return his gaze in the fading evening light, then he paused long enough to demonstrate his indifference in the face of Gunsight's solid threat by calmly, deliberately making a cigarette, lighting it, and flipping away the match, and afterward started for the hotel.

He did not exactly disobey Fred Brand's injunction about appearing in the road with his riot gun; he simply took that weapon in its two parts downstairs to the hotel lobby, on out into the dusk, and carried it across to the vicinity of the livery barn. There, he assembled the gun, loaded it, and put it handily behind a dusty, unused door. Afterward he walked as far as that big cottonwood tree near the town's public watering trough that had a bench formed around its lower trunk, and seated himself. From this place he commanded the entire sweep of Main Street, down past the jailhouse, and on out to the flat country beyond.

Around him full night closed down with its solid formlessness. His eyes, coming as gradually as the darkness also came to their good adjustment to the change away from daylight, missed nothing that happened. It struck him then, as he watched those dwindling groups of men along the sidewalks, that Gunsight's initial surge of raw feeling had atrophied. He smiled a little over this, well aware that he'd been seen sitting up there alone and watching, that the word of his somber vigil had passed around encouraging the faint of heart and the mob-minded among those would-be lynchers to shy away.

Gunsight knew him now as a man who feared no odds. Whatever else it knew about him was unimportant. Yet he thought Brand or that little old man, or perhaps the others who had recognized him, had started a legend. He was not averse to this. Not at all averse. Before he rode out of Gunsight he promised himself there would be enough of this legend to furnish topics of conversation for a long, long time.

He made another cigarette and smoked it. The town was very quiet now, with a held-breath kind of silence. He strained to catch the sound of running horses swinging downcountry from the north. There was no such sound. He gauged the time from a rising moon, and thought those two reward greedy cowboys should have long since reached the Stuart outfit's home ranch with their electrifying tidings — and also, probably, with their strong hints about remuneration.

Moonlight lay gently upon the town, the far-away mountains, the valley floor. The great silver disc itself rode coldly, aloofly across a great curving infinity against that twinkling background of bluish stars. *One more night*, Travis thought, and it would be full. *One more night and probably a lot of things would have happened.* He sat on.

Now, some time later, the roadway was utterly deserted. There were men in the saloons, at the livery barn, in among the stores still transacting business this late in the night. But there were none out in the roadway anywhere to be seen. Travis's eyes glinted at this. *They* were also figuring the time close, estimating the hours yet to pass before all hell broke loose in Gunsight. They were comparing timepieces, heads low and feet resting lightly upon the barroom brass rails, thrilled and fearful both, and the reason they had all drifted in off the sidewalks was because they figured the

Stuart men would be hitting town soon now. *They should know*, Travis thought.

He recollected Jack Wheeler and studied this remembrance as he waited. Wheeler was a type of man. Not at all an unusual type on the frontier: hard and shrewd and sometimes brave, sometimes cautious and sly. Which would he be tonight? Travis thought he knew — he would be impressed by darkness and he would mean to use it as an ally in stalking Fred Brand's jail, in sending men to search out Travis, too.

With that resolved Travis recollected another of the Stuart Ranch people — Barbara Stuart herself. He found it ironic that so beautiful a woman had such a depth of hatred in her. What kind of a trick was this Nature had played. Some admiring man would succumb — probably dozens already had because she was very lovely in Travis's eyes, and therefore in the eyes of other lonely men — only to discover with wrenching disillusionment that beneath this lovely exterior was an icy capacity for hating never associated with beautiful women.

Travis thought back down the years to other women. To their warm laughter and their sometimes misty, sometimes flashing eyes. Being a handsome man he had known his share of girls, yet none had made much impression. He had gone his way always, recalling soft lips and murmuring voices in his many lonely camps, but never had a single woman gotten into his thoughts and remained there.

Travis was essentially a loner. A man who passed through life in a self-sufficient way, capable, confident, asking little, expecting nothing, meeting life head-on, too young yet to feel the compass pull of anything different, satisfied, up to now, with what he was. These things were visible about him now, as he sat waiting in the gloomy, mottled shadows of that old cottonwood tree, thinking his private thoughts and keeping his somber vigil.

CHAPTER
SEVEN

The Stuart Ranch men came into Gunsight on the dawn side of midnight, and, although their horses were blowing hard as though from a steady long run when they came around that intersecting roadway corner northward, all of them were walking their mounts.

Travis saw them long before they could see him in his camouflaging tree shadows. He counted them and came up with seven riders. He counted them a second time and got the same number again. His brow wrinkled over this. He was sure that, counting Jack Wheeler, the Stuart outfit had only six riders. Then he forgot this discrepancy in order to concentrate upon that press of dark shapes passing along wordlessly on their way to Fred Brand's jailhouse. He was entirely unaware that he no longer was alone, there by that big tree, until a soft voice said: "Mister, if I was you, I'd keep out of this."

Travis got to his feet and slowly turned to see who this man was. The first thing he made out in that poor light was the nickel badge lettered *Deputy Town Marshal*. He'd had no inkling Fred Brand had a helper in his law enforcement work. The second thing he noticed was that this stranger was whipcord tough and resolute; he did not know the meaning of the word fear. Travis said in the same quiet tone that the deputy town marshal had also used: "I can hardly keep out of it. I'm the cause of some of it."

"Fred told me," said the deputy, "but we don't need your help."

"Seven to two, and you don't think you need help?"

"Fifty to two, Mister Travis, an' we still wouldn't need your kind of help."

Someone down the road, peering over a saloon door, now saw that advancing black blur of horsemen and let off an alerting shout. Gunsight's deputy marshal made a half turn and dropped his hand toward his gun at the same time. Travis took advantage of this temporary switching away of the deputy's attention; his right hand dipped and rose in a blur. It arced overhand and came down across the deputy's hat, knocking the lawman down to his hands and knees. He hung there on all fours trying to clear fog from his mind. Travis caught him by an elbow, hoisted him up, and pushed him into a sitting position upon the tree bench. He took the deputy's six-gun, started to move forward where the oncoming Stuart Ranch riders were appearing, then swung back and put the deputy's six-gun in his lap, at the same time saying: "Sorry, feller, I had to do that. Your boss doesn't stand a chance. Gunsight is fired-up for a lynching and those riders will take advantage of that."

The deputy lifted a shaky hand to his head. He put a cloudy but clearing look upon Travis and mumbled: "Hell with you."

During this little stretch of time the Stuart men had passed down too close for Travis to run on and take up his shotgun; the deputy had spoiled this part of his strategy, but, because he was no newcomer to the ways of violence, he accepted the alternative at once and planned from there. He permitted those men to ride on past, staying in the tree shadows so as to make recognition impossible, then afterward, when their backs were to him, Travis crossed over, got his shotgun, and paced along through gloom keeping within range of the Stuart Ranch men, but not getting close enough to draw their attention. In this fashion he arrived in the vicinity of the jailhouse, stepped easily into the recessed doorway of a saddle shop, and waited.

Around those riders a little trickle of walking townsmen congregated, a few muted words were exchanged, and Travis understood that Wheeler was eliciting information concerning Bart Hayden. That seventh rider dismounted at the jailhouse hitch rack and Travis got a jolt — it wasn't another cowboy, it was Barbara Stuart herself! Now Jack Wheeler, easily recognizable in the roadway's bright moonlight, dismounted. Around him five more men swung out and down. Wheeler looked at Barbara Stuart, said something to the lovely girl that Travis could not make out, and turned his attention to a townsman standing close by. This time Travis had no difficulty hearing the words and the tone.

"A murderer's got this coming. We all know that. Any o' you townsmen got weak stomachs . . . stand clear.

Any others who favor range law are welcome to come along with us."

No one spoke in the solemn interval of silence that followed, but Travis saw the girl turn as though to address Wheeler, but she didn't get the chance, for Jack Wheeler passed solidly around the hitch rack, trod over the plank walk, and struck the jailhouse door, hard, with his pistol barrel. Now he was under the wooden overhang and Travis could no longer see his face. Out in the roadway men stood like stone, waiting. Some of them had hands lying upon holstered weapons. All of them had their eyes fixed fully forward. Even Barbara Stuart seemed mesmerized.

Brand opened the door and stood backgrounded by office lamplight. He recognized Wheeler immediately and also saw that swelling body of men farther back in the moonlight. From across the road men were coming up, too. Travis watched this silent build-up of Wheeler's strength. He cursed under his breath, angry that Fred had let himself be limned by that inner lamplight. He raised the shotgun belt high.

"I guess you know," Wheeler was saying to Fred Brand, "what we want, Marshal. We think you ought to go along with us and make no trouble."

Brand said nothing for a while. He saw Barbara Stuart standing back a ways and looked steadily at her. He finally spoke, ignoring Wheeler and addressing the girl: "You don't want it this way, do you, Miss Stuart?"

Travis held his breath awaiting her reply. But she did not speak, and Fred Brand then said: "I can't give

Hayden up. You people ought to know that. He'll have a fair trial. I'll promise you that."

Wheeler's right shoulder drooped. Brand's eyes instantly caught this. He said to the foreman: "Don't, Wheeler. Don't force it."

Travis, in his concealed place, could not discern Jack Wheeler's expression, but he knew how it would be — he'd known his share of Wheelers. The wish for combat would be a shine in Wheeler's eyes; it would be visible, too, in the bitter droop of his mouth. Wheeler was conscious of his power and he was hungering for a fight. Only a bullet could halt his intentions now and Travis understood this. He swung the shotgun a little to cover the foreman, but Fred Brand was too close and that troubled Travis.

Wheeler said stiffly: "Back up, Brand. Stand clear of the door and keep your hand away from that gun."

Fred did not move at once, and he seemed to Cole Travis to be weighing his chances of jumping back and slamming the door. Wheeler must have also thought this, for he put out his left hand, resting its fingertips upon the panel.

Back in the roadway near the hitch rack a man said very gently: "It ain't worth it, Brand." His meaning was clear to all.

But a man's convictions, rarely changing, rarely different, now motivated the marshal. He did not spring backward as those watching thought he would do, instead he lunged at Jack Wheeler, lashing out with a wild blow. The foreman, with every nerve alert, sprang away. Brand's fist missed by a country mile and he fell onward, clutching for Wheeler. The foreman went for his gun and Travis, knowing well the kind of man Wheeler was, stepped down from his doorway, cocked both barrels of his shotgun, and yelled: "Drop, Fred!" And fired one barrel.

Men, with no time really to change stance toward this fresh threat, squawked and fell to the ground. One man, slower than the others and slightly to one side of Wheeler's back-pedaling position, was caught by the edge of that shotgun pattern and went staggering out into the roadway in bad pain.

Wheeler dropped like stone, recognizing instantly the position of Travis's weapon, and Fred Brand's headlong rush led him to stumble over Wheeler and go sprawling out into the roadway.

Travis kept moving, sidling sideways or forward or backward but always moving. Gunshots blossomed upward in the night. Well behind Travis there was a quick tinkle of glass. He swung to ground-sluice with his remaining shot and sighted Barbara Stuart standing in stunned immobility in his path. He ran up to her, seized her arm, and roughly flung her aside. He was then too close to those scrambling men in the roadway; they panicked in the face of that murderous weapon he swung upon them, and they fought upright to flee with great shouts. Travis did not let off his other barrel after them. He hesitated, and in that moment three more pistol shots erupted. A slug struck solidly into the hitch rack to the left of his leg. The animals there, badly frightened now, jerked at their reins and tie ropes. Several of them broke away to go careening up the roadway, scattering those fleeing riders and townsmen even more.

There was another and final shot. It came from well up the roadway in the direction of the cottonwood tree beside Gunsight's public trough. Travis swung a little to see this gunman. He could not, so he leaped back to put both shoulders against wood, and whirled his weapon toward the place where he'd last seen Jack Wheeler.

Wheeler was not there. Fred Brand was — face down, half on, half off the sidewalk, but he was alone. Only a hat remained where Jack Wheeler had been. From the yonder shadows across the road a man opened up with his six-gun. Travis heard this slug rip wood. He turned a little, saw Barbara Stuart standing there like stone, and jumped toward her, pushing her toward the open doorway of the jailhouse. She resisted this pressure when another bullet slammed into the siding in front of her. Travis's left arm went up across her in a shielding way. She turned toward him, pressing her body close. He felt the wild strike of her heart through his shirt and turned away, only glimpsing her enormous eyes and twisted mouth, to stand fully in front of her. Now he let off that second shotgun barrel, and across the way a man screamed. After that there was no more firing.

Travis broke his riot gun, ejected its two spent casings, and plugged in two fresh loads. He was closing the weapon when a hatless man ran by him and fell to the ground where Fred Brand lay. Travis, not immediately understanding who this was, cocked his shotgun and covered this man.

It was the deputy town marshal. He turned a twisted face so that moonlight struck it, and cried out: "He's shot! Fred's shot!"

Travis did not move for ten seconds. Behind him Barbara Stuart's rough breathing sounded loud. The roadway was empty and utterly still now. Moonlight shone upon two men — the one farthest out was quite still and flat appearing and he was lying in the dirt all the way across the road. This was the sniper who had taken Travis's second scatter-gun load. He was dead. The nearer man, some twenty feet from the hitch rack, was sitting up in plain sight, rocking back and forth and moaning. It was he who had taken the fringe of Travis's initial shot pattern. He was not fatally injured but right then no one would have believed this because his right side and sleeve were wine-red and dripping.

Travis twisted, caught Barbara Stuart's arm, and led her roughly to that open doorway. He pushed her inside there, and closed the door, cutting off the inner lamplight. He next went to Fred Brand and knelt, holding his shotgun upright in one hand. "Where is he hit?" he inquired of the deputy.

"In the chest. See here."

Travis bent low, then slowly straightened up again. "Fetch a doctor," he ordered. "I'll carry him inside."

The deputy got unsteadily upright. He put a probing look outward, saw the dead man and the injured man, and said: "I want to know who shot him."

"Go get the doctor," Travis repeated, and, when the deputy still did not move, Travis jumped up and grabbed him, gave him a fierce push, and swore at him. "*Get the damned doctor!* I know who shot him. We'll take that up later."

The deputy hurried off.

Fred Brand was a heavy man. Travis might have managed carrying his bulk easier if he'd been willing to put aside the shotgun. This, though, he did not do. So he staggered into the jailhouse with Brand's inert form drooping in his arms, kicked the door closed, and deposited the town marshal upon a wall bunk. After that he went back, barred the door, and leaned the riot gun against the wall. Until he turned, listening for sounds outside, he forgot that he was not alone. Now, seeing Barbara Stuart, ashen and staring at Brand, he said curtly: "One killing is never enough, is it? There always have to be more."

She went slowly forward to stand gazing downward beside the wall bunk. "He'll die, won't he?" she murmured.

Travis shouldered past without answering. He went to work removing Brand's shirt. He used this to sop at the spreading dark stain. Brand's wound was serious; it was a small, puckered hole where the bullet had struck him in the right breast; the flesh there was swollen and a discolored purple. "Get some water," said Travis. "We'll wash him up for the doctor."

"Where?" the girl asked, looking dazed and a little ill.

Travis turned on her. "Look for some," he flared. "Dammit . . . use your head!"

She hurried away, found water, and returned with a bucket and several clean towels. Together they cleansed Brand's injury without speaking or looking at one another until the unconscious man groaned and weakly rolled his head.

"He's coming around," said Travis absently, bending lower over the marshal. He said this as though to himself and was quite unconscious of the girl's presence until she spoke.

"I want him to live," she said swiftly.

Travis raised his head; their faces were close and their eyes met. His were like ice chips. "Get out," he said. "Get out of here . . . now!"

CHAPTER
EIGHT

The doctor returned with Fred Brand's deputy town marshal. Travis was alone when these men entered. He moved aside for the doctor, holding Brand's torn and blood-stained shirt in one hand. The deputy flicked him a resentful look, saying in a bitter-soft voice: "How does it look?"

Travis jerked his head meaningfully at the medical man and crossed to the marshal's desk. There, he eased down and held up the shirt. Brand's badge of authority was smeared with its owner's blood. Travis removed this symbol of office, tossed down the shirt, and wiped the badge clean. He was doing this when the deputy came over to him saying: "The bullet went plumb through, Doc says. He's got a good chance."

Travis finished wiping the badge and looked up. The deputy was staring at him, at the way he was holding Brand's badge. "Well," said Travis, made sharp and irritable by what he had lived through, "what's bothering you?"

"You can't pin that on," said the deputy.

Travis blinked and he looked from the deputy to the badge. He had not considered pinning that badge to his own shirt. Now the idea found lodging in his thoughts.

He put the badge upon the desk, rummaged for his tobacco sack, and gravely made a smoke. After lighting up, he gazed critically upward. "Why not?" he demanded.

"Fred wouldn't stand for it. That's why not."

"He's in no shape to protest," said Travis. "Furthermore, unless he comes around, I'm the only one who knows who shot him." Travis kept watching the deputy. He said: "How about you . . . how would you feel about me wearin' his badge?"

The deputy looked scornful. "You're not that much of a man," he growled.

"How do you know that? You still sore because I had to hit you over the head? Listen, feller . . . if I hadn't done that, Fred would be dead now, and likely you'd be dead right alongside of him." Travis stood up and exhaled smoke. He was feeling better now because a fresh string of thoughts were in him. "I think," he concluded, "you won't be able to do what's got to be done now by yourself."

The deputy shrugged past Travis to perch upon the desk. He put a troubled gaze over where Fred Brand lay, where the medical man was working calmly and efficiently. He said nothing for a while but idly swung one foot back and forth, ignoring Travis.

Bart Hayden in his strap-steel cage across the room had been still and silent. Now he called to Travis: "Why did you let her go?"

Travis looked up quickly, not at once understanding because of other things in his mind.

"She led 'em here, didn't she?" said the prisoner from a white, haggard face. "She's no better'n Wheeler is. Why'd you let her leave?"

The deputy quit swinging his foot. He looked at Travis, also thinking of Barbara Stuart. "Yeah," he queried. "Why did you? She was as much a part of it as Jack Wheeler." He looked grim. "Only she's a sight prettier . . . was that it, Travis?"

Thinking back now, Travis knew why he'd not held Barbara Stuart, and her beauty had nothing to do with it. He simply had been too absorbed in Brand's injury and too wrought up and antagonistic toward her to bear the sight of her. But, in his own mind, these reasons seemed weak and insufficient now, so he said nothing, simply strolled over to lean forward above the doctor and gaze downward. Behind him the deputy sat on, watching Travis's back with his antagonistic gaze, and Bart Hayden lapsed into silence again.

The doctor murmured to the presence he sensed behind him: "He lost a sight of blood. Otherwise, if he's very quiet, he'll probably come along all right. But these things hemorrhage . . . he can't get excited or move. Not for a couple of weeks anyway. And even after that long, he can't do much." The medical man arose, turned, and faced Travis. "I've done all I can. Now, there's another one over at Flannery's with buckshot in him. I've got to go over there."

"One question," said Travis, turning away from Fred Brand. "Did you tend Rock Stuart when they brought him in dead?"

"I did. I'm the only licensed practitioner in the town. What of it?"

"Was he drunk?"

"Drunk? Young man, Rock Stuart was dead."

Travis grunted. "I know that. What I'm trying to find out was whether he'd been drinking before he was shot, or not."

The doctor finished wiping his hands. He began stowing instruments into his bag. When he'd finished with this, he considered Travis with shrewd eyes. "I couldn't rightly say whether Stuart was drunk or not, but I can say that he smelled strongly of liquor when I embalmed him. Does that help you any?"

Travis said: "It does. Thank you."

The doctor buttoned his coat. He cast a last long look downward, and he said: "Now remember, young men, Fred Brand's got to be kept absolutely quiet."

"Yes. I'll have him taken to his mother's place."

"An excellent idea. But be easy about it. Unnecessary bumping can start a hemorrhage."

"We'll be easy," agreed Travis.

The medical man departed.

Travis dropped down into the chair beside Brand's bunk. The office was very quiet; even the town beyond seemed to have lost its taste for excitement for no sounds came from the roadway. Without looking around, Travis said: "Deputy, what's your name?"

"Will Fenwick," came back the sulky reply.

"Will, there's a dead man out in the road. Go take care of him."

The deputy's brows drew down darkly. He did not move off the desk. Travis made a half turn upon the chair. These two exchanged a long stare.

"Now," said Travis gently, "not tomorrow."

Fenwick grudgingly got off the desk and crossed to the door. He passed on out with animus in every line of him. After he had gone, Bart Hayden said: "Mister Travis, you got an enemy in Fenwick. He don't like you at all."

Travis paid no attention to this. He returned to watching Fred Brand. It was a long, solemn vigil, because the marshal did not come around until the moment Deputy Fenwick reëntered the office after having taken care of that riddled Stuart Ranch cowboy. Then Brand looked weakly at Travis and for a full minute made no attempt to speak to him.

Travis said softly: "The doc was here, Fred. He said you'll make it, but you've got to be very still and quiet."

"Yeah," husked the wounded man. Then he took a deep breath, levered up some strength, and spoke again, but so poorly that Travis had to bend to hear. Behind him, Fenwick glided forward also to hear.

"Wheeler . . ."

"I know," said Travis. "I saw him shoot you from the corner of my eye."

"I wasn't going for my gun, Cole. I was trying to get up after I'd fallen over him."

"I said I saw it, Fred. You'd better not talk for now."

"Cole . . . ?" The wounded man appeared insistent, troubled, and anxious. "Anybody else . . . get it?"

"Two Stuart riders. One was hit and another was killed."

"You . . . ?"

Travis inclined his head. "With my riot gun, Fred. I had to. The deck was stacked against you too much for my taste."

"Wheeler," pronounced the wounded man, his voice dropping away. "He . . . he's bad trouble, Cole. If he didn't get hit . . . he'll be back. It won't end here."

"I guess not," murmured Travis. "Now listen to me, Fred. I'm goin' to have you taken to your mother's place. You've got to have nursing. Then I'm going after Jack Wheeler and that girl."

"Her . . . ?"

"She was with them, Fred. You saw that."

"You can't . . . do that, Cole. It's my . . . job. Fenwick'll do it for me . . . My deputy."

Travis put a hand lightly upon Brand's arm. He said: "I'm going to pin on your badge, Fred. I'm going after them. Fenwick's got to stay here. If they think Hayden's unguarded, they can come back. They probably will come back."

Brand's glistening, pale face grew still and thoughtful. He looked away from Travis a while, studying the ceiling. Then he looked back. "Cole . . . ?"

Travis, who had grown up with Fred Brand, knew now what was troubling him. He got up and made a hard little grin downward. "It won't be like you're thinkin'. I'll forget the grudge until this thing is settled, Fred."

"On your word, Cole?"

"On my word."

Brand rolled his eyes sideways. "Will," he said to Deputy Fenwick, "give him my badge."

Fenwick nodded, considerate enough not to argue, but showing in his solid look of dislike that this order stuck in his craw. "Sure," he murmured. "Sure, Fred."

Travis moved quietly back to the desk, took up Brand's badge, and pinned it with deliberation upon his shirt. He looked up as Fenwick came up beside him. They exchanged another long look and Travis said: "All right, Will. You go right on hating my guts. I'm sorry you feel that way but I can't change it. And meanwhile, keep an eye on your damned town because I don't trust it."

Fenwick said grudgingly: "You goin' after those people alone?"

"What choice have I got?"

"Feelin' as you do about this town, Mister Travis, I'd say you got no other choice. If you don't want a town posse, I expect the townfolks feel the same way about you, too."

"That's exactly the way I want it," growled Travis. "One more thing . . . while I'm gone, have Fred moved to his mother's place. But be awfully careful with him . . . you hear?"

Fenwick nodded, running his speculations about this capable-looking man into a composite image and beginning to wonder if Travis might not just bring this thing off. "You better take your scatter-gun along," he said. "They'll maybe be expecting something out there."

"Not at close range, they won't," answered back Travis, making for the door. "You can catch men the same way once, sometimes twice. But not the third time. How, exactly, do I find the Stuart place?"

"Go north to the hills, then swing a little west. You'll see a good trail heading up through the trees . . . stay on it. It'll take you right into the yard." Fenwick's voice dropped. "It may not take you back out, though."

Travis cast a by-passing glance at Fred Brand. He said to Fenwick: "Maybe it won't. But I'll tell you one thing, Deputy . . . I didn't come down in the last rain." Then he crinkled his eyes over where Brand was watching them, calling to him: "Easy now, Fred. And don't worry about that other thing. You've got my word."

He left the marshal's office with nighttime's full measure of pre-dawn stillness everywhere around him, got his horse at the livery barn, and rode leisurely out of Gunsight, northbound. He was conscious of the darkness as an ally. The moon was far down beyond the farthest hills and unless Barbara Stuart had her sentries out, and they were particularly vigilant this night, they would not see him and she would not know he was coming.

Fenwick's directions proved good enough. Travis found the trail with no trouble, and he sat a while letting his eyes search out the way this onward land lay. Then, satisfied which fold in the deeper hills would be big enough to accommodate a mountain meadow ranch, he went forward again. Only now he did not use the trail that Fenwick had directed him to. He instead rode parallel to it, but westerly a quarter of a mile, and kept himself orientated by occasional sashays back to where he could see this trail. He did not think Barbara Stuart or even Jack Wheeler would be considering the likelihood of a lone man pursuing them into their own hills, and yet he knew well enough that in this affair he could afford to be wrong only once — when he rode head-on into an ambush.

The odds, he thought, poking along among stiff-topped pines, had been evened up somewhat. Stuart Ranch had lost one man killed, another injured in the roadway of Gunsight, and a third man, actually the first cowboy to tangle with Travis, also laid low by gunfire. Barring the girl herself, there remained four, perhaps no more than three Stuart riders.

Travis slouched along. If the darkness favored him for just another few hours, providing him with the shroud of secrecy he needed to effect a surprise, he might be able to even up those odds still more. It was a thought, a possibility, and he wished now only that he knew the country ahead better. As a lad he'd hunted these hills, but that was long ago. Even in broad daylight he doubted that he'd remember; certainly in darkness such as he consistently passed through now, there was no possibility of remembering at all.

Once, his horse encountered a granite ledge and made sharp sounds with its shod hoofs before Travis reined clear of that spot. Another time, as they passed from forest to meadow and back to forest again, Travis came erect in swift alarm, thinking a moving shape ahead was a horse and rider. But when this silhouette stopped to turn and peer, he recognized that it was instead a bull elk with a gigantic set of antlers.

He began to wonder, after an hour of this alternating forest meadow forest riding, how close he was to the Stuart outfit's home ranch. He got his answer to that shortly thereafter when a horse loudly whistled beyond the next gang of trees, scenting Travis and his mount.

CHAPTER
NINE

Stuart Ranch lay below Travis in a large meadow that was both broad and deep. Somewhere, northerly, he heard the boiling of an upland creek where it gushed violently over boulders. The buildings were along the course of this ample waterway, consisting of the usual big log barns, the outbuildings, corrals, and incidental smaller sheds such as hen house, smithy, and bunkhouse. A light burned in that latter place, casting outward a nearly square patch of orange glow, but what Travis searched particularly for — a light in the main house — was not visible at all.

He sat in his saddle studying those buildings, thinking how best to approach them. Thinking, too, that unless he could successfully effect this, Fenwick's dour prognostication might prove correct — he might not go back the same way he'd come in.

A number of loose horses came swirling out of the forest east of Travis. He heard their hoofs upon spongy humus only seconds before they broke out into his sight, heads high, eyes brightly curious about this strange man and strange horse, and rammed down to a dusty halt to stand rigid, staring ahead. Travis guessed these to be the ranch's spare remuda. He looked away, returning his attention to the farther buildings. For a while longer he considered his best approach. As he sat there the loose stock, tiring of their vigil, trooped fully forward and downward out of the trees and began following along a trail that Travis could not make out in their onward approach to the ranch yard.

Travis counted the animals — twenty in number — and was struck by an idea that he promptly began to execute. He dismounted and led his own animal shufflingly along behind that loose stock, knowing that in this moon-down darkness a watcher, if there was one, or some listening person who might come out to see about the sounds of that remuda, would not be able to distinguish one horse far back in the dust wearing a saddle.

In this way he got to the ranch yard, veering off behind the main residence where the horses went ploddingly on toward the creek. He left his animal back there in dripping gloom and passed on closer to the house, was almost to its rear porch when a shape whirled up from the ground dead ahead and hurled itself at him. Travis had no time to side-step so he squared himself forward to meet that hurtling form.

The sentinel made no sound as he crashed into Travis, big hands scrabbling for a hold, hatless head dropping low to ram suddenly upward striking Travis smartly along the jaw. Travis had only a second to wonder why this man had not cried out, had not given an alarm to those men at the bunkhouse. Then that fierce blow roared through his skull and he had no further time for thinking of anything except beating off and surviving, if he could, this savage attack.

He shifted his body, seeking to tear clear of those gripping talons. But the other man, larger and heavier than Travis, clung to him fiercely. His breath broke against Travis's face and his wild eyes wetly shone. Travis broke the grip of one of those hands and hit his assailant on the jaw, hard. The man grunted, his knees sagged, but he clung to Travis like a vice, and within a moment he recovered enough to bring his weight to one side, easing it off one foot. Travis instinctively whirled, knowing what was coming, and the cowboy's knee missed his groin and hit harmlessly against Travis's thigh.

This man, Travis found, was very strong. He was also a head taller and easily thirty pounds heavier, which, Travis now felt, was the reason he'd sought to attack Travis instead of shouting an alarm. He wanted the triumph of whipping this man who had broken the back of the Stuart Ranch's attack in Gunsight, single-handed, so he could drag the bloodied form to his companions and drop it there, victorious.

It would be a near thing, Travis thought, trying to break the enclosing powerful arms that were encircling his middle. He would have to fight with everything in him. He tried to lever loose those constricting arms and failed. He rained blows upon the big cowboy's face and head. Still the arms drew tighter. Then Travis did successfully what his enemy had tried to do unsuccessfully — he brought his knee upward and hit the cowboy's crotch with a crashing blow. At once those steel-band arms fell away, the sentinel staggered backward, doubling over. He made little animal grunts down in his throat.

Travis went after him, struck him twice on the head and once in the face. He got one shoulder down with his weight behind it and blasted a vicious strike into the cowboy's chest. This blow would have dropped a smaller man like a stone. Travis's adversary took the blow well, although breath exploded past his lips, and continued to retreat. Travis hit him again and again. Still the cowboy would not go down. Then, as Travis moved in for a sledging strike upon the cowboy's neck, one long arm shot out knocking him off balance and that prepared blow went off in space.

The sentinel drew slightly up and away from his crouch. He spat blood and his little hating eyes shone. He pawed forward keeping Travis off balance. Then he let fly with a whipping overhand strike that caught Travis flushly and jarred him down to his toes. Encouraged by this the sentinel came on with mincing little steps regaining his lost ground and bringing up his freshly recovered strength.

Travis shuffled back, let the cowboy become bold, then ducked in under a looping strike, came upright, and slammed a jolting blow to the cowboy's middle, then, as his adversary involuntarily winced from this, Travis caught him flushly on the bridge of the nose. Claret sprayed, the cowboy's eyes went awry, and both his big arms dropped away. Travis struck his face again, caught the sagging man, and pushed him back upright, caught him folding over and sent him backward with every ounce of his remaining strength. The Stuart rider hit the ground solidly and did not move. His breathing was loud and broken-sounding in the night, and it bubbled inward and outward.

Travis pushed out an arm to support himself, found a little arbor under his hand, and looked at it. There was a bench inside this arbor. He got to it on shaking legs and sank down. There did not seem to be enough air in this night to ease the burning in his chest. He sawed back great lungsful of it while his head swam.

This, he told himself, was no good — he had to find a place to lie down for a while. He had beaten the sentinel but was himself in only slightly better shape. For the time being he would have to forgo his other plan. He arose, groped along to his horse, and was working hard to get into the saddle when a man's soft call came through the night.

"Hey, Pete . . . where are you?"

Travis did not seek the owner of that voice; he instead spun his mount and rammed home the spurs. The beast gave a startled jump and lit running. He had his rider a long two hundred yards through the paling night when a gunshot echoed back behind the house. Travis knew his unconscious adversary had been found. He also knew that in moments the countryside would be alive with riders. He did not spare his beast until, some time later in among forest gloom, he dared to stop long enough for the horse to have a good blow.

That slashing run had brought out every ache Travis possessed. It also cleared his head, though, and brought him back to reasoning thought. He was confident the men probing this night roundabout would not find him now, so he delayed leaving the blackness of that resting place for a time, and meanwhile, far back, he heard two men crossfire to one another in a bracketing way as they searched for him. From this systematic way they were hunting him Travis knew they would not give up. It also occurred to him that if he could let any two of those men go past on either side of him, he would be well behind them. It was this thought that brought to mind still another notion — after the Stuart riders were ahead of him, Travis would have no more enemies back at the ranch — excepting one. If he could not now capture Wheeler, he could, with caution, get back to the main house and capture Barbara Stuart.

Doubts came at once to caution him against this seeming madness. He was physically exhausted, as much from the events of the long day and night, as from the bruising punishment he had recently taken. If he was again caught, he could not hope successfully to withstand more abuse.

He very carefully put aside those warnings and eased his horse around, then sat a while waiting for sounds. They came, in time, enabling him to place the pair of riders nearest to his place of concealment, one on his right side, one on his left side, about equal distance apart and perhaps three hundred yards from him, at the closest spot.

He dismounted, winced from pain in his chest, took his horse by the nostrils and kept that hand lying loosely but ready instantly to clamp down should the horse seek to nicker at other horses, then, when the sounds of those by-passing men moved on, he led the horse back the way it had just come for a hundred yards before remounting it to ride steadily in the direction of the Stuart Ranch main house.

There was now stillness everywhere. Those mounted men were far away and as Travis paused for a look outward and downward into the ranch yard again, not even those loose horses were in sight.

That light in the bunkhouse still glowed. Now, too, there was a light in the main residence. It was toward this that Travis made his way from a fresh direction, and after he hid his mount this second time, he did not stride ahead at once, but instead felt his way, studying each vague shape in the night as he steadily progressed, using considerable caution.

That light that was his compass seemed to be coming from a rear room in the main ranch residence. He stepped along toward it with great care, paused to view ahead the spot where he'd last seen the unconscious sentinel, who was no longer lying there, then made his last hundred-foot advance like an Indian, utilizing each shadow, every natural cover, and scarcely seeming to move at all, sometimes, until he was up to the side wall. Here he remained without moving for a long time. Here, too, he had an excellent sighting of the entire ranch yard, the bunkhouse, the barns, and corrals. He saw one saddled horse drowsing before the bunkhouse, and that orange patch of lamp glow, too, but otherwise he saw nothing, so he turned, finally, felt along the wall to a window, and tried it. It would not budge. He increased the force of his pressure gradually and the window began to give a little. He strained hard, then the sash slid, an opening appeared, grew wider, and when it was wide enough, Travis left off straining. He thought, if that window had ever been opened at all, it had been many years before.

He rested a moment, then, rising up carefully, took a good grip, and eased himself over the sill inside, let himself down upon the floor with extreme gentleness, and turned upon the balls of his feet to see where he was. This was a large kitchen. It had enough white paint to its walls, cupboards, and tables to reflect weak pre-dawn paleness, making identification possible. Where a passageway led beyond this room faint illumination glowed. Travis went forward toward this opening, saw that it was a long hall and that far along it was an opened door. From that room was coming the light.

He held back from additional progress long enough to keen the night for sounds. There was none to be heard, so he drew his handgun and started down that hallway, keeping close to one wall in order to minimize the possibility of squeaking floor boards. There were other doors to be passed. Because he did not know this house and because these doors were not all entirely closed, his progress was prudently slow. Then he got along to that lighted door, took two wide steps across to the opposite wall, and stood stockstill, looking in.

There was nothing to be seen at first, yet clearly someone had only very recently left this room. Travis hefted his gun considering whether to enter or to remain and wait. He decided to wait. No great amount of time passed before there were sounds of movement, of someone coming from one room into another room. Then he saw her — Barbara Stuart. She evidently had only

238

recently dressed and she stood now believing herself alone, running a comb through her hair. This was Travis's first good look at Barbara Stuart. He was pressed for time, and yet he made no prompt move forward.

Beneath strong eyebrows he saw those direct gray eyes again, but with a different look to them now than when they had met before, a troubled look, and a long, full mouth that showed temper, showed that Barbara Stuart could charm a man or chill him to the marrow. A willful mouth, thought Travis, and at the same time a generous mouth, which could be warm and tender to some man. She was slightly better than average height for a woman, and the strength of her figure showed that her frontier life had made her physically hard and active. The white blouse she wore was drawn snugly around the curve of breastline, and lower her stomach was quite flat. Her skin was as flawless as Travis remembered it, as also were the contours of her face, her throat, and shoulders.

Travis's full attention was fixed forward. He estimated her age at twenty-four or twenty-five. He felt sad that she was as he thought she was, because he did not believe he'd ever before met such a complete woman; he knew, too, that forever after, wherever life might lead him, when his lonely man's thoughts turned to women, her image would come up to haunt him. He let his speculations end there, holstered his weapon, and took two long, quiet forward steps and halted in the doorway, waiting.

She saw him at once over her shoulder in the mirror, framed there, looking grim and soiled and used-up. She let her hand with the comb drop down, and very slowly she turned. Not a word passed between them for a long moment. She seemed startled at his appearance in her house, in her sitting-room doorway, but if she felt fear of him, that did not show. She said in a steady voice: "They told me you'd escaped. You didn't leave at all, did you?"

"I left," Travis answered. "Then I came back for you."

Her eyes widened a little. "Why for me?"

"To arrest you."

"Oh. Then we'd better go at once, Mister Travis. Before Jack returns."

He turned her willingness over in his mind, becoming skeptical of her, becoming suspicious.

"While there's no daylight," she added. "We might make it, now. We couldn't make it after dawn." He still said nothing. She put aside the comb, stooped to catch up a light rider's jacket, and put it on. Then she looked directly at Travis saying: "I'm ready."

Travis told himself this was too easy, she had to be up to something. He said: "I'm arresting you for attempted murder, for armed assault, for . . ."

"Anything at all," she cut in. "Only let's get away from here."

Now Travis's puzzlement showed. "You don't understand," he told her. "Two men were badly shot up and another man was killed because you brought those men into Gunsight tonight. Even being a woman under those circumstances won't save you."

She moved closer to him, to the doorway. She said: "Mister Travis, I'm your prisoner. Please . . . let's leave now before Jack and the others return." She looked steadily up into his face. "We'll have to ride double on your horse. There is a guard down at the bunkhouse, and a wounded man. If either one of us tries to go past to the corrals for a horse, they'll shoot. Those are Jack Wheeler's orders . . . shoot on sight."

"Wait a minute," murmured Travis. "Are you trying to make me believe you're a prisoner here . . . on your own ranch?"

She was exasperated at his delaying things. "Believe anything you want, only don't stand there because dawn will be here shortly, and then neither of us will get away." She started to edge around him at the door.

The scent of her hair gave Travis one brief bad moment, aroused all his male instincts. Then he turned and started along the hall, saying: "You walk in front, ma'am. I reckon you've got one of those little black-leg Derringers about you somewhere, but you'd deny it and damned if I'm going to look for it."

She strode out to the kitchen and gazed for some time out a window. Then she said — "Come on." — and took Travis out of the house by the back door and back porch. "Where is your horse?" He pointed the way and she walked out.

Around them darkness was beginning to pale out, turn watery and misty and diluted-looking everywhere except in among yonder forest. There, it remained as stubbornly dark as ever.

CHAPTER
TEN

They got all the way to Travis's horse without incident. He untied the beast, stepped up and across leather, kicked out his left foot, and extended his hand. She toed in, took a strong grip, and rose up to settle behind him. She put both hands about his waist and he reined around making for the nearest tree fringe. There was one bad moment as they crossed three hundred feet of open country, but afterward, in the forest and moving along over a thousand-year accumulation of needles, they made no sound at all.

She said: "I have no gun, Mister Travis."

This no longer troubled him; her willingness did though, and he said so. "If you think you're going to work on men's sympathies, Miss Barbara, you're going to get a surprise. At least as far as the law in Gunsight is concerned."

She waited until they had passed around a huge old deadfall pine, then she said quietly: "I won't deny leading my men to Gunsight last night to avenge my father's killing. Ever since that happened I've had men scouring these hills for that cowboy. I wanted him dead . . . by gun or rope . . . but dead."

242

"You almost made it," he muttered, probing the onward darkness for movement, keeping his right hand lying ready upon the holstered weapon he wore.

"But after the fight . . . after I left Gunsight and got back to the ranch, Jack was waiting. He had a plan to hire more men and strike back." Barbara paused, then went on. "I was even in favor of that, for a while, then I changed my mind. I told Jack we'd done enough . . . that we'd do nothing more until the law tried Hayden, and, if it executed him, we'd consider the episode ended, but, if it didn't execute him, then we'd hire men to hunt him down and kill him."

Travis made a dry comment and Barbara ignored it to continue speaking; it was as though she wished very much to talk this out. Her arms around his middle tightened as her emotions heightened. He, after a time, became acutely conscious of this grip.

"It was here that Jack said something to me . . ."

"Go on."

"He said I was to marry him. He said that my father went out to kill Hayden because Wheeler had told him Hayden had tried to . . ."

Travis's entire attention had been directed to what the girl was saying. He understood now what she could not say to him, too. He pushed out a loud sigh and spoke softly, saying: "Wheeler. It was Wheeler who worked this thing up. That's been the puzzler to me. I never believed Bart Hayden deliberately shot your father. Yet there had to be a reason for your pa to rush out and try to kill Hayden." He considered telling her that her father had been drunk when he'd tried to kill

243

Hayden. Instead, he worded this differently, asking a question. "Did your father see you before he went out to kill Hayden?"

"No, he and Jack rode home from town and my father didn't come near the house. He went directly out after Hayden." Barbara drew in a ragged breath, then said: "If he'd only come to see me first, Mister Travis. Do you understand?"

"Yes," said Travis thoughtfully, "and I also understand a few other things. Miss Barbara, your pa was drunk when he met Bart Hayden. You just said he returned from Gunsight with Wheeler. I can guess what happened and so can you. Wheeler had his reasons . . . he got your pa drunk in town, told him that tale about you and Hayden, then rode back with him all fired-up for a killing, and conveniently split off so's your pa would go on and do his little job alone.

"Wheeler won no matter who lost. If Hayden killed your father, Wheeler had him out of the way for his other plans. If your pa killed Hayden, Wheeler probably had it in mind to prove Hayden had been unarmed, or something like that . . . ambushed perhaps . . . and the law would have convicted your pa of murder. Either way Wheeler came out as top dog."

Barbara said: "Yes. I knew as soon as he came into my room last night after the raid in Gunsight, it had to be something like this, Mister Travis. When he said I had to marry him, I understood perfectly what had happened."

Travis halted the horse to sit a moment, listening. They were deep in the forest now, and far enough along for the tilting land to begin its onward slope toward the yonder town and valley. He heard nothing, considered it likely that the riders had fanned out in a wider sweep to broaden their searching scope, and started forward again.

He said, taking up their conversation where she had left it: "A beautiful girl and a rich cow outfit. I reckon those things could drive some men to murder and worse, Miss Barbara."

She said nothing in response to this, but Travis noticed how her grip around his middle slacked off a little. They came out near the final break of trees before she spoke again. "That man who you fought out behind my house last night . . . Wheeler stationed him there to see that I did not try to get away. After you fought him and got away, Wheeler was in a rage. I never saw him like that before . . . he was insane. He burst into the house screaming that, when he got back from killing you, he'd tie me on a horse and take me over to Forest Falls, the next town north beyond these hills, and marry me. He was frightening, Mister Travis. I've known Jack Wheeler for seven years, ever since my father hired him as our ranch foreman, but I had no idea what he was really like. He left a man at the bunkhouse to guard me and to help that man you whipped . . . he left a saddled horse for him to use if I tried to run away. I heard him tell that man to shoot me if he had to."

"Nice feller," muttered Travis, halting in among the final thin screening of forest. He put his hand backward. "Get down," he said.

Barbara put her hand into his but did not immediately alight. "Why?" she asked.

"I'm going to ride out a little ways. I want to see if Wheeler's got men watching for me. If he has, I'll run for it and you'll hide here until I get back with men from Gunsight. Ma'am, this horse is tired. He'd never carry us both clear to Gunsight if other men on fresher animals were after us . . . too much weight. Now get down."

Barbara obeyed. She stood in the brightening dawn glow looking upward.

Travis considered her gravely for a silent moment, then he too dismounted. "Listen," he said huskily, "a man learns things as he goes through life. I learned long ago when you've got something to say to someone, you'd better say it. Especially if there's bad trouble, because if anything happens to either of you . . . then it's never said." He stopped. Barbara was looking at him. He drew in a little breath. "I don't think I've ever before seen a woman as handsome as you. Even that first day when you ordered me off your land, I couldn't get the memory of you out of my mind. Even though I was convinced you were bad through and through, I still couldn't forget you." Travis reached forth; she did not move away from him, but her lips parted, her eyes widened, and a tiny tremor made her nostrils flare slightly. He placed both hands upon her waist and swayed her to him. He brought his face down, feeling for her mouth. He kissed her, let the hungers that built up in lonely men burn against her.

Unexpectedly she raised both arms, encircled his neck with them, and returned his kiss, first with her own willful fire, then gentler, with an understanding

246

tenderness. Then she pressed both hands against his chest, pushing, and he stepped clear.

"You'll make it," she murmured to him. "We'll both make it." She felt for his hand, hurt its battered knuckles with a quick squeeze, then dropped it. "Now you'd better go."

Travis got back into the saddle. He looked solemnly down. An odd little wry smile came to his lips. He shook his head and reined away, riding on out through those last trees just as dawn's breaking sunlight flashed out over the hills, the valley floor, and the town far along southward.

Travis got clear of the last trees, paced out over the plain a ways, and halted to turn his gaze backward along the rims, the upthrusts, and along that east-west long run of forest fringe. He saw nothing — no men, no horses, no movement. He was critical of this, thinking that a man as sly, as crafty as Jack Wheeler would not overlook the probability of a fugitive coming out onto the valley floor in this area.

But even as this thought ran on, he also considered the possibility that Wheeler, thinking Travis had long since escaped because so much time had elapsed, might be riding into the ranch yard even now, far behind. Or he still might be running the hills believing Travis had forted up somewhere.

Then Travis started back again, riding easy, coming to the sound conclusion that whatever Wheeler was up to was not his primary worry; what must now concern him to the exclusion of all other things, was getting along to Gunsight with Barbara Stuart.

He ran a hand along his mount's neck in an understanding way. He had owned this horse a number of years and it had always served him well and loyally. He knew it was tired now, and hungry. "Another hour," he said to it. "One more hour, then I'll have you bedded to your hocks in meadow hay, old-timer."

He reëntered the forest fringe, saw Barbara watching him, and rode to her with his eyes turning soft, turning warm. She stood on, waiting for him to speak; she was round and full and very lovely in his sight, standing there in quiet shadows. Her eyes, strongly upon him, were shadowed and very dark-looking; he could not read the expression in them but her lips were gently closed, composed and tender-seeming in their fullness, and her breasts lifted and softly fell to her breathing.

"I didn't see anyone," he murmured, relaxing in the saddle.

She said: "What is your first name?"

"Cole. Cole Travis."

"Cole, come here."

He got down, trailed his reins, and approached her. She could call him like that and he would come; he knew this when he stopped a foot away from her.

"Cole, why are you here? Are you just a drifter passing through?"

"You might say that of me, Barbara, although I came to Gunsight for a purpose."

"And that is . . . ?"

He made a little head shake at her. "No . . . it's not working out, so it wasn't important. Not really important, Barbara. I made a mistake, is all."

"Then you will be riding on?"

He saw something in her glance harden against him, something seemingly designed to protect a woman from hurt. He said, with a little shrug: "I guess so. I don't know."

"Is there someone waiting, Cole?"

"No," he told her, understanding her meaning clearly enough. "As a matter of fact there never has been."

"Then I want to know about you. Who you are . . . what you have been."

She was holding herself still. He could see that. She was battling with some kind of intuition perhaps, or an emotion of which he would be ignorant.

"I'm not important, Barbara. I'm just a feller on the loose." He wanted mightily to touch her; her closeness and her beauty did strange things to him; his shoulders drew up a little and he set himself to observe the rules of propriety. "We'd best be getting along now," he said, drawing the horse close, turning to mount it.

She swung up behind him again, and this time, when she encircled his waist, they were both of them very conscious of this as they set out through the trees and came down onto the valley floor.

New day burned with its dazzling brilliance. The heat worked on Travis, turning him loose in the saddle, bringing a drowsiness he fought against, putting totally strange thoughts in his mind, and keeping a peculiar dull ache in his heart at the touch of those tanned arms, at the wonderful scent of that rich, wavy hair.

CHAPTER
ELEVEN

He eventually said to her in a wondering tone: "I don't understand it. Where is Wheeler? He's no fool. He knows I'll head for town. Yet there was no one back in the trees to stop us. I don't understand this at all."

"He might have given up," she said. "Maybe he's come to his senses and is getting out of the country."

"No," contradicted Travis. "Not Wheeler. I know his kind. He wants you. He wants your ranch. He'll never stop trying for those things. Another thing about Wheeler's type . . . they never forget or overlook a whipping, and twice now I've crossed him and come off alive. He won't ever let a thing like that lie still."

"Perhaps he returned to the ranch. He may have thought, since you'd escaped him, he'd go back and get me."

"It could be that," mused Travis. "I only wish I knew."

They went along over the open country through new day warmth, neither of them saying anything for a long time. Once, Travis turned the horse and stopped to put a final long look upon the rearward country. Where sunlight lay upon dark pine needles, there rose up a kind of faint purple glow. Lower, in among those giant boles, were deep shadows and cathedral-like patterns that gave dimensional depth to the forest, yet, aside from the beauty of all that, there was no movement.

He started south again, came to a tiny creekbed, and halted for his horse to drink. They again dismounted. This time Barbara walked a little way off to stand broodingly, looking at the shiny run of water. Travis watched her from below his hat brim for a moment, then went over near her and said: "When I was a kid I used to see how happy animals were and wonder about that. When I was older, I came to the conclusion that being a reasoning animal, man usually uses this ability to pile up troubles for himself."

She turned and said: "Cole, it's beginning to haunt me. What I almost did to that cowboy."

"You came close," he admitted, "but you didn't quite get it done. That's the important thing, Barbara."

"But . . . what about those other men . . . Fred Brand and that rider who was killed?"

Travis pushed back his hat, ran a probing look around, and brought his sober gaze back again. "I killed that rider . . . not you. As for Fred . . . I grew up with him. I know him like a brother. He won't pack a grudge. Anyway, you didn't shoot him."

"I led them there, Cole. I did nothing to stop them."

"Yeah, I know. That's what stuck in my craw last night in the jailhouse when I told you to get out." Travis's eyes crinkled at her. "Anyway, now you know what it's like to be a reasoning animal." His near smile faded. "I'll tell you something, Barbara," he said quietly. "I darn' near made an even bigger mistake than

251

you made. Came so close to it I'll never forget how it was."

"What mistake . . . ?" she murmured, seeing something moving in the depths of his eyes.

He whipped back a big breath and let it out, saying: "Some other time. We had better keep moving along."

"I'm curious, Cole. No, I'm interested. Don't leave me dangling."

"I'll tell you," he replied, and reached for her hand, led her back to the horse. "When things are right I'll tell you."

She squeezed his hand, saying nothing and striding along at his side. He was very conscious of her, of her nearness, of her touch. When they were back astride again, he said almost harshly: "Barbara, by God, I've got to get away from you."

She heard the words, but the manner in which he had spoken them had for her much more meaning. She was a wise person though, with her full measure of womankind's deep wisdom; she said nothing back to him.

They passed on down the valley and into Gunsight. To avoid embarrassing her, Travis rode clear of the town's center and came up a crooked side street to halt at a picket fence where they both alighted and where he tied his horse. The house beyond that fence was old but sturdy; it had a tended flower bed and an old cloth swing upon the porch.

Barbara said: "Who lives here?"

"Fred Brand's mother," replied Travis. "Come along."

They went up onto the porch. Travis knocked and waited and twisted to look around at the other houses, at the bit of Main Street he could see from here, and then Aletha Brand was there in the doorway, gazing from Travis to Barbara Stuart and back again to Travis. Her smile was a little wan. Travis put forth a hand to touch her and say — "How is he?" — meaning the town marshal.

"Resting, son. Come in." Mrs. Brand put that steady gaze upon Barbara again. Travis introduced them. Mrs. Brand was gravely courteous but unsmiling. She led them inside, took Travis's hat, and held it before her with both hands. "Will is with him now, Cole," she stated. "Would you rather wait?"

Travis shook his head. "No, that's all right." He patted her shoulder then, saying — "We won't stay, long . . . don't worry." — and started past with Barbara.

Aletha Brand said, as he swung past: "Cole, where is that man who shot him?"

Again Travis patted her hand. "Don't worry," he murmured to her. "I'll take care of that."

Fred saw them at the doorway and looked uncertain, a little puzzled. He nodded though, saying nothing by way of greeting. Will Fenwick also saw them and arose from the chair he had been occupying. His gaze at Barbara was hard. Brand said: "Cole, darned if you don't look worse than I do. Where you been . . . what all happened to you?"

Travis explained about the fight, his return for Barbara, and their escape to Gunsight together. Then he said: "We've been talkin', Fred. I wish you'd listen to Barbara. I'd consider it a favor."

Brand nodded, moving his attention along and waiting. Barbara spoke out, but there were pauses; she had trouble saying all that had to be said, and, when she was finished, Will Fenwick turned, dropped his eyes to Fred Brand, and let something pass between them.

Travis saw this; his spirit put a testy flash to his glance. He wanted to say something cutting to the deputy but did not, simply stood there waiting, his color high and his jaw tough set.

"That makes things a little different," said the wounded lawman, choosing his words. "Still, though, Miss Barbara's responsible. You know that, don't you, Cole?"

"She never denied it, Fred."

Brand looked long at Travis. He pursed his lips a little. "I know what she said was true . . . at least most of it. That feller you salted down with your riot gun told me after doc picked the buckshot out of him about Jack Wheeler." Brand paused to draw a shallow breath and move slightly under his covers. "I reckon we can't lock Miss Barbara in the jailhouse, though."

Travis said: "She can stay at the hotel. I'll get a room for her."

"No," spoke up Will Fenwick. "If Wheeler's around still, he'll hear of that. Couldn't an army protect her in that hotel."

Travis had an alternative ready. "She could stay here and help your mother look after you, Fred. It'd likely be for only a day or two anyway."

"Oh?" said Brand, gauging Travis's face for the meaning of this remark. "Why for only a day or two?"

"Well, you see, I owe Wheeler something. I owe him for you, Fred, and for Barbara here, and for Bart Hayden. I never knew Rock Stuart but I feel, since you're down flat and can't settle with him for that, maybe I'd ought to pay him in full for Stuart, too."

Aletha Brand appeared in the room. She went up to the marshal's bedside and bent over to study his face. "Are you tiring?" she whispered.

Fred smiled at her and shook his head. "Ma, Cole wants to leave this beautiful woman here with us for a couple of days," he said with a lilting lightness to his voice. "Do you reckon that'd be hard on my blood pressure?"

Mrs. Brand straightened up and made a tart answer that startled everyone in the room. "I think *your* blood pressure is safe, son. I wouldn't want to say about Cole's."

Travis felt his neck get hot and red. He did not look around at Barbara. Will Fenwick gasped, then coughed, and the bedridden man fought back a sudden, erupting laugh.

But the air was clear now.

"I always wanted a girl around the house," said Mrs. Brand, and went over to smile at Barbara. "Of course, I know you by sight, young lady, and I'll tell you frankly the things I've heard lately . . ."

"Give her a chance," Travis cut in swiftly to say. "Just give her a chance."

Aletha turned on Travis, her gaze was tender and misty. "Sure, son, sure. Sometimes having a sharp tongue is no blessing. You know that, Cole. You used to have one yourself." Aletha took Barbara's hand. "Come along," she said, and swept out of the room without relinquishing that hold.

Travis shifted his feet; the silence now became masculine in its stillness. Will Fenwick kicked the chair around and dropped back down into it. He said, referring to Jack Wheeler: "Where is he?"

And Travis replied without hesitation because this was uppermost in all their minds. "I don't know, and that worries me. If he's back at the ranch, he's up to something."

"Will can form up a posse," stated Fred. "You two can ride him down."

Travis ran a hand along his jaw and this made a scratchy sound. He did not want a posse along when he found Wheeler. He did not want Fenwick along, either. He was considering these things when Brand said, from the bed: "Cole, no personal duels. This thing concerns all of us, not just you."

"Why just me, Fred?"

"Cut it out," growled the town marshal. "I saw how you and Barbara Stuart looked at one another. You're standin' there right now thinking how you can even things up for her all by yourself. I won't have it that way, Cole, and you're still wearin' my badge, remember."

Travis shrugged. He went over to another chair and sat down. "How do you want it worked, then?" he asked.

Brand's answer was sharp and immediate. "You get some rest. That's first. While you're resting, Will can go scout the hills, the Stuart place, and anywhere else he thinks Wheeler might be. Then, the two of you can take a posse and go after Wheeler."

"What in hell do we need a posse for?" protested Travis.

"Dog-gone it, Cole, you saw how he hit town last night. He won't be alone. He'll have those hardcases still with him, and, unless you're damned lucky, even with a posse you might get scuttled. Wheeler's no push-over, Cole. Believe me, I know."

Travis uttered a little swear word. "All right," he mumbled. "We'll do it your way." He shifted toward Will Fenwick. "What are you waitin' for . . . an' engraved invitation to get going?"

Fenwick got up stiffly and he glared. "Some one of these times," he began, his tone hard and rough, then Marshal Brand cut in. "Never mind, Will. Just go on. When you locate Wheeler . . . if you do . . . tell Travis. He'll be in a room at the hotel."

Fenwick left the house.

Brand studied Travis, who made a mighty yawn. He said to him: "Cole, have you thought much about the other thing . . . the thing that brought you back to Gunsight?"

"Enough, I reckon," answered Travis. "Listen, Fred, I'm dog tired and sore from crown to heels. Let's talk that over another time."

"All right. Just one more question . . . Barbara?"

Cole got up out of his chair. "I'm going to my room," he muttered, moving doorward.

"Cole!"

Travis turned. He put a critical gaze upon Brand. "You know," he drawled, "for a sick man you've sure got one helluva curiosity, Fred."

"It's not that."

"No? Then what is it?"

"Call it a kind of a hope, Cole. You're the only man I've ever known who could gentle Barbara Stuart, and I think she's the only woman I've ever known who could make you stand hitched." Fred's meaning was naked in his eyes. "Just tell me you're serious about her, then I'll never say another word."

"Hell," grumbled Travis. "How do I know, Fred?" But he did know, and this knowledge made him stir where he stood, feeling both uneasy and deceitful.

Brand watched him, his face gradually taking on a look of understanding, of affectionate understanding. "You know," he said softly. "Cole, you know."

"I reckon I do. I'm serious about her, Fred. I've never been so serious about anyone in my life, and that scares me."

"Why should it?"

Travis scowled, he fidgeted, he plunged both fisted hands deep into his pockets. "Damned if I know why," he replied, "but it sure does." His gaze cleared and went out over the room to Brand's face. "What am I? What can I offer her? Nothing, Fred. On both counts . . . nothing."

Brand shook his head slowly and said: "Cole, you'd be surprised what you've got. It's more than she could ever get in another man. It may not be land or money, but she knows what it is as well as I do."

"You don't know what you're talkin' about, Fred."

"Like hell I don't. Cole, I saw how she looked at you. Like hell I don't know what I'm talking about."

CHAPTER
TWELVE

Travis went along to his room at the Gunsight Hotel. He stood slouched by the street-side window looking pensively out. Gunsight was up and moving, the morning was advancing, and people were abroad. It was as though nothing had happened the night before. Women in bonnets to protect them from sunlight passed into stores and men were visible in two dozen different places. An anvil's good sound rose up from a back street, roadway traffic was increasing, and cowboys in from the range loped by, some inbound, some outbound. He made a cigarette but the thing had no flavor. Suddenly the aches came on strongly to remind him of his battle at the Stuart Ranch. Weariness too, colored his thinking, so, after a moment more of this brooding watchfulness, he left the window, kicked off his boots, and went to the room's washstand. There, he sluiced water over his head from a pitcher, dried himself, and went over to the bed to drop down heavily, push out his legs to their extreme length, and let himself turn loose all over with a delicious sensation of complete carelessness. Around him all the homely sounds of a village rose up, and, after the manner of cautious men, he catalogued each of these — the barking of a dog, the smith at that anvil, the squeak and rumble and jolt of a ranch wagon passing beneath his window, the anxious call of a mother to her child, and the shrill keening of a fretful baby. Sounds that were endemic in towns the world over and that ordinarily held no meaning and no promise to the lonely drifter, but that came to have meaning for Cole Travis, lying there drowsily listening.

They were nostalgic; they got in under his tough hide to remind him mutely of all the things in life he was missing. They told him over and over that he was a misfit. He closed his eyes heeding these odd thoughts, and he slept.

It seemed, when he awakened, that he'd not actually been asleep at all. In fact his mind was fuzzy with a drowsiness that implied a need for more rest. But there was a strong fist working across his door. He gradually drew himself together, swung over, and stood up in stockinged feet, went forward, and opened the panel expecting to see Will Fenwick standing there. Instead there stood three strangers, townsmen from the looks of them, and their faces showed interest and appraising speculation as they gazed upon Travis. He scowled, yawned, and moved aside, saying: "Come in, gentlemen. If you can find three chairs, sit down."

The townsmen entered and remained standing. Cole perched upon the side of his bed to pull on his boots. He then stood up, ran a hand through his hair, and waited.

The foremost of these men was a short and heavy person, once powerful but now running to paunch and soft fat. This man said: "My name is Arthur Bigelow, Mister Travis. These other fellers are Hodding Foster and Jehu Murphy. We constitute the Gunsight town council. I'm the mayor."

Travis nodded, viewing each of these townsmen with wonder, with increasing curiosity. "You know my name, I see," he told them. "What can I do for you?"

"We'd like to swear you in as town marshal."

Travis viewed these men with a look of growing annoyance. "You have a town marshal and he's the best you could get."

"But he's flat on his back right now, Mister Travis."

"Sure is. And he got that way doing his duty."

Bigelow pondered, going silent. One of his companions spoke next, saying to Travis: "We're not exactly replacing Fred. I think you're getting the wrong impression, Mister Travis. All we want, actually, is a replacement for him until it's possible for him to return to his duties."

Travis tapped Brand's badge upon his torn and filthy shirt. "You've got that," he said. "Fred gave me this to wear until he's able to be about, and I'm wearing it. Also, you've got a deputy town marshal . . . Fenwick. You need another town marshal like you need a bullet in the brains. Now get out of here and let me rest up a little more."

Arthur Bigelow made one more attempt. "Mister Travis, we are very much aware of what happened here in town last night. We have been told this man Wheeler is still at large . . . that he might return to Gunsight. All we're asking . . ."

Travis, thinking of other men like these, well-fed and comfortable and safe in their orderly world, from another time, interrupted Bigelow: "I said get out. I meant it." His glare burned against them. "I've got a name for men like you. Brand got hurt upholding the law, and here you are, like a herd of gun-shy nesters, whimpering around for someone else to stand between your lousy little world of bolt goods and stove pipes and an element you don't personally have the guts to face. You are yellow and your town is a nest of hypocrites. Now get the hell out of my room!"

The town council got; it went in a body to the door and squeezed through, closed the door very gently, and hastened away. Travis stood in the middle of his room hearkening to those rapid and diminishing footfalls. He said in outrage and disgust — "Hell!" — and crossed to the window once more to lean there gazing outward and downward. All his wish for rest was gone out of him now and in its place burned a low, fierce anger.

He left the room shortly before high noon, got some food at a café, then went stormily along to the home of Fred Brand's mother. Barbara admitted him. She looked refreshed and cool to him. Her smile was gentle and her eyes held to his through a funny little moment of uncertainty. Then she led him without saying a word to Fred's room and left them together.

"Your lousy town council came calling," Travis growled to the bedridden lawman. "They wanted me to officially replace you, Fred. How do you like that?"

Brand listened, his face composed and impassive.

263

Travis paced the room once, then sat down to scowl over at Brand. "I told you this was a lousy place, Fred. I knew it when I came back here. You said these weren't the same people. They *are* the same, Fred. Maybe not in name, but in all other ways they're as mean and small and vicious and cruel as those other people were."

Brand said: "Whoa, boy, whoa. Cole, I sent those men to see you."

Travis drew up a little in the chair. "*You* sent them?"

"Yes. And you didn't give them a chance, either. They were here not more than fifteen minutes ago. They told me how you called them names and threw them out of your room."

"You sent them? What in hell for, Fred?"

"If you'll simmer down for a minute, I'll tell you," said the marshal, a little bitter-eyed, a little indignant and exasperated. "They called on me this morning to say they'd take care of all my medical bills. They also said, because I'd showed guts in not backing down to Wheeler's band, they were raising my pay ten dollars a month. Then they offered to hire a man to run things until I could be up and around again. I told them to go see you. I said, since they felt that way, they could pay you for the time you're putting in and for the risks you're taking." Brand's brows rolled together, heightening his expression of exasperation. "So they went to see you . . . to make a damned decent offer to reimburse you for your time and your trouble. And you, acting like a spoiled little kid, didn't give them a chance because you'd pre-judged this town years ago, and you threw them out."

Travis turned his hat in both hands, gazing down at it, avoiding Fred Brand's eyes. After a bad moment between them he said quietly: "I guess I made a real fool of myself, Fred."

"You did, for a fact."

Travis continued to sit there turning the hat around and around. "Well, hell," he mumbled, "I didn't know."

Brand came right back, mocking him. "Well, hell . . . you might have heard them out."

Now Travis's head came up. His cheeks were stained dark with hot blood. "I made a mistake. You don't have to keep rubbing it in."

"Yes, I do, Cole. I mean to go right on rubbing it in, too. I think that's the only way I can get this across to you. Even as a kid you were bull-headed . . . you didn't listen even in those days. I don't like to say this to you, Cole, we used to be brothers . . . remember that?"

"I remember."

"All right. I'm going to let you have both barrels then. Sure, you got a raw deal from Gunsight. But you didn't do much to soften it, either. You were sensitive about your pa . . . and your ma. You were always going around looking for trouble. I don't pretend to know what makes people do the things you did, Cole, but I do know for a fact that when a person goes out of his way to be obnoxious . . . he'll find all the grief he's lookin' for."

Travis sprang up, his face drained of color and his tawny eyes drawn out fighting-narrow. He said, in a warning tone: "Fred, you're sayin' things you'll . . ."

"No," snapped Brand. "I won't be sorry about what I'm saying, Cole. I'll only be sorry if you take what I'm telling you in the wrong light. Listen to me . . . my mother and I were the only ones in this town who would put up with you in those days. And by God it was a trial even for us. Cole, you're a man now . . . go for a walk and think honestly about what I've just said to you. Be honest with yourself, Cole . . . for my sake, for my mother's sake . . . for Barbara Stuart's sake." Brand paused, his chest rose and fell with the surging heat of this emotion that gripped him. "Only three people in this town love you, Cole, and only two of those people are from those other days. They wouldn't hurt you for the world . . . you should know that by now. What they'd tell you is for your own damned good. Now do me a favor . . . get out of here. Go for a walk and don't come back until you've done a heap of soul searching."

Brand's breathing was ragged and loud. His troubled eyes, set in a pale and anguished face, fled away from Travis's still, bleak features and went to the overhead ceiling. He said no more until Travis crossed to the doorway and started through.

"Hey!" he called. "Take those keys off my dresser and go see how Hayden is. There's a store clerk over at the jailhouse keeping watch there, but he'll want to be getting back to work."

This was an awkward moment between these two strong men. Brand knew it and so did Cole Travis. It was in Travis's mind to refuse, to fling down that badge he wore and go his way. But because he was an honest

266

man and knew Brand was also an honest man, he put this angry thought aside. Brand had said none of these things to hurt Travis, nor had he said them from spite. Therefore, as bitter as this realization was to Travis, he knew Brand had said them simply because he felt them to be quite true.

As Travis stood there balancing his thoughts, Brand said one more thing. "You might get Hayden some breakfast, too. He'll be hungry."

Travis picked up the key ring and passed on out of the house. He did not see Barbara Stuart standing in the near shadows of a hallway passage. He was not thinking of her at all.

Outside again with morning sunlight beating upon him, Travis hiked along with a hard look to his face. Shortly before coming to the juncture with Main Street he passed two women, home bound, with market baskets. They stopped short and stared. Travis saw this and threw them a scowl. It did not come to him until he was walking westerly past a general store that what had startled those women had been not his hidden feelings at all but his filthy and ragged appearance.

He entered the store, bought a new blue shirt, then took this with him to a barber shop where he had a shave. Afterward, he went directly to Fred Brand's jailhouse and met the interested bright look of the townsman who had been pressed into service as jailhouse guard while Fenwick was busy, Brand was abed, and while Cole Travis, temporary town marshal of Gunsight, was not on hand.

Travis growled at this man — "You can go now." — then ignored the man. He went to a washstand, peeled off his shirt, poured water into a big crockery bowl, and furiously washed. Behind him Bart Hayden stood at the bars of his cell watching this in silence.

Travis's anger diminished but did not entirely dissipate. He felt like a board that had been too long in the summer sun smash — brittle and warped and insufferably hot. He finished washing, put on the new shirt, carefully pinned Brand's badge to it, and turned to find Hayden still staring at him with both hands holding to the straps of his cage.

Hayden solemnly nodded, obviously waiting for Travis to say something. Travis did, he said — "Go to hell." — then dropped down at the marshal's desk, cocked up his feet, and put a smoky gaze upon the wall.

Hayden said, in indignant astonishment: "What did I do?"

Travis ignored this. He took out of his mind those bitter things Fred Brand had said to him. He examined them separately and carefully, and, when in retrospect he saw how it was that others had viewed him in those other days here in Gunsight, he squirmed.

"I'm hungry," said the prisoner plaintively, and watched Travis's reaction to this.

Travis sat on, unmoving.

"Hey, Mister Travis . . . if you're goin' to starve me to death, you just might as well turn me loose. At least with the Stuart outfit I stand a chance. This way none at all."

"Shut up, will you, Hayden? I'm thinking."

268

"Well," muttered the prisoner, "can't you think while I'm eating just as well as when I'm not?"

Travis rose up. He was feeling testy. "All right," he snapped. "All right," and stamped out of the jailhouse bound for the café across from there, and, when he afterward returned with a big bowl of chili and a pot of coffee, he gave these to Hayden saying: "Now . . . be quiet."

Hayden's brow furrowed. He considered Travis for a long time, then he raised and lowered his shoulders and fell to eating.

CHAPTER
THIRTEEN

The jailhouse door opened. Barbara Stuart stood framed there with a napkin-wrapped small bundle in one hand. She paused to look around her, saw Bart Hayden, exchanged a look with him, then faced fully around toward Travis.

He was watching her from his seat at Fred Brand's desk. Her consideration of him was cool, a little appraising, he thought. Then she passed on inside and closed the door before putting the little bundle gently down before him.

"Some lunch," she stated, seeing how his glance rose to her face, catching it and holding it with her own glance until he saw something break in her expression, something meaningful to him.

"Then I want to talk to you," she said. "Alone."

He understood immediately what this meant — she had been with Fred, perhaps with his mother as well. She knew all about him. He drifted his gaze over where Bart Hayden was watching them without finishing his meal.

Barbara went to a wall bench and sat down. In his view she seemed to be judging him, rummaging through him. She sat there quite erectly with both hands lying quietly in her lap.

Bart Hayden said suddenly: "Miss Barbara, I want to tell you . . . I tried to talk him out of fighting me. I swear that to you. I tried my darnedest."

Travis growled at Hayden: "Never mind now. She knows how that was."

"You do?" demanded Hayden, rising up to lean upon his bars. "Miss Barbara . . . ?"

"I said never mind," growled Travis again, this time facing around toward Hayden.

The prisoner stood there with hope shining in his eyes. He seemed not to have heard Travis, but he said no more anyway.

Barbara neither answered Hayden nor looked around at him. She had her grave glance fixed upon Cole Travis, and he, uncomfortable under this stare, pushed back the little bundle of food and stood up.

"Come on," he said to her. "I'm not hungry anyway." He led her from the office to the yonder sidewalk, along it to a dogtrot between two buildings, and down this until they emerged together into a sun-lighted alleyway. Here, where shadows lay and no one was abroad to distract them, he paced along solemnly with her beside him, waiting. She said nothing until they came to the windowless openings in a long-abandoned two-storey building. There, she went into the pleasant seclusion of a hidden old stairway and settled upon a lower step, drawing Travis down beside her. She laced her fingers around drawn-up knees and put a steady look outward over the flow of westerly land to those far-away

271

mountains standing hushed and ageless in dancing spring sunshine. Around them both soft shade lay, layer upon layer of it, making this place where they sat different from the rest of the day, and secret.

She said — "Cole, I talked with Fred and Aletha," — and paused as though expecting him to speak. He did not, so she went on. "I knew nothing about how it was with you here in Gunsight years ago. I probably wouldn't have heard anyway because my father and I came here long after you'd left."

Travis worked up an unwanted cigarette to have something to do with his hands. He sat on, still offering no words, and smoke rose up from his hand into the warm and sparkling air.

She turned at last to look at him. He sat loosely on the step considering that bluish-spiraling streamer of tobacco smoke. His face did not now hold its customary closed away, hard look. It was relaxed, it was moody.

"I can't say Fred was right in all the things he told you this morning, Cole, because I didn't know you those days. I think, though, that one thing he said was very true in those days because it still is. He said he and his mother loved you. They still do, Cole. The worst way for you to repay them for that love would be to destroy it by destroying yourself. Cole, you can't hate a town. You can hate people . . . wish the worst for them. I know how that is, believe me. You know how wrong I was. Can't you also see how wrong you are now, about this town?"

272

He killed the cigarette but sat on still saying nothing. She continued to watch him, and, when this great wall of stillness between them became unbearable, he finally spoke, saying quietly: "I reckon the hardest thing a man ever faces is the truth about himself. I don't believe I was as mad at Fred this morning, as I was . . ."

"Hurt?"

He nodded. "I reckon that's the word."

"I hope for you with all my heart, Cole, that this is the only kind of hurt you'll ever know . . . from your friends."

His face softened. He turned toward her. "Fred was right, of course. And you're right, too . . . about it being wrong to hate this town. Barbara, I think you and I've sort of grown up here, in a way."

"Matured," she murmured to him.

"Yeah. Maybe folks don't mature without some pain to sort of bring it on. I'm sorry for the way I flared up at Fred. I'm sorry if I caused you trouble, too."

Seeing him as he now was, Barbara thought of him as a strong and solid man who was both physically alive and powerfully attractive to her. He breathed deeply and she heard that great whip of wind into his chest. She said: "I had no right to do this . . . to talk to you as I just have."

"No one ever had a better right."

She waited for clarification of this, but he said no more and some confusion came to dwell in this secret place with them. She thought she knew how he meant this, but was not at all sure. She said, then, in the gentlest voice: "When everything is over and straightened out, and you ride on again, we will each have this memory to keep. This time . . . when we came of age at the same time and side-by-side."

He didn't speak. He sat there relaxed, gazing far out, his head still and his hands hanging down. His lip corners were not now being held in, as was usual with him, and this gave his mouth a funny little quirked-up look as though he was near laughing, as though he viewed life and this world with a kind of quiet tolerance. He looked altogether different, even in the way his heavy glance ran on, and in the way his body sagged without any of its customary hard-set wariness.

This, she thought, was the true Cole Travis, this other person under her gaze. This near-smiling, quietly calm, and very gentle man who now absorbed her interest as only a man might who personally meant something to her could do.

He stirred. He said softly: "I'm not going to ride on, Barbara."

"Yesterday you said you would."

"No. I expect I knew all along I wouldn't." He looked around at her, his steady gaze touching her eyes, her cheeks, her lips, and lower down her creamy throat and shoulders. "No, I think not. Because whatever life holds for me is here as well as some other place."

"Maybe," she said wonderingly, "it is here and not some other place, Cole."

"Yes, maybe. Barbara?"

"Yes." She saw his reticence come up now, and obscure that frank and open look in his face. She felt him changing away from what he'd been up to now,

274

under her very eyes, and hunted swiftly in her mind for a way to prevent this from happening.

"Nothing," he said. "It was nothing."

"Let me judge that. What were you going to say?"

But there it was, full up now, closing her out, hiding his man's hard humor, his thorough temper, the hot and the cold of his wants and his convictions.

She took a quiet breath, steadied herself, and said, speaking so swiftly the words all ran together, but having to speak this way in order for her voice to be steady: "Cole, does sitting here with me have any meaning for you?"

"It has," he said softly. "It has an awful lot of meaning."

"Then I want you to tell me how it is with you."

"Well," he drawled, "I guess I'm in love with you." He turned, gazed briefly at her, then swung away saying in wonderment: "I thought it would be harder to say than it was. I knew about it yesterday. Only I wasn't sure."

"When were you sure, Cole?"

"When I talked to Fred early today. He knew. He said you also knew. I guess even his mother knew. That's funny . . . something happens to a man and he's the last to know."

"And . . . it bothers you, Cole?"

"Very much. I'm nobody and I've got nothing but a horse, a saddle, a silvered bit, and a gun with an ivory grip." He smiled. "The whole pile wouldn't fetch three hundred dollars."

Barbara unlaced her fingers and looked at one hand. "So you think we are worlds apart and can never be any closer."

"Yes'm. That's what I think." He ceased speaking and gradually brought his head up and around, his gaze widening upon her. "Barbara . . . ?" he murmured, looking suddenly at her from a changing expression. ". . . Barbara?"

Soberness held her face darkly still. Her profile was to him as she continued to gaze at that hand. She put forth that hand for him to take, and, when he did, her fingers closed around his palm, suddenly strong, holding to him as though seeking to impress upon him in this way her own feelings. The silence ran on like this, troubled and full of bewildering emotions, until she suddenly withdrew her hand.

She spoke now, using once more that gentlest of tones. "Are you certain in your mind, Cole?"

"Absolutely certain."

"And I am also certain in mine," she told him.

"Certain . . . ?"

"That I love you, too." She seemed not as elated by this as she was full of pure wonder over it. She was briefly silent, then she spoke again. "I didn't realize it could happen like this . . . so suddenly. Yesterday at this time I could almost have shot you." She put a liquid dark gaze upon him. "Now . . ." She hesitated before going on again in that same sweet, and clear, and wondering voice. "Now . . . I only know that I want you very much, Cole." She dropped her gaze away, half turning from him.

He pulled her back around. "With nothing?" he demanded in a voice sounding harsh. "With no money and no prospects . . . ?"

"I hadn't considered that," she told him with her face inches from his. "I couldn't consider them . . . they are not important to me. In a man they never would be important to me."

He saw the mistiness of her gaze, the approaching blur of her lips, and it occurred to him in that second that he should be deliriously happy, yet he could not smile, could not show at all how he felt. She put up a hand to touch his face very lightly. Then she closed her eyes and this was the way she sat when he kissed her, with one hand curling along his cheek guiding his mouth to hers, both eyes tightly closed, and the quick flutter of her breath beating upon his cheek.

He kissed her with a heavy, long, and hungry pressure, and, if she had not already seen him revealed as he truly was, his mouth would have told her now, for the things lying still in his heart were there upon his lips — the quick, hot flash of his will, the haunting tenderness, the deep ache of his longing, and the fire of his temper — it was all there, leaving her weak and without resistance, and dredging from deep within her an exploding fire of her own that rose up to meet the flare of his passion, to bruise his mouth with her longings, too, and leave him feeling drained and exhausted when he finally drew back.

She pushed her face against his shoulder, into the curve of neck and shoulder, and kept it there, still with both eyes tight closed. The drumming of his solid heart struck through her; she clung to him, unwilling to have him see into her eyes for this moment. But after a time willing, and therefore she drew slightly away from him seeking his face.

He said: "Barbara . . . I don't know what to say."

"Then don't say anything."

They sat on a moment longer, then she stood up, took his hand, and also drew him up.

"We must go back," she said. "Aletha will be wondering."

They walked along down the shadowy alleyway, back to the narrow dogtrot, passed through it into Main Street's noontime hot glare, and paused for a little time to adjust their eyes, their thoughts, their tempers, to the everyday ways of life. Then he took her hand and led her along to the jailhouse. He stopped outside the door and looked down at her.

"But you can't be sure," he murmured. "Can you?"

"Can you?" she asked.

He inclined his head saying: "Yes. I'm sure."

"And I am, too. Cole, I don't think I've ever been so certain about anything."

They stood close together, unheeding Gunsight's sounds and movements and changing light patterns. Entirely unconscious of all that passed around them — until the shot came, its crashing, discordant explosion raw-sounding and thunderously loud.

Barbara did not move, her eyes simply widened and widened up at Cole, then she very gently wilted and fell forward against him.

Somewhere a man's ragged, startled shout erupted.

278

CHAPTER
FOURTEEN

Cole stood stunned, looking at the red stickiness upon his palm where the bullet had struck her.

Men's shouts were loudly inquiring. Some, seeing Travis pick up the girl in his arms and enter the jailhouse with her, came running. Suddenly Gunsight's thoroughfare was empty of people, excepting those racing for the jail.

Travis took her to the same cot that had formerly held Fred Brand, and there he very gently put her down. The stain across her upper dress was spreading. Men rushed into the office and stopped, staring downward.

"Get the doctor," said Travis. "Hurry!"

Several men left the office, running again. The others milled, uncertain what they should do now that they saw it was a woman who had been shot instead of a man.

She was unconscious and limp, her breathing was a faint flutter, irregular and shallow. Travis knelt there holding her hand.

Behind him a townsman whispered: "Who did it?"

Another man said: "I don't know, but the shot came from between the hotel and the saddlery."

Travis twisted to see these men. "Get your guns," he told them, "and look for whoever did this. Find him if you can but don't kill him. I want him alive. I want to know . . . why."

They left, hit the roadway, and began fanning out. One of them called forth to the town, his voice iron-like and resolute. This call was taken up and men came from stores and shops with weapons to join the hunt.

Travis heard the cries back and forth of the angered men, but he expected them to fail in their quest because he thought he knew who had done this, and he also did not believe the assassin would have lingered for a second longer than was necessary before mounting up and racing out of Gunsight.

The doctor came, anxious-looking and grim. Travis gave up his vigil beside the cot and watched. The doctor made a quick, cursory examination, saw how the bullet had struck Barbara, and said from stiff lips: "Clear out. This will not be for curious eyes." He was unbuttoning the bodice of her dress. "I don't want to be disturbed." The doctor paused, looked up at Travis, and asked: "Who did this?"

Travis said nothing.

The medical man spat out a bitter oath. "Find him. Kill him. A man who would do a thing like this doesn't deserve to live. Now clear out."

Travis wanted the worst way to ask a question but he was afraid of the answer that might come back. He left, crossed to a table where his riot gun lay, picked it up, and left the jailhouse.

280

Gunsight was hushed, seemingly deserted with scarcely a soul in sight along its roadway. Travis lit down into the roadway and strode directly to the hotel. There, he located a badly shaken clerk and inquired if this man had seen anyone near his front window who might have shot Barbara Stuart.

The clerk had not, and, in fact, he told Travis, he had been upstairs when the explosion had come, and, although he'd gone to a window at once and peered out, he had seen nothing.

Next, Travis went to the narrow space between the hotel and its adjoining building. Here, in this dogtrot, where there might have been tracks to follow once, there was now only a mass of churned earth where others had come here ahead of Travis in their eager hunt. He went along to the far alleyway where the dogtrot terminated, and again considered the ground. But again, fresh imprints by the score obliterated what he might otherwise have seen. Near the abrupt curving of the hotel's rear wall, though, he was arrested by a bright twinkling where sunlight struck down. He moved forward and scooped up a brass bullet casing. He smelled it and felt it — the cordite smell was strong. This casing had very recently held a bullet, and because there had been only that one gunshot and none subsequent to it, he knew he had in his hand what remained of the cartridge that had brought down Barbara Stuart. He stood there, examining that casing. It was a common issue .25–.35-caliber shell. It had not resided long enough in the assassin's shell belt to dull out or turn faintly green as those brass casings oftentimes did. But what ultimately held all of Travis's attention was the firing pin imprint upon the center-fire cap set into the base of this shell. Evidently the firing pin of the gun that had fired this bullet had, sometime, been subjected to a hard strike, for a curving portion of that pin was broken off, leaving two-thirds of the remaining bearing surface to detonate bullets. This remainder of the pin was crescent-shaped and its imprint left a very unique impression upon that soft-metal detonation cap at the casing's base.

Travis put the casing carefully into a pocket, hefted his shotgun, and began walking down the alleyway. Near the alleyway's juncture with an intersecting back street, he encountered four men with rifles. They turned at his approach and one raised an arm to point eastward, where scattered homes lay, and beyond town, where there was open country.

"Folks down here," this man told Travis, "saw a mounted man ride hell-for-leather eastward beyond town." The man lowered his arm. "He was putting up a carbine as he rode . . . pushing it down into his saddle boot."

"Anyone recognize him?" Travis asked, expecting exactly the answer he got.

"No. No one seemed to know him. We been among the houses asking. But they all agreed he was a cowboy."

Travis nodded; he was thinking of Jack Wheeler now, and also of the carbine casing with its bizarre firing pin impression in his pocket. "Thanks," he said, and turned to walk away.

"Marshal!" one of the townsmen called. "We'll get our horses. If you'll lead us, I think we might find him yet. At least we can track him."

Travis said: "Not on summer-hard ground you won't. But thanks anyway."

"Well, hell," exploded one townsman indignantly, "it's worth a try!"

Travis looked at those four men, at their smoldering eyes and hard-set jaws. He thought he knew who had fired that shot and he meant to go after him. But he did not wish witnesses around when he and Jack Wheeler met. Still, he knew how these townsmen felt — whatever happened to Wheeler they would approve of, and with true Westerner's reticence they would not speak of it afterward.

"All right," he said to them. "Get mounted up and meet me at the jailhouse." He walked on then, came back onto Main Street, and saw a crowd over at the jailhouse. Several women were in this group. As Travis went on, he saw a large, graying woman leave the office. Aletha Brand. He went along to intercept her where she entered a store.

Aletha saw him and frowned and called to a man inside the store: "Jared, we need more towels and more hot water!"

The storekeeper bobbed his head and fled beyond a back room curtain. Aletha fully turned then, to look into Travis's face. He did not speak, he did not have to, the question was there in his eyes forcing out everything else.

"It's bad," she told him. "I . . . don't know, Cole. The doctor is doing everything he can. He got the bleeding stopped but she'd lost a lot of blood first." Aletha locked both hands together over her stomach. Her voice dropped considerably and she said in anguished puzzlement: "What kind of a man would do such a thing, Cole?"

Travis stood there saying nothing, his mind full of cold hatred again, full of despair and agony and merciless hatred. He was holding the shotgun lightly in one hand scarcely heeding Fred Brand's mother until she broke in upon his thoughts.

"There is nothing you can do here, Cole. I'll do everything in my power for her. So will the doctor. Will Fenwick just rode in . . . he's at the jailhouse waiting for you."

"Did he say anything?" asked Travis.

"No. Only that he couldn't find you at the hotel and that he wanted to see you right away."

Travis coldly nodded. He started to turn. Aletha's work-worn hand went out to arrest him by closing down over his arm. "You do what you think is right," she said softly to him with quiet earnestness. "Only remember, son . . . a man has to live with himself for a long time after his acts are finished. Don't do anything *she* would be ashamed of."

Travis made that cold little nod again and moved away. He got back out to the roadway, saw Fenwick's sweaty saddle horse, and started toward it. The deputy spied his approach, tore away from the murmuring crowd outside Brand's jailhouse, and came to meet him.

They exchanged a long glance, then Fenwick, all his former antagonism gone, said gently: "I'm sorry. Sorry as a man can be, Mister Travis."

Travis let this pass. "What did you find?" he asked quietly.

"There were three men at the Stuart place."

"There should have been four, Fenwick."

Will shook his head. "I thought so, too . . . until I got back here and heard what had happened. I reckon we both know where that fourth man was."

"Anything else to report?"

Fenwick said: "I watched them for a while. It looked to me like they were fixin' to pull out. They'd plundered the house, had two pack horses laden, and were standin' around waitin' for something."

"Yeah," said Travis. "Waiting for someone to do what he'd set out to do, and return for them."

"By now he'll be back. By now they'll be gone, Mister Travis."

"That won't make any difference, Fenwick. There's no place on earth they can go that I can't find them."

Several mounted men drifted along toward the jailhouse. They were heavily armed. Travis saw these men, recognized four of them, and understood that the others had been recruited by these four. "Get a fresh horse," he told Will Fenwick. "We'll wait here for you. Get plenty of ammunition, too."

Travis moved out and around Fenwick, striding toward the jailhouse. He had no difficulty with that milling crowd; his expression stilled questions and opened a path for him to the door.

Inside, Travis saw Aletha and the doctor — in shirt sleeves now — grimly working. Neither of them turned at his entrance and he did not go any closer to the cot than the door. Aletha finally looked around, saw him, and straightened up. She said nothing but her expression of worry, of grave anxiety, was enough for Travis.

"You stay with her," he said, his soft tone sounding loud in the room's complete silence. "Do that for me . . . don't leave her for a second."

"Yes," murmured the older woman. She wiped her hands and watched Cole open the door. She called to him: "Good luck, son!"

Back on the plank walk, still loosely holding his sawed-off scatter-gun, Cole saw that the mounted men in the roadway had become nearly thirty riders. They gazed forward at him and he returned their look. The crowd standing by shuffled back a little, leaving a wide pathway for Travis to pass over. Not a word was said. Will Fenwick came up, looking tired and dusty and sun-reddened. Travis went out to him and said: "Will, you don't have to go. You've been up all night and today. There are plenty of men here. You go on home and . . ."

"I think not," interrupted Will Fenwick. "Even if I went to bed, I couldn't sleep." He waved an arm. "Your horse is there at the rack, Mister Travis. Lead out."

Travis said: "Just plain Cole."

Will's bitter lips softened slightly. "Cole," he said. "And I'm just plain Will."

Travis went to his mount, untied it, turned it once, ran a finger under the cinch, found it snug, and stepped up and across his saddle.

Three men came out of the crowd now to stop beside his animal. The foremost of these people was Gunsight's mayor, Arthur Bigelow. "Mister Travis . . . just get him. Whoever he is, just get him. We've posted a reward. Five thousand dollars."

Travis considered Bigelow and his two companions over a little interval of silence. Then he quietly said to them: "Gentlemen, I owe you an apology. We'll talk about that another time." He nodded, swung his horse, and started along the roadway. Around him rode Will Fenwick and close to thirty-five armed townsmen. He led them at a steady walk to the edge of Gunsight. There, although alive to the urgency of what must now be done, he booted his horse over into a slow lope and rode no faster than that for an excellent reason — he and his posse men had a long ride ahead of them in all probability, and the summertime sun was hot and going to get hotter. A man who rode his horse hard under these circumstances might get close to the outlaws he hunted, but in the end he would lose them because horseflesh, like man flesh, could stand just so much abuse. It was a wise range man who saved his mount as much as he could, for only in this way would he overtake the men he sought.

Will Fenwick eased up to ride stirrup to stirrup with Travis. But he said nothing, only loped along easily, busy with his own thoughts. Around them came on the body of this Gunsight posse. To some those men might have appeared ludicrous, for there were riders with bowler hats and fancy sleeve garters, not more than ten of them wore boots, the others all had shoes. Mostly, too, these men were not experienced riders.

But no one, looking into their faces, would have found anything there to inspire ridicule or laughter. Nor would their armament, which was good, have brought up smiles.

The day was well along and its heat was an increasing pressure. The yonder hills were misted from this warmth and the air itself was heavy from it. Horses began to sweat and men, too, their faces, reddening under this unaccustomed sun smash, turned oily. Travis rode ahead, never turning to look back, never speaking, always studying the lift and drop of those hills, figuring in his mind where this trail might lead him, never once considering turning back from it so long as Jack Wheeler remained alive — Wheeler and his renegade cowboys.

CHAPTER
FIFTEEN

They arrived at the Stuart Ranch near 3:00. The place was completely deserted; even the corralled saddle stock had been turned out. Observing this as they rode quietly into the sun-bright and empty yard, Will Fenwick said tartly: "Wheeler thinks of everything, doesn't he? If we needed fresh horses, we wouldn't get them here." Then Will stiffly got down from his saddle, saying: "But Wheeler can guess wrong, too . . . we took it easy, our animals aren't tuckered." He stood with the others, looking around, seeing signs of hasty departure, of the plundered main house, then he went along to a trough, removed his hat, and used it to scoop up water and sluice it over his head.

Travis, carrying his shotgun, walked to the main house. He stepped past a sagging door into quiet gloom. There, the evidence of eager hands plumbing the depths of closets, drawers, bookshelves was abundantly evident. It looked as though a band of bronco-buck Indians had hit — clothing, books, papers of every description were scattered at random. Even furniture had been upended. He went to the far hallway and there, near the entrance to Barbara's room, found a little painted brooch lying there. He picked it up, found that some unknown artist had delicately and exquisitely captured Barbara's face perfectly, and stood gazing upon this.

He afterward returned to the parlor, found it crowded with posse men standing in deep silence as they viewed the destruction, and worked his way through to the yard again. There, he found Will standing loosely in bunkhouse shade, thoughtfully smoking.

Fenwick turned, saying: "They've been gone, I'd judge, about two hours. They cleaned out the bunkhouse and took food from the main house kitchen. And they rode due north, Cole." Will dropped his cigarette, stamped upon it, and shot Travis a speculative look. "They got those two pack horses with 'em. How fast can men travel loaded down like that?"

"Yeah," mused Travis, considering the rising hills on northward. "How well do you know that northward country?"

Fenwick made a long, lean smile. "Better than Wheeler does, I think. I grew up around here. Furthermore, I've got friends at Forest Falls, the next town northward on over the hills."

"You think they went that way?" queried Travis.

"Their tracks lead out arrow straight, Cole. 'Course, I only walked out a little ways, but I got an idea that's the way they went, all right."

"Let's get mounted up," said Travis, "and find out for sure before nightfall catches us." He twisted, called to the posse men to get astride, then said to Fenwick: "Can we get across the hills before dark?"

Will squinted skyward at the lowering sun. "Doubt it," he answered. "But we can cover a heap of ground after it gets cool."

The crowd of them rode on northward from the Stuart place, climbing higher and higher upon an old wagon road until they came to a place where that brawling creek, which crossed the Stuart Ranch yard, broke from a granite ledge to run both ways, north and south, but with by far the greater spill of water tumbling down toward the Stuart place. Here, several miles from that earlier stop, they paused to permit their animals to tank up. Here, too, in a quiet fold of the hills where shadows lay, they took stock and had a smoke. Will Fenwick scouted on ahead. When he returned, he was wearing a little humorless grin and holding in his hand a near-empty whiskey bottle. He got down where Travis stood, saying — "Whoever emptied this is going to regret it, I think." — and tossed the bottle aside.

A posse man regarded that broken bottle ruefully. He muttered to the men closest to him: "He didn't have to bust it . . . there was still a dram or two in it."

Final sunlight was flaming out beyond the highest peaks, westerly, when they got astride and pushed onward once more. Dust rose lazily and horses repeatedly cleared their nostrils of this. They found very little underbrush, passing back and forth over meadows and forest land to the utmost rise of country, but upon the rimrock top of the divide they encountered some thorny bitterbrush, little else could grow here because eons of wind had scoured away all topsoil.

Travis sat still where they topped out, considering first the onward flow of country, and secondly that disappearing sun far off.

At his side Will Fenwick raised an arm, saying: "See that flicker of light far off there? That'll be Forest Falls, with the last sunlight striking tin roofs."

"Five miles?" asked Travis.

Will nodded. "About that. Why don't I ride on ahead. I could get there in an hour or so, make sure they either passed by or didn't pass by, then come back. It'd save us some time."

"And some riding," agreed Travis. "Go on. And Will . . . watch yourself."

Fenwick looked around. "I always do," he murmured, then eased out over the top out, and began carefully passing along where the old wagon road dropped away steadily toward the low down plain. Within minutes he was swallowed up by a thick stand of red barked pines, and the overhead matting of thick limbs covered him with premature darkness.

Travis twisted to regard his posse men. They looked sun burned and a little hip weary from riding, but he could detect no irresolution among them. He called — "Let's go!" — and followed downhill over Fenwick's tracks.

There were other tracks, too, but only Fenwick still had faith in them. Travis, knowing cattlemen ranged these hills, was skeptical. Still, they had as yet encountered no tracks leading away from the wagon road, so he was content to drift along with Fenwick.

292

When the mob of them got into that tangle of trees where Fenwick had last been seen, the going became harder. There were immense old snags to be wary of, and corpse-colored ancient deadfalls to skirt around. There was also a matting of needles so thick that even the passing of this big body of horsemen scarcely left an impression.

The light, in here, was pearl gray instead of late day red. Several cattle trails were crossed, marked by droppings, and once they started up a she-bear and two cubs. These, they were careful to go far out around. In here, too, the road wound uncertainly in a manner that indicated it had long since departed from its original course, compelled to do this by deadfalls and erosion gulches, and the constant heavings of the loose earth side hills. Night came on slowly, as always in summertime range country. They were down out of the hills when its thickening shadows formed a solid purple wall, passing over the last land swells and foothills.

Travis, coming to a gravelly ford of that two-way creek, called a halt. He got down with barely enough light remaining to see that his townsmen hobbled their animals and in this manner could be certain to have horses to ride on the morrow. Afterward, with the men settling low around him in the night, he detailed a horse guard, one sentry — for whom he thought they had no actual use — then went along to the creek's grassy bank to settle himself upon an outstretched saddle blanket. In this spot he heard the others softly talking. He brought out the little miniature of Barbara Stuart, held it so that its paleness reflected gloomy night light, and studied it. On the brooch Barbara seemed near smiling. He brought the miniature in closer, bending over it, examining the details. It was perfect; he could not fault the unknown hand that had painted it. He considered the way this picture had been meticulously set into its mounting. It was gold, and this made him wonder why Wheeler's renegades hadn't taken it, why they had thrown it aside. The answer to this came slowly — whoever had found the brooch had in fact thought of taking it with him. Then, out in the hall of the main house, he had distastefully cast it down. A man would have to possess a strong reason for doing this. He would have to feel uneasy about looking at the painting of a beautiful girl's face — because he knew she had died violently. Not many men, good or bad, would want to be reminded by a delicate little painting of a thing that, in the eyes of all men, was shameful.

Travis put the brooch into a shirt pocket carefully. He would, he solemnly told himself, cherish this reminder of something that might have been as long as he lived. If it brought pain and melancholy, he would still cherish it because he was not a man who resented life and life's hurts; he was instead a man who, having survived more than one man's share of pain, could live with it, could continue to believe in his irrepressible heart, that some way, somehow, life had another side to it.

He was lying back, gazing steadily upon a star-washed sky when Will Fenwick returned in the late night. Will's coming brought up the sentry. But this man, after ascertaining it was the deputy town marshal, faded back out into the night again. Others, mumbling sleepily among themselves, also returned to sleep.

Fenwick cared for his animal, went to the creek, and lay a long time drinking, then rose up to fling off residual water, and stump along until he found Travis alone upon his blanket apart from the others. He dropped down as only a tired man would, and he said: "One of 'em's in Forest Falls with a bad headache."

"The one that had old man Stuart's bottle of whiskey," said Travis.

"Yeah."

"And the others?"

"Gone on. They hit town about the time we were at Stuart Ranch. They still got those two pack animals."

"Wheeler with them?"

"I think so . . . at least when I described him my friends said he was with the ones that pushed on northward."

Travis turned these things over in his mind for a while, then sat up and reached for his hat. "All right," he said matter-of-factly. "Let's ride. You can guide us on in, can't you?"

Fenwick scowled. "A couple hours' sleep won't hurt, Cole. *They'll* be sleepin', too, you know."

"That's why we won't sleep. We want to close the gap, Will." Travis stood up. "I'm sorry. I know you're dog-tired," he said.

Fenwick jumped up, saying: "Tired? Me? Hell's bells, I'm like a coyote. I can close my eyes for ten minutes and feel as refreshed as though I'd had hours' sleep."

Travis looked into the stubbled, gray, and putty-slack countenance. He put forth a hand to brush Fenwick's shoulder gently, then he passed onward, carrying his saddle blanket. Fenwick turned and made for the dark lumps low upon the still-warm earth, his voice breaking the slumber of those resting men like a bugle call.

"Up. Up, you boys. Get your horses. Come on now . . . dammit all, let's get a-going."

It took a little time for Fenwick to accomplish his purpose and even after he had all the townsmen stumbling after their horses in the moonlight, they muttered and groaned aloud and mildly cursed.

Twenty minutes later the body of riders was plodding along through quicksilver moon glow, mostly nodding, sagging, drowsily weaving in their saddles, but reconciled, too, and thoroughly understanding.

Will Fenwick rode ahead with Travis. "It'll not be so easy to track them beyond Forest Falls," he said. "The country thereafter gets pretty rocky."

"But you've got an idea where they'd go," said Travis, knowing his statement was true.

Will made his long, thin smile again. "They don't have much choice. If they don't swerve off from due north, they're going to end up in Crow country . . . and if there's one thing Crow warriors like, it's little bands of renegade whites running from the law with plunder."

"Does Wheeler know that, though?"

"He knows," said Fenwick. "Anybody who has been in this part of Colorado for over six months knows that. He's got to swing either east or back south."

"Why not west?"

"More Indians. Sioux this time, and they're even worse than the Crows."

"He won't try doubling back," said Travis. "Not unless he's absolutely desperate and has no alternative."

"He'll go east," stated Will, with strong finality. "Eastward, he can travel five hundred miles through settled country. He can rope fresh horses off the range, and, if he wants to, he can hit a town or two."

Travis nodded. It occurred to him that a wise thing would be to send Fenwick onward again out of Forest Falls, eastward, to pick up and relay back to the main posse, the route of Wheeler's band. He said this, too, and Fenwick was silent while considering it. He finally answered Cole, saying: "Afterward, if it's all right with you. After we settle with that one who stayed behind to rest his splitting head."

Travis nodded and they continued onward.

The moon was now fully up and very bright. It was almost like daylight, passing slowly over that immense plain. There were shadows on the far sides of sage clumps and also drawn out, long and narrow, where they passed an infrequent, low down growing pine or fir tree.

They were well within sight of the village of Forest Falls when Fenwick said carelessly, his gaze fixed ahead: "This one's name is Pat Mullaney. He's an old friend of Wheeler's."

"They all had to be friends of Wheeler's," said Travis. "Ordinary riders wouldn't have been a party to any of this."

"They were," assented Fenwick. "He imported them one at a time. Old man Stuart didn't object . . . why should he? They were all top hands. 'Course, he had no idea what else they'd been."

CHAPTER
SIXTEEN

They came into the village of Forest Falls, over thirty of
them, tired to the bone and likely to be short-tempered.
Will Fenwick galloped ahead to the town marshal's
office and was waiting out in the roadway when Travis
came up with the others.

Forest Falls, named for a little creek width that
passed behind town and fell over a stony wash, was a
cow town such as Gunsight, lacking the insularity of
the latter place because it was out upon a broad plain.
This early hour of morning there were not many men
abroad. Saloons, several gambling houses, and one
variety house, or dance hall were still doing business
but otherwise Forest Falls was abed.

Travis stopped and was introduced to Forest Falls'
lawman. His name was Cal Horton. He was an elderly,
stocky man with a tough face and piercing blue eyes.
He listened calmly to what Travis had to say, then
quietly informed Travis that he had previously heard
the same story from Fenwick, and had, since that time,
made a discreet investigation. He now would, he said,
lead Travis to the man who he thought would be the
person Travis was hunting.

The men from Gunsight left their horses and went along in a body behind Cal Horton. They stopped, piling up behind Travis and Fenwick, when Horton paused outside the entrance of a saloon.

"He's not using the name of Pat Mullaney," Horton told Travis. "But I'm sure he's your man. He arrived in town about the same time those others rode in, and he's been carousing ever since." Horton studied Travis, then he shrugged. "If I'm wrong, you'll leave him be . . . right?"

"Right," agreed Travis, and stepped into the saloon. He had no idea that he would recognize this Pat Mullaney, and in fact when he entered the saloon and Horton nudged him, saying softly — "That's him at the bar." — Travis looked, and did not know Mullaney at all, from the rear.

Something close to a sigh passed over the saloon's carousing patrons when that heavily armed body of men came stepping quietly into the smoky room, ranged out along the walls, and halted to look around, saying nothing. All noise stopped. A man at a piano sat twisted doorward with both hands poised in midair. Men along the bar turned and stood and showed wonderment, speculation, and growing wariness. The particular man Cole Travis was watching was one of the last to come around. He did this very slowly, as though a warning had belatedly flashed out to his nerve ends. Then, when he was fully around, his eyes moving down that line of armed men, Travis recognized him. He was the cowboy with whom Travis had battled out behind the Stuart residence.

Travis felt relief over this. It had troubled him before entering the saloon that they might have trouble getting some unidentifiable rider to admit he was a Wheeler henchman. Now, this problem was resolved. Travis waited until those shifting eyes came to rest upon his own face; he saw Mullaney stiffen, draw clear of the bar, and drop both hands very gently to his sides. These were the movements of a man who was getting set for trouble. Mullaney would make no attempt to deny his identity — he couldn't. Therefore, he would fight.

People, watching this long exchange of stares between two big men and understanding very well what that fierce exchange promised, sidled quietly away from the bar, from the likely pathway of bullets, and halted only when confronted by hard-eyed posse men who stood athwart each exit.

"You're under arrest," said Travis. "We'll take you back to Gunsight, Mullaney."

The cowboy's dirty face showed fading bruises from their earlier fight. He kept probing Travis, studying him and teetering back and forth between drawing and not drawing. He said: "What for? I didn't do anything."

"You didn't shoot her?" asked Travis quietly, baiting this man in whose eyes he saw a dawning hopelessness.

"No. Wheeler did that."

"Why?"

"He said if he didn't get her, no one else was ever going to."

"He rode to Gunsight?"

"Yes. We waited for him."

"Yeah. You plundered the ranch while you waited. Mullaney, you knew why he was going to Gunsight, but you didn't try to stop him. That makes you as guilty as he is."

"How? How, I'd like to know. What could I do?"

"Warn me in town. Get word to Barbara . . . to anyone . . . that he was riding to kill her." Travis called Mullaney a fighting name, then he said: "Shuck your gun . . . you're going back."

There gradually formed in Mullaney's eyes a strong brightness. He was not an intelligent man but he did not have to be to understand what would happen to him back in Gunsight for having been part of a band of woman-killers. "No," he said softly to Cole Travis. "I'm not going anywhere with you."

Travis watched Mullaney's color pale, saw how the cowboy's jaw set with blind stubbornness. Mullaney had made his decision and he knew he would not leave this room alive. He also knew death here would be swifter, more merciful than it would be back in Gunsight. Mullaney was many things but he was not a coward.

Travis was no stranger to the position he now found himself in; an instantaneous flash passed through him, alerting every nerve and leaving him cold, leaving him entirely prepared. He saw Mullaney clearer, each detail of the other large man's face stood out sharply to him, every wrinkle in his clothing, the way Mullaney's right hand hung gently curving. The walls of Travis's belly closed down; his heart set up an even beating. He scarcely breathed at all. His brain was like ice, every thought, each stray notion, squeezed out of it by this intense concentration that held him.

"All right," he said, in a way so quiet only those nearest him heard it. "All right, Mullaney. It's your choice."

The renegade rider hung there, feeling nothing at all, balancing between drawing and holding off, waiting for an eyelid flicker, a twitching muscle to divert Travis for the thousandth of a second. None of these things occurred; they would not occur. It came to Mullaney that he was facing, not a cow-town lawman at all but an accomplished gunfighter. That was when he made his move. One shoulder, already down, dropped lower the smallest bit. Mullaney's right hand moved scant inches in a blur.

Travis, no novice at this, had been watching for something else, for that instinctive tiny tightening of a man's lips. He saw it just before Mullaney's arm moved. Travis went for his gun. Those closest to him, including Will Fenwick and Calvin Horton, sensed rather than actually saw Travis draw.

There were two explosions, one a full second ahead of the other one. A burst of powder-fine sawdust blew upward three feet in front of Mullaney from that saloon's floor, and Mullaney struck hard against the bar front. He flung out both elbows to hook himself there and remain upright. Then he put a disbelieving stare upon Travis and fell, making a little rustling sound as he crumpled face down upon the floor. There was absolute silence for fifteen seconds. Travis's checked short breathing was clearly audible to Will Fenwick.

Will stood there staring at dead Pat Mullaney, thinking with utter detachment that it was a shame Travis had killed Mullaney before they'd found out from him where Wheeler and the others were.

Then Forest Falls' town marshal spoke, shattering all the accumulated tension. "Red, how about you an' Owen carryin' him around to doc's embalmin' shed."

Two men came forth from the motionless crowd, bent to grasp Mullaney at armpits and ankles, and heave upright with his sagging body between them. In this manner he was borne out of the saloon. With his passing went something intangible yet quite real, and people began once again to stir, to murmur to one another, and to seek and discover the moods that had held them before that armed mob of men had entered the saloon.

Travis turned on his heel and went out into the night. Fenwick, also moving, halted Town Marshal Horton in the doorway. "Let him go," he said. "You know how it is."

Horton knew. He put a long look upon the Gunsight posse men, apparently estimating their numbers, then he said loudly: "Beer's on me, boys. We all could use it."

Outside, Travis plugged out that spent casing from his handgun and pushed in a fresh load from his shell belt. He afterward stood quietly in full darkness taking in deep breaths and putting a willful glance beyond Forest Falls eastward. Some ten minutes later he reëntered the saloon, caught Fenwick's eye, and beckoned. They went together back out into the night.

"You'd better ride on," said Travis quietly. "How far will they be, you reckon?"

"Horton told me when I rode in earlier, they were plumb tuckered out. That's why I said, back at camp, they'd be resting, too. I'd guess they'll be maybe five, six miles on east."

"You know the country?"

Fenwick nodded. "Well enough. There's a good spring about where I figure fatigue overtook them. I'm gamblin' that's where we'll find them."

"You better scout them up, then, Will."

Fenwick said: "Let the boys finish their beer. All right?"

Travis nodded.

Fenwick sighed, hitched at his trousers, and started down through ghost light toward his horse. He got astride under Travis's watching look, wheeled away from the rack, threw outward a careless wave, and went loping out of Forest Falls.

Travis stood there in half light, half shadow, the aftermath of that fight still a smoky flare in his glance.

Horton came up, after a time, saying easily: "Be no more than three left now, Mister Travis." Horton took two cigars from a pocket and offered Travis one. Travis refused with a headshake, so Horton lit up alone. He rolled out a gray cloud; he examined the pleasant night and the benign sky. "Your boys were telling me, in the saloon, about that shooting down in Gunsight. If you wish, Mister Travis, I can get up a posse and ride after Wheeler with you."

"No thanks," said Travis.

"Sure," murmured Horton. "Some things a feller likes to do alone. Well, I wish you luck, an' I know you'll have it. Maybe those townsmen of yours don't look like much, but they mean business." Horton stepped down into roadway dust and went plodding along toward his lighted jailhouse. He did not look back.

Travis waited a little longer, then passed back into the saloon and caught the eyes of the nearest Gunsight posse man. He jerked his head at this man, then returned to the roadway, went along to his horse, untied the animal, and got astride grimly to wait.

The Gunsight men came shuffling out to their mounts, got astride, and, when Travis turned northward, they dutifully trailed along in his wake.

Travis rode for a long time deep in thought. Then, where the roadway forked, he took the easterly route and kept on going. Once, passing a ranch house, a dog ran out to yammer at this large, silent body of riding men, and a silhouette appeared beside the house, rifle in hand to stand still, watching. Otherwise, the men from Gunsight passed along through soft and uneventful moonlight to the next juncture of several trailways. Here, Travis halted, got down, and stood idly making a smoke.

One of the posse men said to him: "Will said he thought Wheeler'd be at Box Springs. If you want, Mister Travis, I'll take you there."

Travis smoked and considered this man. It had been his intention to await Fenwick's return at this spot.

306

Now he changed his mind. "Lead out," he said, killed the cigarette, and got back into his saddle.

The eastward route eventually left behind on its forward run every vestige of humankind. Even that road they were following petered out into a number of forking saddle-horse trails, and after another hour even these disappeared. That leading townsman rode steadily, as men ride who know their course and destination. Travis was satisfied and slouched along with others around him also slouching along.

The moon was nearly down now. Off in the dim east night's final last dark stain was beginning to alter away from total darkness. Daylight, thought Travis, was not more than two hours off.

"Someone's coming!" called the guiding townsmen, out a hundred yards ahead. "Probably Will."

It was indeed Fenwick. He came on at a weary jog and slowed when the posse came even with him. "They are at the spring," he told Travis. "Like I figured." Fenwick made a little ironic head wag. "They still got those damned pack horses with them, too. How do you like that? Nobody in his right mind would trail along a slow, damned pack horse when he's runnin' for his life."

Travis grunted. "Wheeler thinks like that. He doesn't give up without getting *something* for his troubles."

Fenwick, adapting his mood to Travis's, said next: "There are all kinds of fools, but I reckon a greedy fool is the least admirable. In Wheeler's case . . . it will cost him his life."

Travis was thinking ahead. He still had it in mind to face Wheeler alone. He was not, however, sure just how this could now be managed. Finally he said to Fenwick: "Listen, Will, can we surround them?"

"Yes . . . they're dead to the world, all lyin' close to the spring."

"Then you pass among the men and tell them to be as quiet as mice . . . to cut far out and around this place, and close up on it in a big circle. But not to shoot unless I tell them to. Be sure you tell them that, Will, it's important."

"Sure," said Fenwick. "What you got in mind?"

Travis did not reply.

CHAPTER
SEVENTEEN

The land onward was beginning to buckle; there were long, rolling ribs of land, swales where night's darkness lay thickest, and now and then a clump of trees. The spring that was their destination lay in one of those swales. Green grass was there, too — excellent horse feed.

It was the hobbled animals Travis saw first as he came up, quite alone, to halt within sight of the lumps upon the ground, and he sat there with both hands crossed upon his saddle horn, gazing at them. It would, he thought, be good if he could get to those animals and remove their hobbles, then the last hope for Wheeler's renegades to escape would be gone. He did not, however, get down to attempt this. Conceivably he might succeed with one or two of those animals, but not with all of them. Range horses were totally unlike farm horses — they would not stand to be touched by strangers.

Travis got down, turned his horse away with a light slap, and dragged forth his booted carbine as the beast trotted back. Down in the swale a man coughed, cleared his pipes, and spat. He afterward rolled upright off his saddle blanket, mightily stretched with both arms, then turned to gazing at the still dark landscape and heartily scratch his stomach at the same time. Travis got down flat, pushed forward his carbine, brought this man to him down the Winchester's barrel, and waited.

It would take time for the posse men and Will Fenwick to get into position. Travis meant to shoot only if something alerted the renegades to peril before the surround was in place.

The standing renegade put a grumpy look around him at his slumbering companions. He spoke, and in that depthless silence his voice carried clearly up to Travis in the rank grass above the swale's curving lip.

"Hey, you guys, let's get moving. Hey! Get up, dammit."

The renegade accompanied his final words with several light kicks. Then, as other shapes firmed out of earth shadow, the wide awake man sat down to tug on his boots.

"Jack," someone said in a whine, "I'm for takin' a rest at one o' these little towns."

The man tugging into his boots said carelessly, "Sure, Rufe, sure . . . after we got about three hundred miles between us an' Gunsight. Now get your damned bones to movin'."

Travis's finger closed very gently around his carbine trigger. He knew now which one of those men was Jack Wheeler and he had no intention of removing his eyes from the shadowy figure at all, nor did he, not even when one of those silhouettes sprang up, crying swiftly: "What was that?"

310

"What?" said Wheeler, coming upright in one graceful sweep.

"I heard something . . . sounded like a gun barrel bein' dragged over stone."

All of Wheeler's men were up now and wide awake. They became wholly still, listening. Travis heard nothing. The pre-dawn pulsed on deathly still. Jack Wheeler turned away, finally saying disgustedly: "Oh, hell . . . come on, let's get saddled up. You fellers are gettin' as jumpy as old women." Wheeler stamped away from the spring, heading for those hobbled horses. He hadn't progressed fifty feet when one of the men behind him let off a sharp little cry and grabbed his gun. This man fired twice, rapidly, at the farthest lift of land above him.

Travis saw Wheeler instantly drop down, roll over, and come up onto one knee with his six-gun cocked and poised. "What the hell . . . ?" he yelled back at the others. "Who done that?"

A panting voice answered quickly: "There's someone up there on the prairie, Jack, east of us."

Wheeler was like stone. He seemed half inclined to blast his man who had fired with profanity and scorn. Before he could do this, though, a third voice spoke out. Travis at once recognized this voice as belonging to Will Fenwick.

"He's right, Wheeler!" called Fenwick. "There are over thirty men surrounding you down in there."

Travis's finger was curling tighter; he had Jack Wheeler dead-on in his buckhorn sight. That other renegade gave off a great shout and threw himself sideways toward the rank weed growth beside the spring. His companions also whirled frantically away.

Only Jack Wheeler did not move. He hung there on one knee, still holding up his cocked pistol, looking totally astonished. He was, he knew, caught well away from any cover at all. If he made a dash back down toward the spring — he would be riddled.

Wheeler got heavily upright. He planted his big legs wide and lowered his gun hand. "Come out where I can see you!" he yelled toward the east. "If there *are* thirty of you, I give up."

Travis stood up off to one side. Wheeler, looking in a different direction, did not at once see him. Travis said, almost casually: "All right, Will. That'll do. Keep the other ones covered."

Wheeler turned only his head. He saw Travis moving toward him. "Who the hell are you?" he fiercely demanded of Travis. "What right you got to bust in on a man's camp like this?"

"Drop that gun," said Travis, stopping twenty feet away, covering Wheeler with his carbine.

"I will not. Who are you, anyway?"

"You got a poor memory," drawled Travis, and moved the slightest bit so that dying moonlight touched down under his hat brim showing Wheeler his face.

Wheeler said: "By God, the feller with the shotgun." He was recalling Travis from the fight at Gunsight's jailhouse. Then his surprise passed and Wheeler said jeeringly: "How come you've got a Winchester now . . . shotgun man?"

"For better range," answered Travis, his cold gaze steady. "Drop that gun, Wheeler."

"Yeah? Who says so? Why should I drop it?"

Travis carefully considered his answer. "I don't really care whether you do or not. But if you don't, I can kill you legally."

"You cannot!" exclaimed Wheeler. "You're no lawman. That badge don't mean nothing. Fred Brand's the lawman."

"You shot him, Wheeler. You shot him without him having a chance."

"And you want me to drop this gun so's you can do the same to me," snarled Wheeler.

"You also shot Barbara Stuart. You did that the same way . . . without any warning. You planned Hayden's lynching the same underhanded way by engineering him into a shoot-out with Rock Stuart. You think it'd bother me to shoot you without a gun in your hand? Don't push your luck, Wheeler."

Travis could see from the edge of his vision that Fenwick and the others were filtering down over the swale's lip from all directions, that Wheeler's henchmen, recognizing the hopelessness of resistance, were grudgingly coming upright around the spring with their arms high overhead. Travis heard the quick utterances back down there, and the answers these commands got back, surly but complying replies. He said of these things to Jack Wheeler: "It's all over. You made your play and you lost. Now drop that gun or use it . . . I don't care which, because I'm going to kill you either way."

Wheeler stood on in silence. From farther down Will Fenwick called up: "Hey, Cole, you want any help up there?"

"No, stay out of this, Will."

"Sure. We'll take care of these."

But the men down in the swale, renegades and posse men alike, made no move; they were watching that deadly drama being played out upon the distant side hill.

Wheeler said, his eyes crafty, his face a setting for shifting thoughts: "Travis, I seen you two walkin' hand in hand. I seen how she looked at you. Well, now neither of us get her and . . ." Wheeler didn't finish; he had never intended to. He launched himself across that intervening twenty feet with unbelievable swiftness. He had one big arm outflung to strike aside Travis's carbine. The arm struck sideways at the same moment that gun exploded. Then Wheeler crashed into Travis knocking him violently backward.

Wheeler grunted under that impact; he also grunted when he threw a looping punch at Travis's jaw. Travis could not entirely get clear of that blow; it made lights burst inside his skull. He pawed at Wheeler, seeking to hold him off long enough to regain his balance. He was not successful at this, though. Jack Wheeler was fighting the greatest battle of his entire lifetime and he knew this. He dropped his head and went wheeling in, both huge arms flailing. Travis turned partly to deflect these strikes. They hurt him, and then his side became numb and he went sidling far around. Wheeler, head down, did not immediately see this maneuver. When he brought his head up to peer, Travis's bony fist ripped through his guard and cracked him on the jut of his jaw. Wheeler winced and dropped his head again.

Travis had his balance back but his ears echoed with a roaring and his arms felt like solid lead. Twenty-four hours of merciless punishment was now coming on to overtake him.

Wheeler's big arms whipped in and out, not always landing, but getting through to Travis often enough to heighten his sense of numbness. Wheeler grunted when he struck out — he was a large, heavy man. Now, he was putting everything into these blows, for it had suddenly come to him that, if he could whip Cole Travis, could beat him down senseless, he could use Travis's inert shape as a shield for his own body, perhaps even as a hostage to get his men safely away from the posse.

He dropped low, squared around, found Travis's mincing silhouette in the watery dawn, and shoved himself toward it, low and fast. Travis did not side-step or move at all out of the way. He had a fist up and cocked. When Wheeler's right arm lashed out, Travis dropped under it and let go. His fist caught Wheeler flushly on the mouth. Wheeler wilted. His arms dropped for a second and water gushed from his eyes. Then he recovered and swung around wide to come at Travis again. This time he hurt Travis with a strike under the heart. To follow this up Wheeler ran in recklessly again, smothering Travis's blows. He hit Travis a glancing blow under the ear, and Travis, his breath sawing fiercely in and out, caught Wheeler again in the mouth. This time claret sprayed. This time, too,

Wheeler's arms dropped away and did not come back up so quickly.

Travis jumped at Wheeler, stood close, swinging his hard fists like clubs, striking the big renegade in the face again and again. Then shifting, striking Wheeler in the belly, in the chest, in the ribs, his fists sinking to their wrists in Wheeler's soft parts. It was a savage, merciless attack, wickedly effective. Wheeler began to give ground, to weave a little, and to bring up a ragged guard. He was gasping for breath.

Down where the posse men and renegades stood, a sigh went up.

Wheeler was stumbling now; he was trying stupidly to get away from that deadly punishment. He whimpered once and flung out a pawing hand that was not even curled into a fist. Travis abruptly dropped both his arms, watched Wheeler a second, then came at him, aiming high, aiming with everything he had left.

Wheeler took this final blow over his high-bridged nose. Bone and gristle flattened. Wheeler plunged over and struck the ground and rolled fully ten feet before coming to stop upon his back, both arms outflung, his mutilated face dim in the diluted early light.

Travis sat down. He hung both arms out, hands limply dropping over both knees, hatless head low, mightily inhaling and exhaling. Thirty feet farther down Jack Wheeler twitched, blinked, rolled over to retch, then sighted Travis sitting like that. He reached for his gun, had it out and moving when Will Fenwick, who had started up the little hill toward them, cried sharply: *"Cole! Look out!"*

Travis went groggily sideways, driven by instinct and the two-edged shrillness of Fenwick's cry. He drew his own gun as he rolled, and once, coming up on his side, he shot.

Wheeler never fired at all.

Travis's bullet hit Wheeler flush in the breastbone; he went on over very gently, flattened out with a rattling sigh, and never moved again.

Fenwick came on. He toed the dead renegade over and knelt. Moments later he straightened up, saying in quiet awe: "He did that on purpose. He deliberately did that, Cole."

Travis got unsteadily upright. He walked down to stand above Wheeler, looking at him. "What are you talking about?" he asked Fenwick.

Will untangled Wheeler's fingers from his gun. "Broke," he stated. "His hand's broke all to hell. He couldn't have pulled that trigger if he'd had all day to do it."

Travis, putting up his gun, said — "Go get the horses," — to Fenwick, and, after the deputy had moved off, he considered Jack Wheeler for a long time without moving. When they were quite alone, he said to the dead man: "All right . . . you wouldn't go back to be hung, and now you don't have to. But you're going back anyway."

When the horses came up, half a dozen posse men secured big Jack Wheeler across his saddle. Other silent men lashed his companions to other horses, excepting that these men rode astride.

Travis had trouble getting back into the saddle, but when Will suggested a layover, Travis lifted his reins, nudged his animal, and led out southward, saying nothing to anyone.

They ambled along spent in body and drained in spirit, a wilted cavalcade of Gunsight men and their completely used-up leader. From time to time Will Fenwick put a thoughtful look on Travis, but he never once offered to break in upon Travis's thoughts.

They plugged along like that all day, stopping only once to water the stock, then got back astride under Travis's unrelenting scowl, and resumed their homeward way.

They saw Gunsight late in the afternoon, having by-passed Forest Falls and the southwesterly rise of those hills over which they had come the night before.

Sunlight burned against them, adding its torture to exhaustion, to saddle-weariness, to minds filled with somber thoughts.

This was the way they re-appeared in Gunsight to be hailed as heroes, feeling as unheroic as men could feel, wishing only for twenty-four hours of rest, some food, some cold water, a bath, then another twenty-four hours of rest.

They split off from Travis and Fenwick at the jailhouse, riding away silently in pairs or alone, leaving Jack Wheeler's survivors to be locked up by Will and Cole.

When this had been accomplished, under the wide-eyed look of Bart Hayden, Cole said: "Will, you're a damned good man. Now head home and go to bed."

Fenwick nodded, made his lean, long grin, and said: "Cole . . . I can't say what I feel. See you later."

Travis turned, viewed the cowed renegades in their cell and their defunct leader where he had been dragged into a corner, and started doorward without a word.

Bart Hayden, for this brief moment forgotten by Travis, said in loud awe: "My God, Mister Travis, you're a mess."

Travis crossed to the hotel, called for bath water, laid out fresh clothing, and, when the tub was ready, descended to it in the back room, stripped down, and climbed in. He at once fell asleep. A timid clerk awakened him past 10:00p.m. Travis dried off, got dressed, and left the hotel bound for Fred Brand's mother's place. He stopped briefly on the way for a quart of black coffee. It buoyed him up at once, and, by the time he was on Aletha Brand's front porch, he felt almost human again.

Aletha opened the door and her eyes sprang wide open. "Good heavens," she gasped. "Cole, you look like a locomotive train met you head-on."

He smiled, winced from this, and stepped past. His eyes were darkly haunted-looking; even the attempt at a smile did not conceal this. "How's Fred?" he asked, holding his hat before him. "I want to tell him . . . we got them all. That Jack Wheeler is dead."

"Yes," said Aletha Brand. "He'll want to know those things, son. But first, would you like to see Barbara? I brought her here, too."

Travis stood stockstill, hardly breathing. "Barbara? I thought, by now, from what you and the doctor said . . ."

Aletha Brand seemed shocked. "No," she said swiftly. "Why, no, son . . . she lost a sight of blood, but we got the bullet out. She's going to be fine. 'Course, it'll likely be a month before she can do much moonlight buggy riding. But she'll . . ." Aletha took Travis's hand, tugging him along. "Come with me . . . she's still awake. You can see for yourself."

Barbara's room had a little bedside lamp, turned low. She had heard Travis's voice and was intently watching the doorway. When he entered, being drawn along by Aletha Brand, Barbara smiled softly at him.

Travis stopped at the bedside. Aletha released him and looked at them for a little time, then she took Travis's hat, saying fretfully: "Land sakes, Cole, you've twisted this hat all out of shape." She left the room softly, closed the door, and hurried along to her son's room, still carrying Travis's hat.

"It was too much to hope for," Travis told Barbara Stuart. "Life never dealt me a good hand . . . didn't seem likely it would deal me one now."

She took his hand, held it lightly with cool fingers. "I couldn't let a little thing like a lead bullet hurt me now, Cole," she told him.

He saw the tears suddenly blur her vision and knelt, touched her full mouth with his lips, and drew upright again. "You need lots of rest. I'll come back tomorrow."

"And . . . the other tomorrows, Cole?"

"Yes, for as long as I live, Barbara. If you want me to."

"I want you to, Cole."

320

He touched her lips with one finger, and he afterward left the house, halted outside with star shine around him brighter with promise than he'd ever before seen it. Then he strolled back toward his room at the hotel.